CHRONICLES OF MILLER'S CROSSING:

SLEEPING DOGS

LINDA L. CHONTOS

Chronicles of Miller's Crossing: Sleeping Dogs
by Linda L. Chontos

ISBN: 978-1539674771

To Steve, my forever love

Dear Suzanne -
We have a natural
friend in MaryAlice. She has
been a special blessing in my
life. I hope this little book
will bless you in some
small way.
With love,
Linda

~ TABLE OF CONTENTS ~

~ PROLOGUE—1978 ~

She hesitated before stepping onto the wooded path. The sun had dipped below the horizon trailing soft rays of light in its wake. It would soon be dark.

The meeting had lasted longer than planned, and her mother would wonder where she was. Not that it mattered all that much, but she wasn't in the mood for another argument. The shortcut would shave a good ten minutes off the time it took to get home. She turned off the road and onto the path.

The familiar surroundings took on a sinister appearance as darkness closed in around her. She picked up her pace, walking as quickly as her platform shoes would allow.

As she approached the spot where the remains of an old rock wall bordered the path, she heard a noise—the sound of someone running. Her heart began to pound. She turned and stood fixed to the spot. The sound grew louder. Then someone called her name.

She recognized the voice, and anger quickly replaced the paralyzing fear.

"Oh, it's you. You nearly scared me to death. What do you want?"

Moments later her lifeless body lay crumpled in the dirt.

~ CHAPTER 1 ~

Matty set her suitcase on the sidewalk and stared up at the darkened windows. The house looked cold and forbidding. She stood rooted to the spot for long minutes before hefting the suitcase and climbing the porch steps.

A biting wind swirled around her legs as she fumbled for the keys in her purse. She began to wish she hadn't decided to come home without letting anyone know. She pulled the doorknob while turning the key in the lock. It had a frustrating habit of sticking. Joe had promised to add it to his to-do list.

Inside felt almost as frigid as the outdoors. The air smelled damp and musty. Matty flipped a switch, and the small overhead light illuminated the foyer. She closed the door and sank down on the little loveseat, wrapping her coat around her. This place that had once been her safe refuge seemed foreign and unfamiliar.

She longed to let the tears come, but they were stopped up somewhere deep inside, refusing to give her relief. Though still trim, her sixty-two years weighed heavily as she got up and made her way into the kitchen, flipping light switches as she walked through the dining room and down the little hallway.

The old house creaked and moaned when the heat came on. Her body relaxed a bit with the familiar sounds. A cup of tea sounded good, but the effort required was more than she could muster. Instead, she wound her way back down the hall, back through the dining room where she paused for a moment. The oil painting Joe had given her for their last anniversary was crooked. Wondering if she should bother to straighten it, she shrugged and headed up the stairs to the bedrooms, feeling like a stranger in her own home.

She stood at the doorway to their bedroom and looked at the neatly made bed. Without looking, she knew Joe's side of the closet and his bureau drawers were empty. Every trace of her husband had been removed. Their daughter, Jenny, had insisted on taking care of this difficult task after the funeral, before they left for a three-week stay at her home on the island.

Matty hadn't had the energy to protest. She closed her eyes for a moment, then turned and walked away.

Joe's study had escaped Jenny's ministrations. Matty stood on the threshold and thought back to the days right after the funeral. Jenny had been working in the bedroom when Matty slipped into the study to look for the papers their lawyer had requested. It looked just as it had the day he died—books and papers piled on the old roll-top desk, wastepaper basket overflowing, his golf clubs standing in the corner.

She had been after him to get organized.

"How can you work like this, Joe? It would drive me crazy. I don't know how you get anything done." Her own voice echoed in her head.

He had come over to her and wrapped his arms around her.

"I know where everything is, honey. You're the neatnik in the family. I like a little ordered chaos."

She had given him only a half-hearted hug, annoyed that he didn't seem to care about the mess. *"Ordered chaos is still chaos,"* Matty had muttered.

"I'm sorry," he said, holding her tight despite her response. *"I promise to work on it."*

What she wouldn't give to have him sitting there in the middle of it all. Why couldn't she have held her tongue?

With so many details swirling around the funeral arrangements that week, Matty couldn't bear to move a single thing in the study. Instead, she walked to the antique filing cabinet Joe had found at the thrift store and opened the top drawer. Her heart sank when she saw the neatly arranged files. Obviously Joe had been keeping his promise to get things in order. The last time she'd checked, the file drawers had looked just like his desk.

She began looking through the drawer for the required papers and had just about given up hope of finding them when she saw the marked folder way in the back. She pulled it out and noticed a little red spiral notebook tucked away in the farthest corner of the drawer.

Her heart had begun to pound. A hidden notebook seemed so out of character. They had never kept secrets from each other. She sat down, clutching the notebook in her hand. Warily she opened it to the first page. In big block letters, Joe had written "BILLY TAYLOR."

There was only one Billy Taylor she knew of, and he was serving a life sentence for murder. Why would Joe have a notebook with his name in it? She had been so deep in thought she jumped when Jenny popped into the room.

"Did you find the papers, Mom?"

Matty nodded and held up the file. Before they left the room, she slipped the little notebook back into the drawer. That was four weeks ago.

Alone in the house now, after her stay with Jenny, Matty was drawn to Joe's space. She stepped down into the room and closed the study door behind her. For a brief moment she thought about getting out the notebook. *No, I can't do it. It's too soon.*

Instead, she turned around to face the back side of the door, praying it would be there. *Yes.* He had worn that old tan sweater for years, balking whenever she suggested buying a new one. Taking it off the hook, she walked over to the old couch and sank down. Its sagging cushions and threadbare cover seemed to close in around her. She buried her face in the sweater and breathed in his scent. Finally, the tears came.

❖

Rain spattered against the study windows in waves driven by the wind. Long seconds passed before Matty remembered where she was. Her back ached and her eyes felt as though they were filled with fine grains of sand. Still, she lay there, not wanting the day to begin. Perhaps lying still would keep it from coming.

I should pray. The familiar thought nudged its way into her tired mind, but the words wouldn't come.

A loud banging echoed up the little staircase. Someone was at the kitchen door. *No one knows I'm home. If I just keep quiet, whoever it is will go away.*

"Matty! Matty Amoruso! I know you're in there. I'm gettin' soakin' wet. Open the door."

It was Willa-Mae. Matty's next-door neighbor never missed a trick. She must have seen the lights in the windows last night.

Matty groaned and stretched. She felt a bit stiff after spending the night on the old couch. She made her way down the back stairs that led to the kitchen. Jenny used to call it her secret stairway. The study had once been Jenny's bedroom, and she always said it felt like her own little apartment with its very own entrance.

The old house needed a major overhaul when they bought it. During the renovation work, Joe realized the bedroom, along with the kitchen, small porch and large walk-in pantry, must have been a later addition. He felt that explained why they needed to walk through the bathroom to reach the study. The kitchen door that opened onto the smaller front porch was the one used most often by friends. The large front porch had a more formal feel. The family tended to use the door on the lowest level of the house—the one that led to the downstairs family room.

Matty closed the stairway door and peeked out the kitchen window. She stepped back when she saw Willa-Mae's face peering in at her.

"There you are. Hurry and let me in. I'm freezin' out here."

Willa-Mae stormed into the kitchen, wind and water in her wake. She set a big basket on the counter. Then, without bothering to take off her raincoat, she opened her arms and wrapped Matty in a soggy hug. Matty rested her head against Willa-Mae's chest and put her arms around her. She could feel every rib in the strong, slim back.

Willa-Mae stepped back, holding her at arms' length.

"I'm so glad you've come home."

Whenever there was trouble of any sort in their little community, Willa-Mae was one of the first people there.

"Why on earth didn't you call and let us know you were comin' home? We would have gotten the house ready for you, stocked the fridge, made a hot meal. How did you get home from the airport? Don't tell me you rode all that way in a cab."

Matty waited for Willa-Mae to pause for breath. "I didn't

want to bother anyone..."

"Bother? Since when have you ever been a bother? Matty, you're just too sweet for your own good."

"I'm not sweet at all. I just needed a little time to—"

"Well, lucky for you I baked last week, so I pulled some biscuits out of the freezer. Then I whipped up one of my breakfast casseroles this mornin' and popped it into the oven."

She continued to talk while bustling around the kitchen, unpacking the basket and searching the cabinets for plates and silverware. Without missing a beat, she took off her wet coat, hung it on the back of one of the chairs and turned to face Matty.

"I left part of it home for Jason, but this should tide you over. Bless your heart, you must be starvin'."

Matty suddenly found herself caught up in another huge hug.

Willa-Mae's eyes were brimming when she released her. She pulled her handkerchief out of her apron pocket and wiped her eyes. "Will you look at that. I was in such a hurry I forgot to take off my apron. And where in tarnation are my glasses? I can't see a thing without them. I know I had them on when I drove down here."

Matty pointed to Willa-Mae's head.

"Oh for heaven's sake!" Willa-Mae reached up and plucked the glasses off the top of her head. "Sometimes I think I need a keeper."

She gave them a thorough cleaning with her damp

handkerchief before putting them on. Wincing a little, she kneaded her hands together. "This weather is makin' my arthritis act up somethin' wicked. Well, let's don't stand around here lettin' everything get cold. Here, I even brought a thermos of coffee. Come and sit down, honey. You look like you could use a good meal."

They sat facing each other, seated at the table Joe had crafted from a huge pine slab. Willa-Mae filled their plates and poured the coffee. Then she said a simple grace, thanking God for Matty's safe return and asking Him to comfort her with His peace and love.

Neither woman spoke as they picked up their forks and began to eat. The old schoolhouse clock on the kitchen wall ticked a steady rhythm. Water gushed off the eaves.

"This is delicious, Willa-Mae. You shouldn't have gone to so much trouble."

"It was no trouble at all, honey. I want so much to help you, and I just don't know what to do. My Daddy used to say I could talk the legs off a chair, but I can't think of a single thing to say."

"You don't need to say or do a thing. Just knowing you're here helps."

Willa-Mae reached across the table and squeezed Matty's hand. They quietly finished their breakfast.

"Well, time for me to head home." She stood and gathered up the dishes. "If I'm not there, Jason is liable to forget to feed the calf. I swear, that husband of mine would forget to breathe if I wasn't there to remind him."

Matty managed a strained smile and nodded.

"We'll expect you for supper—5:30 sharp."

"Oh no, really, Willa-Mae. I have so many things I need to do today."

"Five-thirty sharp. You don't have to stay; don't even have to make conversation. You know you won't bother cookin' for yourself, and from where I'm standin' you look like you could use a good home-cooked meal."

Thrusting her arms into her raincoat, Willa-Mae opened the door and let in a blast of frigid air as she made her way outdoors. The door slammed, and quiet descended.

Matty sighed deeply. "When am I ever going to learn to say no?"

She loaded the dishwasher and shuffled down the hall, through the dining room and up the main staircase.

"I have to do this." The sound of her own voice echoed through the hall. She stepped into the bedroom. It looked bleak and sterile—not the warm, welcoming room it had once been. One by one she opened and closed the drawers of the old dresser not knowing what she hoped to find. She went into the bathroom and ran the water for a hot bath.

The phone began to ring as she stepped out of the tub. She grabbed a towel, wrapped it around herself and hurried into the bedroom. She felt certain it was her daughter calling to check on her.

"Mom, it's Jenny. How are you?"

"I'm fine, honey. Just got out of the tub."

"Oh, I'm sorry. I waited as long as I could, but I just had

11

to know you were okay."

Matty smiled wearily and tightened the towel around her. "Willa-Mae stopped by with breakfast a while ago, and I'm to join her and Jason for supper tonight. So you don't have to worry a bit. I'll be well taken care of."

"I wish you had stayed a little longer."

"It was time for me to come home."

"Well, I want you to think about what I said. Pete and I want you to come and live with us. The kids would love it. We all would."

"I need to take some time, Jenny." She sat on the edge of her bed and closed her eyes.

"Okay, Mom, but please remember you have a home here with us."

"I will. I love you. Give my love to Pete and the kids. I have to run. I need to get some groceries and stop at the Post Office to let them know I'm back. Although now that Willa-Mae has been here that probably won't be necessary." Matty sighed and said, "I do love her and don't mean to complain, but she certainly has a way of taking charge."

"Well, I'm glad you're going there for supper. Tell her I said hi. Love you, Mom."

"Love you too, honey. Bye."

Her Bible caught her eye as she hung up the phone. She hadn't taken it with her to Jenny's. What had once been her source of comfort now made her feel forsaken. Fighting the anger that simmered just below the surface, she went back to the bathroom and got ready to go into town.

~ CHAPTER 2 ~

Holding her breath, she turned the key in the ignition of the new SUV. It had been sitting for weeks but started up on the first try. Matty uttered a little prayer of thanks.

The rain had stopped. Fluffy clouds skittered across a brilliant blue sky. March had decided to modify her behavior and act a bit more like a lamb. Carefully, Matty steered down the long driveway and out onto their little country road. She wasn't used to driving this car. They'd purchased it when Joe retired, after much discussion about whether or not they needed a bigger car. They wanted to do some traveling, so the SUV won out. Now Matty wondered if she would ever have use for such a big vehicle.

Over the bridge and down to the corner, past the little white church she and Joe had pastored for over thirty years, Matty noticed several cars parked out front and remembered it was Tuesday morning—women's Bible study. She turned the car in the other direction toward town, not wanting to face them just yet.

She pulled onto the highway and drove the short distance to the Post Office. It wasn't quite as old as the church but had been there as long as anyone could remember. A sturdy little wooden building, it also served as a grocery store of sorts. There was even a gas pump out front. Anna and Art Williams had taken over the place years ago after old Mr. Burns passed away. Matty knew she could get the staples there and decided to put off going into town.

Unexpected tears stung her eyes when she walked through the door. The neat rows of mailboxes faced her, and behind the little counter, Anna was sorting stacks of mail. To her right, Art was stocking shelves with homemade baked goods. The sun shone through the windows making pretty patterns on the old wooden floor, and the smell of coffee and dried herbs filled the air.

Anna looked up, and their eyes met.

"Matty. Willa-Mae said you were back. I...I'm glad you're home. We've missed you." She came out from behind the counter and gave Matty a tentative hug. Art joined them and quietly patted her shoulder.

"It's good to be home. I've missed all of you, too. I just stopped in to let you know I'm back and to see if there was any mail for me. Could you let Mel know he can start delivering my mail at the house from now on?"

Anna nodded. "Sure, Matty. I don't have anything for you right now. I forwarded the last batch of mail to your daughter's house yesterday."

"I should have let you know I was coming home. I'll have

Jenny send it back. I need to pick up a few things, so I'll just do a little shopping."

Feeling rather awkward, Matty made her way down the short aisles and gathered the things she needed.

Art rang up her groceries on the old cash register. "I'll give you a hand out to the car, Matty."

"Thanks, Art, but I think I can manage."

"Nonsense. There's too much there for you to carry by yourself." Art scooped up all but one of her bags and led the way outside.

"Good-bye Matty," Anna called. "You take care now!"

After the groceries were loaded, Art turned to Matty. Looking somewhere over her head, he said, "Pastor Joe was a good man, and I'm gonna miss him." With that, he scurried back inside.

❖

She could hear the phone ringing as she juggled the grocery bags and tried to get the door unlocked. By the time she got inside, it stopped. The answering machine had been turned off before her trip to Jenny's, but Caller ID announced that Nancy had been trying to reach her.

A nice long talk with her best friend would be good, but weariness plagued her for weeks since Joe's death and the thought of talking felt like a monumental task. How could she possibly get through an evening with Willa-Mae and Jason?

"I'll call Willa-Mae and tell her I'm not feeling well." She spoke the words out loud, startling herself with the sound of her own voice. "No," she continued, "that would only make it worse. Willa-Mae would be here in a flash, fussing and lecturing. I'll go, but I won't stay long. Surely they'll understand."

By the time the groceries were put away and the house straightened up, it was lunchtime. Nothing sounded appealing. She climbed the back stairs to the study and sat down on the old couch.

Joe's sweater lay crumpled in the corner. When she reached to pick it up, the filing cabinet caught her eye. Holding the sweater against her chest, she got up and walked over to it. She opened the drawer and spotted the notebook in the corner, right where she left it before leaving to go to Jenny's a few weeks ago. She picked it up and carried it to the couch. Heart pounding, she opened to the first page: "Billy Taylor" written in big block letters. This time she turned the page.

What followed was a detailed account of a meeting between Joe and Billy Taylor at the state prison. Matty read through the first few pages and discovered that Joe met Billy the first time he visited the prison with a fellow pastor who conducted a Bible study with some of the inmates. Billy must have been part of the group. From what he had written, there was something about Billy's demeanor that drew Joe's attention.

They met several times over the following months. Casual

conversation eventually gave way to discussions of the crime—the reason Billy had spent the past thirty-six years in prison.

Matty put the notebook down and thought back to their first weeks in Miller's Crossing just two years after the murder. That passage of time had done little to dim the collective memory. There had never been a murder in their little village. Something fundamental had changed—a loss of innocence.

Beatrice Smythe Campbell had called the local sheriff in a panic when her sixteen-year-old daughter Karen hadn't come home from an after-school meeting at church. They found her body in the woods behind the Taylor farm. Her skull had been crushed. Witnesses testified they had seen Billy Taylor with her shortly before the murder.

Joe hadn't written much about the crime itself. Instead he had recorded his impressions of Billy, his increasing belief in his innocence:

"I have been trying to get Billy to remember the day of the murder," he wrote. "He struggles with the memories; they are so painful. He just keeps saying he didn't do it. We've gone over those hours again and again. On this last visit he began to recall some of the details. I'm trying not to get too excited, but I think we may have a solid lead.

"I haven't mentioned any of this to Matty. I don't want her to worry. But we've never had any secrets between us, and I don't want to start now. I must tell her soon."

The notebook ended there.

"He never got the chance to share this with me. Oh, Joe." She sat holding the notebook in her lap. "Is it possible Billy Taylor is innocent—and what is the lead? And what am I going to do with this now that I've read it?"

She stretched out on the couch and laid her head on Joe's sweater. Before drifting off to sleep, she tucked the notebook under the makeshift pillow.

❖

Fighting her way up through the darkness, Matty struggled to open her eyes. They felt glued shut. When she finally managed to get them open, she just lay there as if drugged.

The rays of the setting sun shone through the window and cast shadows across the old oak floor.

"What time is it?" she wondered out loud. Slowly unfolding her body from the depths of the old couch, she made her way over to the desk. "Five o'clock! How could I have slept so long? And I really have to stop talking to myself. It can't be a good sign."

She ran her hands over her slacks and shirt in a vain attempt to press out the wrinkles while racing to the bathroom. Splashing some warm water on her face and combing her hair made her feel a bit better. Makeup was only for special occasions. A little bit of lip gloss, and she was ready to go.

Looking at her reflection in the mirror, she was startled to see the dark circles under her eyes. In spite of herself, she spoke to the woman staring back at her. "You look every minute of your sixty-two years, Matty old girl."

She turned from the mirror with a sigh and lowered herself onto the little chair, the one Joe had made for Jenny when she was just a toddler. "I can't do this, Joe. I can't..." Tears flowed down her cheeks, rolled off her chin and landed softly on her shirt. She sat for a few minutes until the tears subsided. The anger she'd felt faded; despair seemed to settle in its place.

She returned to the sink to wash away the evidence. As she came down the stairs, the phone began ringing. The temptation to let it ring was overwhelming, but her innate sense of integrity won out. Not bothering to check Caller ID, she picked up the receiver.

"Are you alright, Matty? We were beginnin' to worry. It's 5:45."

"I'm fine, Willa-Mae. I took a nap and somehow overslept. I'll be right there. I'm so sorry."

"You want Jason to come pick you up?"

"No. I'd like to walk. I could use the fresh air."

"In the dark?"

"It isn't dark yet, Willa-Mae. I'll be fine. See you in a few minutes."

She grabbed her jacket off the hook by the door and quickly walked the length of the long driveway. The sun still hung low in the sky. Matty stepped out onto the lane and picked up her pace. Although they were next-door neighbors, several acres separated the houses. It took a few minutes to cover the distance.

Jason was waiting for her and had the door opened before she had a chance to knock. His gentle smile and warm hug threatened to start the tears again. He held her away from him, looked deeply into her eyes and said, "Thank you for coming, Matty."

Willa-Mae bustled into the room, drying her hands on a dishtowel.

"Here you are. Supper is all ready. Come on in and sit down." She gave Matty a quick hug and led the way into the kitchen.

She looked around the familiar space—at the collection of ceramic roosters on the shelf over the stove and the cast iron trivet shaped like a pig that hung on the wall. The smell of fried chicken and warm rhubarb pie reminded Matty that she hadn't eaten anything all day. For the first time in a long time, she felt like eating.

After supper, they sat around the table and talked about everything that had happened while Matty had been away. She felt herself relaxing—a long exhalation after holding her breath for what seemed like an eternity. Willa-Mae chattered non-stop, and Jason smiled fondly at both women. Matty felt a deep gratitude for these two dear friends.

"Time for some coffee and pie."

"The pie smells wonderful, Willa-Mae. You make the best rhubarb pie in the county."

"We're about to make that official," said Jason.

"What do you mean?"

"Tell Matty about the contest, hon."

Willa-Mae set the perfect pie on the table, turning the pan slightly for Matty to have the best view, and went to get the coffee pot. As she poured, she filled Matty in.

"The Youth Group is raisin' money for summer camp. As soon as it's warm enough they plan to have a few car washes."

Matty could sense her excitement.

"They're gonna have a couple of Saturdays where they do chores and such for folks, too," Willa-Mae continued, "but the big event will be the Fourth of July celebration. All the money they raise will go toward helpin' kids who can't afford to go to camp."

"So where does your rhubarb pie come in?"

Willa-Mae took off her apron and sat down next to Matty. "There's gonna be a contest to see who bakes the best pies, cakes and cookies. The winners will be auctioned off. There'll be first, second and third place in every category and grand champion of the whole shebang. Since it's for a good cause, they figured the bids will be real high."

"She's got her sights set on that grand champion ribbon," Jason said. "She's been baking pies and tweaking her recipe for weeks now. I'm about rhubarb-ed to death!"

Willa-Mae stood again and started slicing and serving. "Hush, Jason. I'm just gonna do the best I can, and may the best pie win."

Matty glanced at Jason. He winked.

Willa-Mae didn't notice as she slid a plate to her friend.

"Well, give it a taste, Matty. I added a little extra butter before I put the crust on. See what you think."

Matty lifted her fork, and both Willa-Mae and Jason leaned in to watch. Matty smiled and took a bite, chewing self-consciously as they stared. Willa-Mae nodded hopefully and raised her eyebrows, awaiting a response. Matty nodded reassuringly, trying to swallow. "Absolutely delicious. I wouldn't change a thing."

"Well, thanks, honey. But I'm thinkin' about experimentin' with just a touch more sugar next time." She finished her coffee and pointed a bony finger at Matty. "You should enter one of your apple pies."

"Oh, I don't know, Willa-Mae. I'm not much for baking these days."

"You really should. You make a terrific apple pie. What kind of apples do you use?"

"I always use Macs. Joe didn't like any other kind—especially not Red Delicious."

"Is that so? I use Red Delicious in my apple pies. Didn't Joe like my pies?"

"Of course he did." Matty could feel her face getting red. "I just meant he preferred my pies with Macs." It sounded lame even to her. Why couldn't she just let well enough alone? Hoping to get Willa-Mae's mind off of apples, Matty jumped up from her seat and began clearing the table. "Come on, let me help you with these dishes."

Matty finished drying the last pot and hung the towel on the hook in the pantry. She felt the familiar weariness set in.

She loved these two but longed for solitude. Seeming to sense her mood, Jason put an arm across her shoulders and said, "Why don't I walk you home, Matty. You must still be a little tired after your trip."

"Oh Jason, you don't have to do that. It's just a short walk."

"Nonsense. Get your jacket on, and we'll brave the cold together."

Willa-Mae hugged Matty and handed her a covered plate of rhubarb pie.

"I'll talk to you soon, honey. Get a good night's sleep."

"Thank you for supper, Willa-Mae. It was scrumptious."

Jason tucked Matty's hand under his arm and strolled quietly beside her. She longed to pour out her heart to this good man, but words wouldn't come. Together they climbed the porch steps. Jason waited while Matty unlocked the door.

"If you ever need anything, Matty—anything at all."

"I'm all right, Jason," she said, sensing what he was struggling to say. "Joe left me well provided for."

She reached out, squeezed his arm and walked into the dark house.

~ CHAPTER 3 ~

It was much too early to think about going to bed. In any case, her long nap ensured she was anything but sleepy. As she made her way downstairs to the basement family room, the smell of the old brick fireplace greeted her. Sitting in Joe's recliner, she picked up the remote and began flipping through channels hoping to find an old movie she could lose herself in for a while. All thoughts of the notebook were pushed aside.

"Why is it there's never a good movie on when you're in the mood, and why am I still talking to myself? Because there isn't anyone else here, Matty. You have to try to accept the fact that he isn't coming home."

The only answer was the silence of the old house. It seemed to close in around her.

"Maybe I can find something to read. I think I still have that mystery Nancy lent me weeks ago." She walked over to the little bookcase and picked up the book lying on the bottom shelf.

A loud crash just outside the basement door shattered the

silence.

"What in the world?" Carefully making her way to the window, she pulled the curtain aside. The pitch darkness made it impossible to see, and she realized she was going to have to be brave and go out there to investigate. In all likelihood a raccoon had gotten into the trash again, but the possibility of an intruder did cross her mind. Armed with the old golf club they left in the corner for such an emergency, Matty opened the door and stepped outside, flipping on the outside light as she went. A sudden movement in the corner where they kept the trashcans made her legs go weak.

"Who's there?"

A pair of eyes appeared just a few yards from where she was standing, followed by what looked like a coyote.

"Go! Get out of here! Shoo!"

She stamped her feet up and down and waved the club wildly in the air. The coyote shot past her and down the driveway. He had gone only about halfway when he turned and looked at her. Then he sat down. It wasn't a coyote—just a big dog. A rather thin, mangy dog at that.

"Well, go on. Don't just sit there looking at me. Shoo!"

Arms akimbo, Matty watched in amazement as the dog dropped down onto his belly and began to crawl toward her. His eyes never left her face as he made his way over the rough gravel, stopping just a few feet in front of her.

"Please go away. The last thing I need right now is a dog. Go on home."

She realized what a ridiculous comment she had just

made to the poor dog. Go home? He probably hadn't seen a home in weeks—or a meal either, for that matter. She stared at him. He stared back, eyes wide. "All right. You stay right where you are. I'll see what I can find for you to eat. Just stay right there—don't follow me."

She raced into the house and upstairs to the kitchen. The pantry was always well stocked with canned goods. She searched the shelves for something the dog might like. Grabbing a large can of stew, she popped the lid and poured it into an old plastic bowl. She filled another bowl with water and hurried back outside.

He lay right where she had left him. Setting the bowls down on the ground, she stepped aside. "Okay. Come and get it."

He didn't move a muscle—just looked at her. She felt her heart softening. "It's all right. I'll just go inside, and you come and eat."

Closing the door behind her with as little noise as possible, she ran to the window and peeked out. The dog gobbled down the stew as if he hadn't eaten in days.

"Okay, Matty. You've done your good deed for the day. Turn off the light, and hopefully he'll go on his way. Someone else will probably give him a home."

She knew the chances of that happening were slim. All of the farmers had dogs that were essential to their work. They wouldn't take kindly to a stray getting into the farmyard. If this dog got desperate enough, he could prove to be a real problem.

"Matty Amoruso, you do not need a dog." She picked up the mystery, turned off the light and went upstairs.

With the book tucked under her arm, she climbed into bed. It seemed huge without Joe beside her. She propped the pillows up behind her and tried to settle in with her book. The words she'd been looking forward to reading seemed flat and dull. After a few false starts, she put the book down.

Leaning her head back and closing her eyes, Matty replayed the conversation about apple pies over and over again in her mind. *I hope I didn't hurt Willa-Mae's feelings. I never seem to learn to think before I open my big mouth.* She got up and walked over to the window.

It was hard to see two stories down, but the driveway looked empty. Instead of feeling a sense of relief, she felt a twinge of disappointment. "I guess the poor old thing has moved on."

She turned and walked through the bathroom and into the study. The worn sweater lay where she had left it, crumpled in a corner of the old sofa, and as she picked it up the notebook fell to floor. An image of Joe sitting with Billy Taylor went through her mind. She reached down and picked up the notebook. So many of the things she loved about him seemed to somehow be wrapped up in that little book—his compassion and ability to see clear through to the heart, his courage and his passion for truth.

Climbing back into bed, she placed the sweater on Joe's pillow—the little notebook nestled underneath.

27

❖

Shadows danced across the wide wooden planks of the bedroom floor. Sunlight streamed through the open window, and a cool breeze stirred the curtains. Matty drew the quilt up to her chin and huddled down into the warmth. Keeping her back to the empty side of the bed, she could almost feel the weight of Joe's body beside her. A deep ache centered in her chest grew and rendered her immobile.

I can't face this day, she thought. She longed just to fall into a deep sleep—to never have to wake up to another empty day.

The bedside phone rang, startling her into consciousness. She tried to ignore it, but her sometimes annoying sense of responsibility wouldn't let her.

"Hello."

"Matty. It's Nancy. I've been trying to reach you for the past couple of days. How are you, honey?"

"Oh, Nancy. I'm so sorry I didn't call you back. It's been a bit hectic since I got home, but I'm all right."

"Matty, this is me—Nancy. How are you *really?*"

Drawing the old sweater onto her lap, she began to pick at the pills. "I miss him so much, Nancy. I don't think I can do this." A single tear dropped onto the tan wool.

"What are you doing right now?"

"I'm ashamed to tell you...I'm still in bed."

"Well, get up, get dressed, and come on over here. Buddy's out mending fence, and I have to wait for a delivery or I'd come to you."

Matty ran her hand over the sweater. Nancy's practical, no-nonsense approach to life made her a natural leader, and her wisdom and compassion made others want to follow.

"Give me a half hour or so, and I'll be there."

"Don't bother with breakfast. I've got a fresh pot of coffee on the stove and cinnamon rolls right out of the oven."

"Thank you, sweet friend. See you in a little bit."

She hung up the phone and carefully folded the sweater before setting it on top of the little notebook on Joe's pillow. She couldn't resist a quick peek out the window. No dog in sight, but maybe he was hiding? A quick look under the porch and behind the trashcans confirmed that he was gone. After taking a quick look down the road, she went back inside to get dressed.

Another beautiful day. Pale blue sky and a fresh, cool breeze—perfect weather for the half-mile walk to Buddy and Nancy's farm. Walking down the little country road, she remembered toting milk bottles to the farm with Jenny, who felt as safe with Nancy's six kids as Matty did with Nancy.

Cresting the hill, she stopped for a moment to catch her breath. The fields rolled away on either side, brown and silent waiting for the turning of the season. She walked slowly toward the old farmhouse. It seemed to reach out to her. How many hours had she spent in that big kitchen with her dearest friend, talking, laughing, crying—sometimes sitting in companionable silence working together on their needlework projects?

She closed the gate behind her and climbed up the porch steps. The door opened before she had a chance to knock. Nancy reached out and drew her inside. Without a word they walked over to the old plaid sofa that had been part of the kitchen for as long as Matty could remember and sat down.

Smiling weakly, Matty tried hard to hold back the tears, but since the dam had finally broken it seemed nearly impossible to hold them back. Nancy gathered her into her ample embrace and just held her tightly until she had cried herself out.

"I'm sorry. For weeks I couldn't cry, and now I can't seem to stop."

Nancy handed her a tissue. "Come. Let's get something warm into you."

Over steaming mugs of coffee and warm cinnamon buns the two friends talked of everyday things—kids and grandkids, local news, how the farm was doing. Nancy got up and poured them each a second cup of coffee. As she sat down, she reached over and took Matty's hand. "We never had a chance to really talk before Jenny took you home with her. Would you like to now?"

"Oh, Nancy, it all seems to be stopped up somewhere deep inside. I don't even know where to begin."

Matty stopped. A quietness settled over the house. Through the open window they could hear the sound of chickens gossiping in low clucks. Somewhere in the distance a dog barked. Nancy leaned closer to her friend and gave her hand a gentle squeeze.

"I keep going over those last days before he died," Matty continued softly. "He was so tired, but I thought it was because of all the extra work he'd been doing around the house. I should have known something wasn't right. Why didn't I insist he go to the doctor?"

Matty gently pulled her hand free and rubbed her legs in an effort to stop the trembling. "But the worst is...that last day I fussed at him to take the Christmas decorations down to the basement. I dropped a not-so-subtle hint that it really was about time he straightened up the mess down there while he was at it. He was gone for hours. I finally went down to see what he was doing and to tell him to come get washed up for supper. I saw him lying on the floor in front of his workbench. I wanted to run away and pretend it wasn't happening. I knelt beside him and begged him to wake up. I felt for a pulse, but I couldn't find one. I ran to phone for help. Then I raced back to him and tried to do CPR. The EMTs came so quickly. They worked on him for such a long time before they put him in the ambulance. I kept hoping for a miracle."

Nancy just nodded, not willing to stop the flow.

"I prayed so hard, Nancy. I screamed for God to help us. I pleaded with Him. Why didn't I go downstairs sooner? Maybe I could have saved him."

"The doctor said there was nothing you could have done."

Tears rolled down her cheeks, and her voice shook with emotion, "But God could have."

Getting to her feet, Nancy gingerly got down on her knees

in front of her friend. Taking her hands in her own work-worn ones, she said, "And you're angry that He didn't?"

"I was. Now I'm...just deeply...hurt. He was such a good man, Nancy. I've never known such an honorable, godly man. He was absolutely selfless. I think his heart just wore out. We had such plans for his retirement. We were going to travel for a while. Then he wanted to do some small mission trips and some speaking. Why couldn't he have had just a few more years?"

Neither spoke for several minutes.

"I've sat beside so many people who've lost loved ones," Matty whispered, "and I thought I had all the answers. I knew better than to say them out loud. I just thought that when the time came I would be able to get through it with my faith intact. I feel so lost—as though the ground has given way beneath me."

"Why don't we pray together, Matty?'

"I can't. I haven't been able to pray since the day he died. God feels so far from me right now."

"It's all right. I've been praying for you."

The sound of a truck slowly making its way up the long driveway startled them.

"That's your delivery. You'd better take care of it. I need to get going anyway."

"Well give me a hand up then." Nancy laughed as she struggled to her feet. "I love you, Matty, and I'll be praying."

"I love you, too."

Matty waved to the driver as she went down the porch

steps and out through the gate. Daffodils were beginning to push through the earth in Nancy's flower bed. Matty inhaled the fresh, clean air. Instead of heading back down the hill toward home, she began walking in the opposite direction, slowing her steps as she passed the familiar farms and fields. This peaceful place was a tonic to her. From the moment they arrived at the little parsonage, she had loved it. She had always lived in town, but there was a country girl living deep inside who blossomed and grew in this land of wide pastures and distant mountains.

Matty turned the corner and stopped. Set back from the road, the Campbell house stood like an elegant Victorian lady. Sunlight reflected off the windows. A thin line of smoke curled up from the brick chimney and the scent of burning wood filled the air. Tiny spears of grass appeared on what would soon be a lush lawn, and in her mind, Matty saw the magnificent roses set against the gleaming white walls of the house.

Matty had been inside only once. When they first arrived in Miller's Crossing, Beatrice Smythe Campbell invited them for tea. Joe and Matty quickly understood that not much happened in their little village, or the neighboring towns for that matter, without Beatrice's approval. Her family owned several large slate quarries and had amassed a fortune over several generations. As the only living heir, Beatrice was the wealthiest woman in the county. However, her wealth had done little to make her a happy woman. She had never been sociable, and after the tragic death of her daughter, she had closed herself off completely from everyone.

Matty thought about Billy Taylor. *I wonder how Mrs. Smythe Campbell would feel if it turned out he had not murdered her daughter? This could affect so many lives. I'm not brave like you were, Joe. I don't know what to do.*

As Matty passed the paved driveway, a dog came running past her so fast he nearly knocked her over. Beatrice Smythe Campbell trotted behind him, waving her arms and yelling at the top of her lungs.

"Get out, you stupid mutt. Get out!!"

She stopped short when she saw Matty, drawing herself upright and moderating her tone. "That horrible creature chased my cat up a tree and got into the trash. It's spread all over the backyard."

She smoothed her perfectly coiffed hair and glared at the dog. "I'm going to call the sheriff and have him picked up."

In what seemed like a dream, Matty watched as the dog, the very one she had fed the night before, came and stood behind her.

"Is that your dog?"

"Yes." She could hardly believe the lie had come from her own lips. "I'm terribly sorry, Mrs. Campbell. I'll take care of the mess."

"Never mind. My man will take care of it. Just get that dog out of here and see to it that he stays away from my house. By the looks of him, he could use a good bath and something to eat. Don't you ever feed him?" She picked an invisible piece of lint off her mint colored linen slacks and adjusted the matching silk scarf.

"I'm so sorry. He ran off last night, and I didn't know where he was. I'll..." she began stumbling over her words. Beatrice Smythe Campbell turned her back on her and marched up the driveway and into the house without another word. Not one mention of Joe.

~ CHAPTER 4 ~

Matty strode down the road, the delinquent following closely at her heels. He at least had the decency to keep his head down and his tail between his legs.

"I can't believe I told her you were my dog. What do you think you were doing? Don't you know she could have you put away for good?" She sighed and shook her head. "What am I going to do with you?"

He looked at her with what seemed a bit of a sheepish smile, ears perking up a bit. One ear anyway. The other seemed to droop at a jaunty angle.

"Oh, all right. You may as well come on home with me. But you'd better behave. Honestly, the last thing I need in my life right now is a dog."

She noticed a definite spring to his step as he passed her and began loping ahead—head up and tail wagging.

"Of course...you know the way home." She shook her head and grinned.

Once they were home, Matty couldn't decide what to do

first.

"I'm sure you're starving. Wait right there while I go look for something for you to eat. Although I have no idea what that will be."

He sat and looked at her expectantly.

"I'll be right back."

The pantry didn't offer much in the way of dog food. Another can of stew would have to suffice for now. When she took it down she saw a can of chili way back in the corner of the shelf. *That ought to do,* she thought. *At least it's something different.*

He downed the entire can almost before she had filled the water bowl.

"You poor thing. Who left you here, and why would they do such a mean thing?"

He lifted his head and gave her a questioning look.

The wind had begun to pick up and she could feel the temperature dropping. "It's getting too chilly to give you a bath outside. How about I take you to see my friend Jess? She's a vet, and she'll know just what to do for you. What do you think?"

Looking for all the world like he understood every word, he came over and licked her hand.

"That won't get you anywhere." She tried using a stern tone of voice, but the words came gently and ended with a smile.

Grabbing an old blanket from the laundry room shelf, she spread it across the back of the SUV and motioned the dog in.

Without a bit of hesitation, he jumped in and faced forward—eager for a ride.

"I sure hope you don't have fleas."

He looked innocently out the window.

The ride to the vet's office was short. There were only a couple of cars in the parking lot, so Matty was hopeful that Jess would have a few minutes to see them. She hadn't thought about finding a leash, but it wouldn't have mattered. Jenny loved cats—there had always been at least two curled up on her little bed at night—but they never owned a dog.

Deciding to leave the dog in the car while she checked in with Jess, she breathed a sigh of relief at the sight of the empty waiting room. Jess's assistant Elizabeth looked up from her computer.

"Matty! Hi. I didn't know you were back. I'm so sorry about—"

Matty cut her short. "It's all right, Elizabeth. Is Jess busy? I have an abandoned dog in the car I'd like her to take a look at."

"Just a minute. I'll go check."

A short time later Jess walked through the door. She walked straight over to Matty and gave her a hug. No words, just a teary smile that spoke volumes.

"Now, what's this about an abandoned dog?"

"He just showed up on my doorstep last night. I thought he had gone away for good because he wasn't there this morning. However, I ran into him again at the Campbell mansion and saved him from certain death."

Jess laughed. "I can only imagine. Well, bring him on in, and let's have a look."

It didn't take long for Jess to examine him. He was so patient and trusting, Matty had to resist the urge to wrap her arms around his neck.

"He's malnourished for certain. He's got a few cuts and bruises—probably had to fight for what little food he managed to find. Other than that I think he's a healthy young fella."

"Does he have fleas?"

"No, Matty. He doesn't have fleas. I think it's been too cold for fleas up until a couple of days ago."

"How old do you think he is, and what kind of dog is he?"

"I don't think he's a year old yet. As for his breed, I think he's a happy shepherd mix. He probably needs his shots and a good deworming. And a bath is definitely in order. What would you like to do, Matty?"

"I don't know. The last thing I need right now is a dog."

"Oh, I'm not so sure about that. I think a dog might be the very thing you do need right now. He certainly seems to like you, and he's got a sweet disposition. He's been through a lot, this poor guy, and yet he's as gentle as can be. He'd make a wonderful pet."

"Do you know of anyone who might be looking for a dog?"

"Sure don't."

Matty sighed. "Well, go ahead and do whatever needs to be done. How long will it take?'

"Why don't you pick him up in a couple of hours?"

"All right. And thanks, Jess."

"My pleasure, Matty." Jess grabbed the dog just in time to keep him from jumping off the examination table and running after Matty as she was pulling the door shut. She stroked his head and whispered, "Don't worry. I think you've got a home." Matty stuck her head around the door and called out, "I can hear you."

❖

Matty decided to run into town to get groceries while Jess took care of the dog. *I need to get a few things*, she told herself. During the fifteen-minute drive she tried not to think too much about the dog. Maybe Jess would come up with someone who could give him a home.

She had to drive around the parking lot for a while before she found a place to park. Their own little village consisted only of the combined Post Office and General Store, the church, and a little diner. Everyone from Miller's Crossing came into Centerville to do most of their shopping.

Hoping she wouldn't run into anyone she knew, Matty grabbed a cart and fairly flew up and down the familiar aisles. She knew she would have to face people at some point, but not right now. *It doesn't help to put off the inevitable,* she scolded herself. *But I just don't want to talk to anyone yet.*

She found herself slowing down at the pet food aisle. Examining the different kinds of dry dog food, she bent down to pick up one of the large bags, mentally scolding herself.

What are you doing, Matty Amoruso? Nevertheless, she added a half-dozen cans of dog food to the pile and walked over to examine the collars and leashes. Soon, a brown leather collar and shiny new leash rested atop the food. Just before leaving the aisle, she snatched a box of dog treats and tossed it in the cart.

Loading the bags into the back of the car, she checked twice to be sure the receipt was tucked safely in her pocketbook in case she wanted to return anything.

The dog was lying on the floor next to Elizabeth's desk when Matty walked into the waiting room. Before she had taken two steps into the room, he was on his feet, rushing over to greet her. He looked like a different dog, his dark brown coat clean and shiny. He still looked painfully thin, but that could be easily remedied. Bending over, she took his face in her hands.

"Look at you. You look like a different dog." He gave her a slobbery kiss on the cheek.

Just then Jess came out of the back room.

"He cleans up real well, doesn't he?"

"Thank you so much, Jess. I hardly recognized him. Please send me the bill."

"What would you like me to do with him, Matty? I can probably keep him for a little while, but if no one wants him I'll have to take him to the shelter."

Matty felt her heart beat just a little faster at the thought of the shelter. "I've decided to take him home with me."

For a minute the three women just looked at each other.

Jess began to laugh. Elizabeth pressed her lips together, trying to stifle a giggle. Before they knew it, they were all laughing. The laughter bubbled over until they had tears rolling down their cheeks. The big dog looked from one woman to the other and did something Matty hadn't heard him do since the night she found him. He started barking.

~ CHAPTER 5 ~

That evening Matty sat in the family room watching the news. The temperature had dropped steadily since lunchtime, and they were predicting snow flurries for the next day. She looked down at the dog softly snoring at her feet and watched his chest gently rise and fall, thankful he would have a warm bed tonight.

He woke up when she turned the television off. She looked at him, that one silly ear flopped over, and smiled.

"I think it's time we give you a name. Don't you? I can't keep calling you 'the dog.'"

He cocked his head.

"Let's see...how about Rin Tin Tin? You look sort of like him. I could call you Rinty."

He lowered his eyebrows.

"You're right. Too silly. How about Prince? No...you don't look like a Prince." She leaned back in the chair trying to think of something original. "I'm really not good at thinking up unique names. I always let Jenny name the cats. She came up with such exotic names, like Cleo for Cleopatra."

She looked into his solemn brown eyes, and suddenly the name was there. "Shep. We'll call you Shep. Do you like that name? Shep?"

Tail wagging furiously, he came over and put his head in her lap. Had someone once cared enough about him to give him a name, and did they name him Shep? The name fit him perfectly.

"Come on, Shep. You can keep me company while I sort through Joe's papers. I've put it off long enough."

She climbed the stairs, the dog right at her heels, then drifted over to the old couch where she sat rubbing Shep's soft head. "This is the one job I've dreaded."

The dog looked at her with sympathetic eyes.

"He spent so many hours bent over that desk studying the Word. Jenny tried to get him to use his computer to research his sermons, but he refused. He loved searching the pages of his old study books." She scanned the shelves for his favorites, and then her gaze shifted to his desk where his "#1 Dad" mug sat full of pens. "He wouldn't even use the computer to write the outlines for his sermons. He said there was something special about moving the pen across the page that he couldn't find by tapping keys."

She buried her face in the soft fur. Shep sat quietly. When she lifted her head, he proceeded to lavish doggy kisses on her already wet cheeks. She laughed and pushed him away.

"Come on. Let's at least get started."

Matty sat in the big swivel chair and began to sort through the papers covering the surface of the big desk. The laptop sat on top of the books on a shelf near the desk, the printer tucked away inside the side drawer.

She decided organizing the sermon notes and putting them into folders in the antique filing cabinet was a good place to start. Joe had been working on a series he hoped to teach in the state prison—something he never had the time to do while pastoring full time.

She looked over at Shep. "It's no good, boy. I can't concentrate on these old sermons. I keep thinking about that notebook. Maybe the pastor in charge of the prison ministry could give me some more information."

Hurrying into her bedroom with Shep right on her heels, she pulled the notebook out from under the sweater. Clutching it to her as if it could somehow give her strength, she opened the drawer of her bedside table. The little address book lay buried under a pile of papers. Under the "Rs" Joe had written Pastor Reed's phone number. She punched it in before she had time to think too much about it.

"Hello."

"Hello Pastor Reed. This is Matty Amoruso. I hope I'm not calling too late."

"Not at all Matty. How are you?"

"I'm doing well." She hurried on not wanting to have to talk about how she was really doing. "I wondered if I could ask you a couple of questions about the Prison Ministry."

"Of course. How can I help you?"

"I know that Joe was particularly interested in one of the inmates, and I wondered how he was doing." *Oh that sounds so lame, but I don't want to say more than I should. If Joe didn't confide in him, he must have wanted to keep things quiet for a while.*

"Ah. You must mean Billy Taylor. I know that he and Joe had developed a good relationship, although Joe didn't talk much about it. Was there something in particular you wanted to know?"

"Oh, not really. I just wondered if he knew what happened to Joe, and if so, how he was handling it."

"I told our whole little Bible Study group about Joe, Matty. Everyone was deeply saddened—Joe was well liked—but I could tell Billy was more upset than the others. I tried, but I couldn't get him to talk to me. He hasn't come back to the study since Joe died."

"I see. Well, thank you Pastor Reed."

"Not at all Matty. Is there anything else I can do for you?"

"Thank you, but no. I'm fine."

She hung up the phone and turned to look at her furry friend. "Well that wasn't much help. Come on. Let's get you outside for a few minutes before we call it a night."

Placing the notebook back under Joe's sweater, she turned and followed the big dog down the stairs. They walked through the kitchen and into the pantry. Matty could hear the wind howling through the bare branches of the trees. She grabbed a jacket off one of the hooks and opened the back door.

Shep ran out ahead of her disappearing into the darkness. They never had the money to fence in their five acres, and she worried that he would take off into the woods. Long minutes passed; she stood peering into the darkness willing him to come back. She thought about going back inside to get a flashlight so she could look for him, but suddenly he appeared, tail swishing back and forth, looking at her with shining eyes.

"It's freezing out here. Come on, let's get back inside."

Something wet hit her cheek. Carried by the wind, tiny white flakes stung her hands and face. She turned to go inside and stopped in amazement. She watched as her exuberant pet jumped into the air in a vain attempt to catch the snowflakes. He turned in circles, leaping higher and higher, snapping at the air.

Matty threw back her head and laughed—it started deep inside and bubbled up to the surface. In that moment, head tilted heavenward, she saw a small opening in the clouds. The moon shone through, radiant. A brief glimpse and it was gone. Something moved in her heart, and she whispered into the wind, "Thank You, Lord, for this moment and for sending this sweet friend."

❖

Matty opened her eyes and was startled to see a pair of brown eyes only inches from her own.

"Shep! You scared me!"

He licked her nose. She laughed and pushed him away.

"Okay, okay. Time to get up." She caught herself just

before turning to talk to Joe. The familiar weight returned and settled around her heart. *Will I ever get used to this?* she wondered. *It aches so bad. Please help me, Lord.*

She brushed her fingers over the worn sweater before heading downstairs.

Peering through the kitchen window, she squinted. The morning sun had turned the thin covering of snow into a field of dazzling diamonds. She decided Shep could be trusted outside on his own. He was back in a matter of minutes.

"Cold out there?" Matty ran her hand along his back and shook her head. "Just when we thought the warm weather had come to stay. I should know better. March isn't to be trusted."

She had just poured herself a second cup of coffee when the phone rang. After a brief conversation she headed for the stairs.

"That was the new Pastor. He wants to come over for a visit," she said. Shep sat at attention, prepared for anything. "I've got to get dressed. He'll be here in forty-five minutes."

When the doorbell rang, Shep ran into the hall to investigate. Not sure how he would react to strangers, Matty grabbed his collar before opening the door.

"Hi. Come in, come in. It's so cold this morning."

The young pastor and his wife hesitated a moment before taking tentative steps inside. Following their gaze, Matty tried to reassure them. "He won't hurt you. I know he's big, but he's a sweetheart."

"I didn't know you had a dog." Mrs. Schmidt stepped

behind her husband and grabbed hold of his arm.

"I didn't. I mean, I just got him. He turned up on my doorstep the other day and made himself at home." Matty loosened her grip on his collar.

Mrs. Schmidt edged her way past him, still hanging onto her husband's arm. Pastor Schmidt held out his hand for Shep to sniff, then patted his head. Satisfied with that simple greeting, Shep decided it was time this other person got to know him. He went up to Mrs. Schmidt and gently nudged her free hand with his moist nose. Matty watched as the younger woman put a tentative hand on his head. Shep returned the favor by licking her hand. She laughed and gave him a more substantial rub around his droopy ear.

Matty grinned and said, "Please, take off your coats and make yourselves at home."

She led the way into the living room. The Schmidts sat, shoulders touching, on the small love seat; Matty settled across from them in an upholstered armchair with Shep at her feet.

"Can I get you a cup of coffee? I'm afraid I don't have anything in the way of baked goods to offer. I've just been home for a couple of days, and I'm still a bit disorganized. How are you settling in? Do you like the parsonage? Joe and I..." Seeing the look of sympathy on their faces, she stopped mid-sentence.

Pastor Schmidt spoke, his voice clear and earnest. "We're fine, Mrs. Amoruso. We just wanted to see how you're doing and to ask a small favor of you."

She had only seen them a few times, but Matty felt drawn to this young couple. They were warm and outgoing—brimming with enthusiasm. Joe had been delighted when the church voted to make this young man their new pastor.

"I'm doing well," She reached down to stroke Shep's head. He looked up at her and leaned against her leg. Matty felt an unspoken invitation from Laura Schmidt as she tilted her head. "The truth is," Matty continued, "it's been hard. I feel so lost without Joe. I miss him every minute of every day."

No one spoke. Matty looked down at her hands, wishing she hadn't said quite so much. Shep panted contently beside her. "Now, tell me about this favor."

The Schmidts looked at one another, hesitant to begin.

Matty suggested, "I don't know about you, but I could certainly do with a cup of tea. I can't seem to get warm this morning. Come into the kitchen while I brew us a pot."

They filed into the kitchen, Shep bringing up the rear, tail wagging, delighted with the idea of a tea party.

Matty reached for the teapot and smiled at the younger woman. "Would you mind getting the teacups, Mrs. Schmidt? They're in that first cabinet on the right."

"Laura. Please call me Laura. I'd be happy to."

Pastor Schmidt sat down at the old table and looked around the room. The handmade curtains, the antique brickwork around the oven and stove, and the rag rug on the tiled floor combined to give the space a warm, cozy feel. The women chatted as they set the table and prepared the tea.

"You have a beautiful home," he said.

Matty set the sugar bowl on the table and stopped to look around the homey room. "Thank you. You should have seen it when we first bought it. Everyone thought we were crazy."

"Did you do the work yourselves?"

"We did." She walked over to the refrigerator to get the milk and filled the little blue creamer.

"It took a long, long time. Come and sit while I get the tea, Laura."

Matty continued talking as she filled their cups.

"We made the decision to stay in Miller's Crossing long before Joe retired. We thought we'd build a house while we were still living in the little parsonage, but we couldn't find land we really liked." Matty sat down across from Laura and looked at the embroidery she'd stitched and hung on the wall years earlier. "There was something about this old house that just sort of drew me."

"Was someone living here?"

"Yes, an elderly couple. They weren't able to keep it up, and it got pretty run down. After they passed away, the family put it on the market. The price was reasonable, so we took the plunge."

Laura smiled. "You've certainly put a lot of love into this home. It's so warm and welcoming."

"There were some days we did question our sanity," said Matty, smiling. She poured milk into her tea and then slowly stirred in a spoonful of sugar. "In the end it was worth all the hard work."

They sipped their tea and continued to talk, carefully

avoiding the real reason for the visit. Pastor Greg filled her in on some of the changes they had made to the parsonage.

"We converted one of the little upstairs bedrooms into a craft room for Laura." He turned and put his hand on his wife's shoulder. She's more than a talented musician—she's a seamstress, too. She helped make the costumes for the last musical we put on in our other church."

"Oh, I admire you for that, Laura. I'm not much of a seamstress."

"Thank you. My grandmother taught me. My mom wasn't much for sewing either. I made some new curtains for the kitchen, and Greg put up some shelves in the laundry room for me. We're enjoying our first little home."

Matty got up and refilled their cups.

"Did you have a good visit with your daughter?" Laura blushed and hurried to add, "I know it was a difficult time I just meant..."

Matty came to her rescue. "I love visiting Jenny and Pete. And, of course, I love spending time with my grandkids. They're growing up so fast. I know it sounds like a cliché, but it's so true. It seems just yesterday they were toddlers."

"Don't they live on an Island?" asked Greg.

"Yes. It's a tiny Island off the Connecticut coast. Pete grew up there. Beautiful beaches and lovely country roads. The best part? It's never crowded. Except during summer weekends, when there can be as many as two thousand people on the Island. They love living there, and I love visiting, but I like coming home, too."

When there was a lull in the conversation, Matty leaned forward and said, "Now, tell me what it is you would like me to do?"

They both started talking at once, looked at each other and laughed. "You tell her, Greg."

"Mrs. Amoruso..."

"Please call me Matty. 'Mrs. Amoruso' makes me feel as ancient as I am."

"When we first came to Miller's Crossing, Matty," he paused, then continued when Matty gave him a smile, "we were a little concerned when we realized you and Pastor Joe would be staying here in your home. We wondered what it would mean for the church—whether people's loyalties would be divided."

Matty wrapped her hands around her teacup and nodded slowly.

"Your husband set all those fears to rest. He said I was now the pastor of Miller's Crossing Baptist Church, and he would be simply one of my neighbors. He told me in order to make things easier, the two of you would be attending another church."

Matty nodded again, pressing her lips together and blinking back tears.

"Your husband was a wise, generous man, Matty. I knew I had some big shoes to fill. He did everything he could to make it easier."

Matty set her teacup back in its saucer. "He was very fond of you, Pastor. He told me over and over again he was sure you were God's choice for our little church."

"We know how much the church means to you—meant to both of you—and we'd like to invite you to come back. I don't see any reason you shouldn't. We would love to have you there with us."

A tear rolled down her cheek. She picked up her napkin and held it against her eyes. Shep came to her and rested his head on her jeans. Laura came around to Matty's side of the table and put her arm around her shoulders.

Pastor Greg spoke softly. "I didn't mean to upset you, Matty. If you don't think this is the right thing for you to do, we'll understand. We just wanted you to know you are loved and missed."

Matty dried her eyes and wiped her nose with the crumpled napkin. "I'm sorry." She smiled up at Laura. "Lately I can't seem to stop the tears. It's true. I've missed the church—the people. I didn't know what I was going to do about church. I wasn't sure I would go at all. I've been struggling..."

Laura gave her shoulder a gentle squeeze. "Whenever you're ready, we would love to have you come back."

Pastor Greg stood up and walked around the table. Placing his hand over Matty's, he began to pray. She closed her eyes and felt at peace.

~ CHAPTER 6 ~

Matty had just put the last teacup into the dishwasher and was closing the door when Willa-Mae charged into the kitchen.

"I could hardly wait for them to leave. I—" she looked down just in time to avoid stepping on the big dog, who, startled by the sudden intrusion, began to bark furiously.

"What in tarnation? Where did that critter come from? Call him off before he takes off my leg!"

She grabbed hold of the kitchen chair and put it between herself and the critter. Matty reached down and grabbed Shep by his collar. Willa-Mae continued to yell, and the barking got louder. Matty had to shout to make herself heard over Willa-Mae's exclamations of "blood-thirsty mongrel" and "savage monster."

"It's all right, Willa-Mae. He won't hurt you. Hush, Shep. Hush." She managed to get him into the pantry and out the back door while Willa-Mae called him a crazy varmint. Saying a silent prayer that he wouldn't wander off, she returned to the kitchen where Willa-Mae had taken a seat at the table and was smoothing her skirt and picking off dog hairs.

"Don't tell me that mangy critter belongs to you."

"He does. Someone abandoned him, and I've taken him in. He's a sweet, gentle dog."

"Coulda fooled me."

"Oh, Willa-Mae, you frightened him. I'm sure the two of you will get along just fine. Now tell me what's wrong. You burst in here as though someone was chasing you."

"I saw Pastor Greg's car in driveway when I was comin' home from the Post Office. What was he doin' here? Is he tryin' to get you to take his side in this thing?"

Matty just stared at her.

"You know. The music thing and the other stuff. I didn't bring it up the other night. It was too soon to bother you with such nonsense. Besides, I knew Jason would kill me if I did."

"Willa-Mae, I don't know what you're talking about. Pastor Greg and his wife very kindly came to see how I was and to invite me back to church."

"I knew it! They're tryin' to get you on their side."

Matty sighed and sat down across from Willa-Mae. "I have no idea what you're talking about."

"Well, they're probably just bidin' their time. They'll start workin' on you the minute you come back to church. You mark my words."

"Why don't you tell me what's going on?"

"It started a few weeks ago. You know his wife plays the piano."

Matty nodded.

"Well, in the mornin' service he decided to teach us a chorus she had written. It sounded like some rock song, Matty. And the words—same couple of lines over and over again. It went over like a lead balloon."

"So, no one liked it?"

"Well, to be honest, some of the younger folks seemed to think it was okay. And of course the kids liked it, but that's to be expected. It just wasn't right for church. It was all I could do to keep quiet."

Matty tried her best not to smile.

If Willa-Mae noticed, she chose to ignore it. "And as if that wasn't bad enough—he showed up at the evenin' service in jeans and a sport shirt. I couldn't believe my eyes. Then, instead of the usual hymn singin', he whips out his guitar and starts with that chorus again. His wife sat in the front row...clappin'. I ask you—clappin'? You'd a thought it was a rock concert or somethin'."

Matty started to ask how the rest of the service had gone, but Willa-Mae was in full cry.

"A few started clappin' along with her and tryin' to sing the words—which wasn't all that hard since there sure weren't many of 'em. I thought he'd quit after that and go back to singin' hymns like we always do—but not him. No, sir. He starts in with another one of those choruses. I had a good mind to get up and leave."

"Oh dear. What did you do, Willa-Mae?"

"Nothin'! I sometimes think Jason has ESP. I was just

thinkin' about gettin' up, and he grabbed ahold of my arm and wouldn't let me move. I think most everybody would have left, but we're all too dern polite."

"I'm sure he just wants to introduce some new things. Contemporary worship music is very popular now..."

"We don't need popular. What's wrong with the hymns? We didn't hire him to come here and make changes. We like it the way it was."

Matty sat silently praying for wisdom. *What I really need,* she thought, *is the courage to tell Willa-Mae to stop being so critical and give that poor man a chance. Why is it I'm always so afraid of offending people?* She heard Shep whimpering to come inside and gratefully got up to let him in.

"Excuse me a minute, Willa-Mae. The dog wants in. It really is awfully cold outside today."

"I've got to get on home, honey. I shouldn't have bothered you with all this. It's just too soon. Don't you worry about it. I'm on it."

Willa-Mae straightened her skirt, gave Matty a quick hug and marched out the door.

✤

Willa-Mae's visit had upset Matty more than she cared to admit. Her to-do list sat on the kitchen counter, but the morning's events had left her emotionally and physically drained. She climbed the stairs to her bedroom, gathered up Joe's sweater and carried it into the study. Seated with Joe's sweater cradled in her lap, she stared into space, twisting a loose piece of yarn around her finger.

Thoughts of late-night talks, when Joe seemed to open up about the things pressing on his heart, filled her mind. She could hear his voice, feel his hand reach out to grab hold of hers as they lay in the dark, moonlight painting shadows across the patchwork quilt.

On one such night, he drew her close and told her how discouraged he felt. He had been concerned about a sense of complacency in the small church. Attendance at Wednesday night prayer meeting had been reduced to the same faithful few. On visitation nights he was thankful if two or three people showed up. More often than not, Jason was his only companion as he went to visit families who were in need of help or to invite folks out to church.

The people who had labored faithfully for years were still the ones who bore the burden. And most painful of all, some of the younger families had begun to leave, preferring a bigger church that offered more activities and a more "modern" service.

Any changes he proposed were met with stiff opposition from those who had been members since the beginning of time.

He brought in vibrant speakers for revival meetings, and for several weeks after, folks seemed to be energized. But inevitably they slipped right back into the old routine.

"I think he was just worn out," she said aloud. Shep lifted his head from his paws at the sound of her voice. "He never said so, but I think it's the reason he retired when he did. He must have felt it was time for someone else to pick up the mantle."

She thought back to last night and that moment when the moonlight shone through the clouds; this time there was only the darkness blotting out the light. Recalling her conversation with the Schmidts, she knew the peace she thought she had found was gone.

"Where were You, Lord? He wore his heart out serving You. And now this trouble for Pastor Greg. Are You there? Are You real?"

Never in all her life had she doubted God. Now everything she had believed seemed somehow suspect. Never had she felt so lost. She lay down on the couch and slept the rest of the day away.

✣

In spite of the chilly temperatures, the air held the promise of warmer days to come. The daffodils she and Jenny had planted years ago danced in the April breeze. The maple trees showed off their tiny green leaves, and the lilacs were heavy with buds. Before long she would have to cut the grass.

A few weeks passed since her visit with the Schmidts, and Matty still had not gone to church. Every Saturday evening she promised herself she would go, but when the morning arrived she simply couldn't do it. Everyone had been understanding. Even Willa-Mae seemed to be giving her time—with forceful encouragement from Jason, no doubt.

Matty spent her days taking long walks with Shep and organizing Joe's papers. The little notebook lay untouched under Joe's sweater. She hadn't pursued it further since her phone call to Pastor Reed. When that hadn't proven fruitful, she had left it at that, not having the energy for anything more.

Once the papers were sorted, she began going through the boxes of pictures stored on the top shelf of the closet. She sat for hours, reliving the years—the precious moments of life with Joe. A big box was now ready to mail to Jenny—filled to the brim with pictures and mementos from her childhood. They talked every day—Jenny always urging her to come.

This Sunday morning was so beautiful Matty couldn't bear the thought of staying indoors. She packed a little lunch, got Shep in the car and took off in the opposite direction of the century-old white church. She had waited until after eleven to leave, not wanting to run the risk of seeing anyone from church.

"Not that we're doing anything wrong," she informed her happy companion. "It's just that this old people-pleaser can't bear the thought of anyone thinking ill of me." She smiled at his image in the rear-view mirror.

She rolled down the windows and breathed in the fresh, clean air. The trees were a haze of fresh green, and wildflowers grew in abundance on the sides of the road. Newly plowed fields lay waiting to receive the tiny seeds that held the promise of new life. Behind it all a bright blue sky formed the perfect backdrop.

Matty hadn't planned to stop, but when she came to the cemetery, she slowed the big car and turned in the gated driveway. She hadn't come since the day of the funeral.

She clipped the leash onto Shep's collar and walked the short distance to the edge of the cemetery. The new headstone looked stark under the huge branches of the towering oak. She stood reading the inscription etched into the stone—hardly remembering choosing the words. It had all been like an awful dream.

"Well done, thou good and faithful servant."

Just those words and, underneath, his name and the dates. Her legs felt like they were about to give out from under her. She dropped to the cold ground and rested her head against the smooth stone—her big dog leaning against her.

She shivered and got to her feet. Pulling a tissue out of her pocket, she walked to the little bench someone had placed not far from the gravesite and sat for a long time without moving.

"I'm sorry I didn't come sooner, Joe. I'll bring flowers next time—lilacs. I know you love the way they smell."

Shep had walked as far as his leash would allow. As she watched him explore this unfamiliar territory, a cloud passed in front of the sun and cast a deep shadow over them. Matty felt the darkness settle around her heart.

"God, please help me." The wind began to pick up a little, and she shivered in her thin jacket. Hugging herself in an effort to keep warm, she started to get up. Then, a voice. It wasn't audible, yet it came to her as clearly as if someone had spoken out loud.

"I have never left you, Matty."

She looked around to see if there was anyone there, knowing all the while she was alone. Listening intently, she willed the voice to speak again, but her heart hammered in her ears drowning out any other sound.

She waited. There was only the sound of the wind in the trees.

"I know, Lord," she spoke into the stillness, "but I feel as though You have." Then questions tumbled out. "If You are good, why do You allow suffering? Why didn't You answer my prayer? Are You real, or is it all just an illusion?"

Her words sounded harsh and strident in her own ears. How dare she speak to God in that way! Yet, she wanted to know. After doubting, she craved answers.

Desperate and straining to hear, a gentle whisper brushed against her heart.

"Will You leave Me, Matty?"

The words pierced her soul, and in the piercing came the answer.

"Where would I go, Lord? Who have I in heaven but You?"

The words, memorized from scripture long ago, came from somewhere deep inside. She knew they were true. Apart from Him, there was nothing—no hope, no joy, no purpose, no life. Apart from Him there was only loss and despair.

With doubts still clinging to the edge of her soul, she got

up and began walking. Yes, they were still there, but something had been settled. She was making her way back.

~ CHAPTER 7 ~

Monday was her day for grocery shopping and getting caught up on laundry. It was the one routine she had maintained. With Joe gone, the whole pattern of her life had changed. He had been at the very center of everything. Even when they were apart, their relationship anchored her. She felt adrift, unable to find her place.

It had started out sunny, but by late afternoon the clouds began to roll in. After supper Matty took the leash from the hook by the back door and called to Shep.

"Come on, boy. You've been cooped up all day. Let's go for a walk and get you some exercise before it starts pouring. We don't want you to get fat and lazy."

She scratched his head, his floppy ear soft against her hand as she clipped the leash to his collar. This happy dog barely resembled the emaciated, mangy-looking dog who had crawled into her life a little over a month ago. He had filled out and, unless she was mistaken, had even grown a little. Jess had figured correctly. He wasn't much more than a big, overgrown puppy. They set off at a quick pace down their country lane.

Just before they reached the corner, Shep trotted to the side of the road to make a pit stop. Just a few feet away, Matty spotted the path Karen Campbell had taken the day she was murdered. She glanced up at the dark clouds and made an uncharacteristically bold decision.

"Come on, boy. I think we have just enough time to explore this path, but we'll have to hurry."

She tugged his leash and set off. Delighted with the new adventure, he shot past her—she had to jog to keep up with him. Light barely penetrated these dense woods. It was easy to imagine the chill Karen must have felt when she realized someone had followed her onto the path.

They came to the spot where the old stone wall bordered the path. She called to Shep to stop. "I think this is where it happened," she whispered. He came over to her, and they stood still for a moment.

The wind picked up, and the branches dipped and swayed over their heads. It reminded her of waves rushing to shore. Underneath the swooshing sound, she thought she heard a noise and turned quickly to look behind her. Shep barked. Had he heard it too? She didn't see anything but couldn't shake the feeling that they weren't alone.

"Let's get out of here, buddy." She walked as fast as she could, glancing back over her shoulder every now and then. She felt such relief when they came to the place where the path diverged. They took the one on the right—the one that came out by the old Taylor farm. The rain began just as they turned into their driveway. Matty quickened her pace, and Shep, full of energy even after their long walk, began running. She was out of breath by the time they reached the shelter of the downstairs entrance.

As she unclipped his leash, her furry friend shook himself from head to tail, soaking her already damp clothes. She brushed herself off and stepped into the little vestibule. Shep trotted into the family room, circled his blanket and lay down in front of the empty fireplace.

"It's almost cold enough for a fire, isn't it, boy? Tell you what. Let me go upstairs and get the rest of those old letters I need to sort through. When I come down, we'll have a little fire. There's dry firewood out in the shed, I think."

He looked as though he approved the plan, put his head on his paws and fell asleep.

The box of old letters was in the closet in the study. Now that all of Joe's things had been taken care of, Matty had decided to organize the rest of the study. She got the box down from the shelf and was leaving the room when she stopped. Walking the path and standing on the spot where that poor girl had been murdered had shaken her. *It's time. I need to look at the notebook again.*

She retrieved it from its usual spot on Joe's pillow. Placing it on top of the box, she made her way downstairs.

The previous owners had turned the basement level into a small apartment when painful knees made climbing the stairs to the second-floor bedrooms a challenge. What had been their living room became the family room. Joe had lined the walls around the fireplace with bookshelves and placed a TV in the corner. Matty had him put the piano in the little alcove under the stairs, and they installed a used refrigerator and stove in the kitchen. Art and Anna gave them their old washer and dryer when they upgraded to new ones. When the house filled with company, the extra kitchen and laundry room came in handy.

Matty moved deftly through the spaces, balancing the box and notebook all the way. She set them on Joe's chair before heading into the woodshed to retrieve some firewood.

The woodshed was just off the downstairs kitchen. It had two entrances an old wooden door on the outside and another inside, right beside the old refrigerator. When the freezing winds of winter were howling around the house, the second door made it easy to reach the wood without having to go outside.

Stepping cautiously into the little shed, she turned on the light and grabbed an armful of firewood. Less than half of what Joe had chopped last year remained. She would have to think about getting in a supply before next winter.

She barely stifled a scream when something brushed against the back of her legs. She spun around, dropping the load of wood in the process. There stood Shep, looking up at her, his tail fanning the air, ready to explore the woodshed.

"You scared me to death, you silly dog." He jumped up and licked her chin.

"Oh stop, you big lug." She picked up the wood and shooed

him back into the kitchen.

Joe had been the one to build the fires—carefully constructing the wood to burn down evenly. She stacked the kindling on rolled-up newspapers the way she had seen him do it then added the bigger logs. Wiping her hands on her jeans, she got to her feet and set a match to the paper. The flame caught and the kindling began to burn.

"There. Not bad for a beginner."

No sooner were the words out of her mouth when smoke began pouring out of the fireplace, filling the room. Shep barked at the fireplace.

"The damper!" She smacked her head. "Matty Amoruso, you are such a dummy!" She raced to the kitchen and grabbed an old towel. Running back to the fireplace, she wrapped the towel around her hand and pushed the lever to open the damper. It immediately began to draw the smoke up and out through the chimney.

Eyes streaming, she rushed to open the windows, then raced upstairs and closed the door to the first floor—Shep right on her heels the whole time. Outside the rain fell in sheets and cold, damp air seeped into the house.

Collapsing into the sagging armchair, Matty put her head in her hands. She fought back tears. Smiling weakly, she shifted her gaze upward.

"All right, Lord. You see what a mess I've made of this. You're going to have to help me. There are so many things I took for granted when Joe was alive. The least of them was building a fire in the fireplace, and I can't even do that right."

When the smoke dissipated, she got up and began closing the windows. The fire crackled, warming the room. Darkness pressed against the windows, but it was cozy inside.

"Well, I did get the damper opened, and that's a pretty nice fire, if I say so myself. Not so bad after all, Matty, old girl."

Shep resettled himself on his blanket and let out a contented sigh. Matty picked up the notebook and sank into Joe's chair. It swallowed up her small frame. Joe had always laughed when he saw her like that.

"You look like a little girl sitting in a big people's chair, Sweetheart."

He liked to tease her about her height. Even in heels she barely reached his shoulder. But the words he whispered when they made love assured her he loved her exactly the way she was.

Instead of trying to push the memory away, this time she let it wash over her. She closed her eyes and remembered the way it felt to be wrapped in his arms. He was a big man, standing over six feet by nearly four inches. And gentle. Matty often thought if she could actually feel the arms of God around her, it would feel something like his embrace, combining love and security and an understanding that he would give his very life for her. This time, no tears—just a deep sense of gratitude.

She picked up the little notebook and began to read, slowly this time, trying to put herself in Joe's place. Conjuring up images from television and movies, she pictured the visitor's room at the prison with a small table that separated the prisoner from family members or friends. She imagined the cacophony of voices, the atmosphere charged with emotion—or maybe they sat facing each other separated by glass, speaking into telephone receivers, trying to somehow connect.

In her mind's eye she saw Joe lean in, listening intently to the words of a man who had long since given up hope. How long had it been since anyone had looked at him in such a way, with respect and compassion?

He began to take form as she read:

"Billy is a slow, quiet man—slow in his actions and his thoughts. It takes him time to process what he wants to say, but there is an innate wisdom I can't quite explain. He is not intelligent by the world's standards. Yet I think Billy has an understanding of life that goes beyond that. His world is a simple one. He may not be able to articulate a philosophy of life, but he lives by a moral code that is at once both simple and profound. I cannot believe such a man capable of murder."

A log burned through and softly fell, scattering tiny sparks on the hearth. Matty got up and rearranged the remaining wood with the old poker. She stood transfixed by the dancing flames, remembering a conversation she had had with Nancy.

She and Joe had already been in Miller's Crossing for a few months. They heard about the murder from several people, but Nancy was the first one to make the people involved come to life for her.

Sitting in the now familiar kitchen, Matty had asked about Karen Campbell and Billy Taylor. "Nancy, I hope you don't mind my asking you a question about the Karen Campbell murder."

"No, Matty, I don't mind—although I'm sure by now you've heard it all. It was the biggest thing to ever happen here in Miller's Crossing."

"I've heard the story, but I don't know much about the people involved. What were the Campbells and Taylors like?"

"Well I'm older than both Karen and Billy, but I know the families fairly well. I think I'd have to say they were both pretty dysfunctional. As far as social standing went, they were worlds apart, but they did have that much in common.

"Beatrice Campbell was an only child. John and Opal Smythe were middle-aged by the time she was born, and they just doted on her. She was rather plain and painfully shy—a brilliant student but very much a loner. I don't think she had a single date the whole time she was in high school.

"Her first year in college she met Charlie Campbell. He was handsome and outgoing and as shallow as they come, but he was smart enough to recognize a good thing when he saw it. He swept poor Beatrice off her feet. She didn't seem capable of seeing what was obvious to everyone else. As far as Charlie was concerned, her only attraction was her money.

"Before the year ended, Beatrice dropped out of college and announced to her distraught parents that she and Charlie were getting married. She was already a few months pregnant. No amount of pleading could get her to change her mind. I'm not certain, but I think they even tried to buy Charlie off.

"So, not wanting to lose both their daughter and their future grandchild, her parents gave their reluctant blessing. Beatrice and Charlie were quietly married, and they moved into the big house with the Smythes. Mr. Smythe found a job in the company offices for Charlie. Karen was born several months later.

"The Smythes were killed in a plane accident when Karen was about two years old. Beatrice inherited the entire fortune, and Charlie gave up all pretense of being a loving husband and conscientious businessman. He began drinking heavily and seeing other women. Beatrice chose to turn a blind eye.

"It wasn't until after the trial that she finally kicked him out of the house. I don't know anything about the terms of the divorce, but she hired the finest attorney in the state.

"When Charlie was gone, Beatrice retreated inside the walls of that lonely house. She rarely has any visitors and almost never goes out. That's not to say her influence isn't felt. I'm sure you're aware of that."

Matty nodded and asked her about Billy Taylor. She recalled the look of sadness that swept across Nancy's face as she sighed and answered:

"Billy was always what we referred to as slow. He struggled to keep up with the other kids his age and got held back a few times. He was big for his age and towered over the other kids in his class. But considering his home life, he didn't do too badly. His mother left when he was just a little guy. She got tired of being his daddy's punching bag. I have a hard time forgiving her for leaving that poor boy behind."

Matty asked about Billy's father. Nancy said, "He didn't ever abuse the boy, as far as anyone knew. He simply ignored him. Billy pretty much had to fend for himself. The neighbors and people at church tried to help, but Zach Taylor was a proud man. He wouldn't accept anything that smacked of charity. Whatever we did for Billy had to be done quietly.

"I was shocked when they arrested him for Karen's murder. He seemed such a good-natured kid, but apparently there was a darker side to him I never saw. Several witnesses at his trial said he could get violently angry when frustrated. The prosecutor theorized he followed Karen when she took the path through the woods. At some point he tried to get close to her, and she rebuffed him. In a fit of anger, he picked up a rock and hit her. He said Billy had a crush on her for years and kept trying to get close to her."

Matty leaned in close. "Where was Billy's father in all of this? Did he stand by his son?"

Nancy shook her head. "He told anyone who would listen that Billy had always been trouble—just like his mother. The only time he showed up at the trial he was so drunk he could hardly stand. After it was all over, he went back to his farm and slowly drank himself to death."

"What happened to the farm? Is it for sale?"

"Beatrice Smythe Campbell owns the farm, Matty. She

foreclosed on it shortly after Zach Taylor died."

At that point they had been interrupted by the children bursting in from outdoors and never discussed it again.

I'll go and talk to her tomorrow, she thought as she closed the notebook. *I have a few more questions, and I'll feel as though I'm letting Joe down if I don't at least try to find out a little more.*

The fire had burned down to ashes. She congratulated herself for remembering to close the damper and made her way upstairs—Shep leading the way.

After a hot bath, she got into bed and plumped up the pillows behind her back. The small lamp on her bedside table glowed softly. Taking her Bible from the shelf, she held it on her lap for long moments, not knowing where to begin.

"I feel a little lost here, Lord. I don't know where to start."

The worn Bible fell open to the Psalms. She read the familiar words:

Praise the Lord! Oh give thanks to the Lord for He is good; for His lovingkindness is everlasting. "Praise and thanks. I give You praise and thanks, Lord," she whispered, "even when my heart is aching."

❖

A weak sun shone from a pale blue sky, and brisk breezes tugged at Matty's sweater as she scaled the steep hill. Feeling a twinge of guilt for leaving Shep at home, she walked toward Nancy's house, promising herself she would get him out for some exercise later in the day. With all of the potential hazards at the farm, their dogs being the least of them, it felt like a wise decision. But she missed his company.

Nancy walked out of the barn just as she reached the gate.

"Matty! Come on in. I've got a fresh pot of coffee on the stove."

There was always a fresh pot of coffee on the stove, it seemed—coffee to match the warm hospitality that drew everyone in.

"I haven't seen you in days. We've been so busy. Buddy will start plowing next week if we don't get another freeze." She poured their coffee and sat across from Matty, smiling. "How have you been?"

"Better. I'm doing better."

"I can see it in your face. You look more...at peace."

"Yes."

They had never felt the need to fill the silence with small talk. Minutes passed before either of them spoke. When Matty broke the silence, Nancy put her cup down and leaned in to listen. Matty's legs trembled as she told her about her time in the cemetery. Nancy reached over and rubbed her arm.

Eventually the conversation turned to more mundane things, so Matty asked the question that had been on her mind since last night. "Nancy, do you remember the day you told me about the Campbells and the Taylors? It was when we first moved here."

"I do. Why?"

"We never finished the conversation. Why did Billy get a life sentence? It didn't sound like premeditated murder, and he was only nineteen years old at the time."

"I believe Beatrice Campbell had a lot to do with that. She has a lot of influence, and she wanted Billy Taylor put away for good. She testified that her groundskeeper found him hanging around the estate a few times and had to run him off. She never doubted Billy's guilt. She believed he had been stalking her daughter for a long time and when Karen resisted his advances, he killed her. Every time he comes up for parole, she goes to the hearing. She's determined to see him 'rot in prison.'"

"Do you have doubts—about Billy's guilt?"

"I don't know. It seemed so out of character to me. I didn't know the people who accused Billy of having a dark side. No one ever even hinted at such a thing before the trial. I just don't know. He was the only one there that afternoon. The witnesses who testified about seeing him are good, honest people. I don't doubt Billy and Karen were together at some point..." Nancy shook her head. "Why the curiosity now, Matty?"

"Oh, I don't know. Joe met Billy on one of his visits to the prison, and I got to wondering about it. That's all."

"Did he say anything about Billy?" Nancy asked.

"No. I just found a note he had written about meeting him. He never mentioned it to me."

Buddy burst into the kitchen. "Hey, babe! Can you give

me a hand out here in the barn?" When he saw Matty, he pulled off his John Deere cap and tossed it onto the couch. Wiping his hands on his jeans, he came to the table and leaned down to give her a hug. "It's good to see you, Matty. You doin' okay?"

"I'm doing well, and it's good to see you, too. I'm going to get out of your hair now so you two can get something done. Thanks for the coffee, Nancy."

She stood, and Buddy put an arm around her shoulder. "We miss him too, honey. He was the very best of men."

Matty leaned into him for a moment. He smelled like fresh air and the farmyard, and she felt comforted. "Yes," she nodded. They walked to the door together, and she promised to visit again soon. When she reached the gate, she looked back. They were standing on the front porch, arms wrapped around each other's waists. She gave them a little wave and closed the gate behind her.

~ CHAPTER 8 ~

Matty woke early Sunday morning. Her jittery stomach refused to settle down. Throwing back the covers, she nearly stepped on her sleeping dog in her haste to get up. *If I don't get moving, I'll change my mind about going to church this morning and go back to bed,* she thought.

"Come on, boy. Time to get going."

Shep watched from the doorway as she straightened the old quilt. "I'll be right with you, pal. I can't stand a messy bed." Joe's sweater lay on his pillow. She held it close for a moment, then set it on the rocking chair in the corner, smoothing it a little. Before leaving the room, she moved the little notebook to her nightstand.

They walked out the back door together. Matty watched as Shep raced to the edge of the woods. She wrapped her bathrobe a little tighter and took a deep breath of the cool, fresh air. The sun was just peeking through the trees, and the birds were singing—a harmonious morning choir. Shivering, she called for Shep to come back inside.

"Time for breakfast." The dog food clattered into the bowl. He dove in before she had time to close the bag. "I'm glad someone's hungry. I don't think I can eat much."

A cup of coffee and a slice of toast were all she could get down. She put her cup and dish into the dishwasher and hurried upstairs to get ready.

"Hmmmm...what shall I wear, Shep? According to Willa-Mae, things are a bit more casual at church these days." She shook her head at her friend's criticism of Pastor Greg. "I hope things have worked themselves out. Nobody's said a word, but I don't imagine they would. After all, I'm the former pastor's wife."

The light wool skirt and matching sweater seemed like a good compromise. She looked at herself in the full-length mirror before going downstairs. She had lost weight, and the skirt hung a little loose. Her face looked thin, making the lines and wrinkles more prominent. She ran her hand through her short curly hair. "I didn't realize how grey I'd gotten," she said to the strange woman in the glass.

Matty picked up her pocketbook and started down the stairs. At the front door, she turned to Shep and caressed his head.

"You won't be able to come with me today, buddy. I won't be too long, and when I come home we'll go for a nice long walk. Promise."

He looked at her with sad eyes and lowered his head.

Even though she had gotten an early start, the church parking lot was nearly full. Heart racing, she grabbed her pocketbook and looked around for her Bible.

I must have left it home. Good grief, Matty. You'd forget your head if it wasn't attached.

She made her way slowly up the familiar steps and through the ancient doors. People were scattered throughout the little sanctuary. Some were already seated, while others were still standing in small groups discussing everything from world news and weather reports to corn prices and plowing techniques.

For a couple of minutes, Matty stood quietly at the back. Then Nancy spotted her, and before she had a chance to be overwhelmed by all the emotions roiling in her heart, she found herself surrounded by friends. She didn't notice until she was already seated with Nancy and Buddy that Willa-Mae and Jason hadn't been among the ones to welcome her back. In fact, now that she had a chance to look around, it looked as though their whole Seniors Sunday School class was missing from the service.

Turning her attention to the front of the church, she watched as Laura Schmidt walked up the steps to the platform. Pastor Greg came next, followed by a young man Matty didn't recognize.

She leaned over to Nancy and whispered, "Who's that?"

"He's our new drummer." Somehow Nancy managed to keep a straight face.

Peering around the person sitting in front of her, Matty took in the keyboard, guitar and drum set. *No wonder Willa-Mae is conspicuously absent,* she thought.

The music began, filling the little sanctuary clear up to the old rafters. Even though Matty wasn't familiar with the song, everyone else was on their feet singing and clapping in time to the music. The words were projected on a screen behind the now vacant choir loft. In place of the choir, a small praise team had joined the musicians on the platform.

Matty felt a bit uncomfortable as she attempted to sing along with the others. She thought she might understand why Willa-Mae was so upset. The music blared through the speakers and the beating of the drum vibrated inside her chest. The final chords hung suspended in the air as Pastor Greg stepped forward.

"We're so glad to see all of you this beautiful spring morning. Turn and greet your neighbors and tell them how glad you are to see them."

Matty found herself surrounded by friends, some stepping across the aisle to give her a hug and welcome her back. There were quite a few unfamiliar faces, and she smiled as they looked her way.

Following another lively song, Laura began to play a slow, haunting melody on the keyboard. She sang softly, a few simple lines taken from scripture. Pastor Greg invited everyone to sing the chorus. They began tentatively, but as they became familiar with the words, the music swelled in a beautiful harmony. Matty stole glances at the people around her. Most stood with eyes closed and heads tilted up toward heaven. Some raised their hands in worship.

"There is the sweet presence of the Lord here with us,"

Pastor Greg whispered softly.

Yes, thought Matty.

As soon as the worship service ended and everyone had taken their seats, Matty heard a slight commotion in the back of the church. She couldn't resist turning to peek. To her dismay, in strolled Willa-Mae, Jason and what looked like the whole Senior Group. They took their places in the back pews, eyes fixed on a spot somewhere over Pastor Greg's head.

He began his sermon, and Matty whispered a prayer—for him, for this church family so dear to Joe's and her own heart, for healing. She tried to concentrate on the words, but her mind kept wandering back to the very first time she had entered this little sanctuary.

After a lengthy interview with the search committee the previous day, Joe would be preaching as a candidate at the morning service. The following week the congregation would vote on whether or not to invite him to be their pastor.

Joe sat on the platform with the Chairman of the Board of Deacons. After settling Jenny in the nursery, Matty self-consciously made her way down the center aisle. She slid into the pew right behind the organ. Willa-Mae sat ramrod straight on the worn seat with her back to the congregation—but she had installed a rearview mirror at eye level to keep track of everything going on behind her.

The ancient organ operated by means of a bellows pumping air into the chamber; however, the pedal on the bellows pump had broken years ago. The cost of a new pump was beyond the means of the little church, so an enterprising trustee came up with an innovative solution. He hooked up a bus heater blower motor to operate the bellows.

Unfortunately, the bus motor didn't have the capacity of the original bellows pump. Willa-Mae had to turn it on well in advance of the first hymn in order to get sufficient air into the chamber. In the quiet of the sanctuary it sounded like an angry swarm of bees.

Matty watched in fascination as Willa-Mae flipped the switch and the motor revved up. The hum made its way up from the depths of the organ and around the hushed sanctuary. A smile tugged at her mouth. Her stomach contracted and her shoulders shook. She tried desperately to stifle what was threatening to erupt into full-blown hysteria. *Why is it,* she thought, *that everything is twice as funny in church?* She lowered her head, her body shaking with suppressed laughter.

Gaining a bit of control, she looked up and to her horror realized that Willa-Mae was looking right at her. Yet, she could see Willa-Mae wasn't the least bit offended. They laughed about it later, and it became a standing joke between them. Whenever they heard a hum of any kind, they looked at each other and giggled like children.

The old organ expired right about the time the arthritis in Willa-Mae's fingers made it too painful for her to play. When a piano was donated to the church, Matty was officially installed as pianist—with Willa-Mae's blessing.

So why is Willa-Mae having such a hard time with all of this?

She was startled back to the present when everyone stood for the final song. The familiar melody of an old hymn filled the sanctuary, and Matty felt both relief and sympathy: relief in the hope that the older crowd would be appeased and sympathy for this earnest young minister. She felt a bit of sympathy for her contemporaries, too. Change isn't easy at any age.

Turning to leave, Matty was once again surrounded by people welcoming her back. With so many new folks, it would be impossible to remember all the names. By the time she reached the back of the church, Willa-Mae and Jason were gone. Disheartened, she made her way to the parking lot.

"Matty! Matty! Wait!" She turned to see Donna Johnson running toward her.

"Oh, Matty. I wanted to catch you before you left. It's so good to have you back." She set down the big basket of art supplies she'd been carrying and tried to catch her breath.

"It's good to see you, Donna."

An old farm tractor rumbled past the church. The farmer tipped his cap to the two women, and they waved back.

"I had nursery duty this morning, so I had to wait for all of the parents to come get their babies. I wanted to invite you to our knitting group."

Matty waited for her to continue.

"I started a little group to make blankets for the folks in the nursing home. I visit them every week. They get cold in that drafty old place and could really use some nice warm blankets."

Matty tried in vain to make eye contact with her. Donna seemed to have such a difficult time looking people in the eye. *She tries so hard to fit in,* Matty thought, *but seems so insecure.* "That sounds nice, Donna. What time do you meet?"

"We get together every other Tuesday evening at around 7. We had a meeting last Tuesday, so we won't meet till the week after next."

"I'll try to make it, Donna. Thank you."

"Oh, that will be great! We meet at my house. Hope to see you there."

She grabbed the basket and walked toward her car then abruptly turned back to face Matty.

"I'm so sorry I didn't come to visit you—you know, when you first got home. Willa-Mae thought it best we wait a while. I wanted to bring you a meal or something, but I just wasn't sure what to do."

"Please don't worry about it, Donna. Willa-Mae was right. I needed some time."

"Well, I just didn't want you to think I didn't care."

Matty gave her a reassuring smile. "I would never think such a thing."

❖

Shep strained at the leash, as Matty tried to keep from tripping over her own feet.

"I think I left you alone too long."

They were trotting past Jason and Willa-Mae's house

when she spotted Jason coming up from the barn.

"Jason!" She waved to get his attention. Pulling hard, she dragged Shep over to the fence just as Jason spotted her.

"Shep taking you for a walk, Matty?"

Matty laughed while she tried to get her energetic friend to sit. "He was cooped up all morning while I was in church. I'm sorry I didn't get to visit with you and Willa-Mae."

Jason thought for a moment before speaking. "I'm sure it was very obvious to you what's going on. I can't seem to reason with her, Matty. She's made up her mind that Pastor Greg is taking the church in the wrong direction."

"Well, I admit the music is different—and loud. But, Jason, it seems most of the congregation likes it. You should have seen them. They were singing from their hearts."

Jason turned to look at the house. Then, putting his hand on Matty's arm, said, "I love that woman to death, but you know how it is when she digs her heels in. I think for now I just need to go along with her. I haven't given up. You pray, hear?"

Matty reached up and patted his cheek. "I have been." Shep pulled at his leash, eager to get moving. "Give Willa-Mae my love."

Oh, I hope I didn't say too much, she thought as she watched Jason walk toward the house.

They walked a long time. Spring was definitely putting on a show. The trees wore a mantle of fresh green, and the lilacs were beginning to bloom. The whole world brimmed with new life, but Matty scarcely noticed. She was preoccupied—

images of a faceless man sitting in a prison cell filled her mind. A man her husband believed was innocent.

What did Joe mean by a "solid lead"? I wonder if he told anyone else about it? Oh, I really don't want to get involved in this, but what if the poor man is truly innocent? He's already spent thirty-six years in prison. It's unthinkable.

"I can't do this," she spoke the words aloud, "but I can't just pretend I don't know. What do you want me to do, Joe?" She already knew the answer.

The minute they walked in the door, she took out the telephone book and looked up the number for the state prison.

~ CHAPTER 9 ~

The huge facility, encompassed by a 3,000-foot wall, appeared on the right as Matty drove down the two-lane highway. The moat on one side of the wall and the forest on the other gave it a sinister appearance. For a minute she was tempted to turn the car around at the next exit and drive home. Her fingers felt like ice.

She signaled the turn into the parking lot and drove past several buses and vans parked outside the visitor's center. She found a spot to park the car, turned off the motor and watched as women and children climbed out of the buses and vans. There were a few older women—mothers, perhaps—but most were younger with little children in tow.

Matty took a deep breath, got out of the car and walked toward the others. She took her place in line behind a young Hispanic woman holding a baby in her arms. A little girl, who looked to be about three, stood next to her. Matty smiled down at her, and she buried her face in her mother's skirt. When the young woman turned to see who was behind her, Matty smiled again and said, "It's a little chilly this morning."

"Yes." Her smile softened the lines of exhaustion. "The sun is barely up. I think it's supposed to get warm later on."

The line moved forward, and they were admitted into the visitor's waiting room. The guard handed each person two forms to fill out. Matty took her forms and sat at a nearby table to fill in her own information on the first form. On the second form she filled in the details about Billy, the prisoner she was visiting that day. Then following the lead of the others, she brought the forms to the guard seated at the desk. He took them and asked to see her I.D.

She found a seat next to the young mother, who glanced up at Matty as the squirming baby began to cry. At the same time, her little girl began begging for something to eat from the table filled with breakfast snacks, coffee and juice.

"Why don't you let me hold the baby while you get your little one something to eat?"

Matty saw the hesitation and hurried to offer assurances. "I don't blame you for being cautious, but I promise to take good care of him. I'll sit right here where you can keep an eye on us in case he needs something."

She gave Matty a grateful smile and placed the baby in her arms. She pulled a bottle out of her huge bag and said, "Oh, thanks. He's just hungry."

The crying stopped as soon as Matty put the bottle to his mouth. He looked up at her with watery brown eyes. Her anxiety lessened as she watched him take big gulps and felt his little hand grab hold of her fingers.

All around her women were talking and laughing. It was nothing like the gloomy, depressing atmosphere she had expected. Many of them had gone into the restroom and changed into dressy clothing they'd brought with them.

"Can I get you something to eat?" They were back—the little girl contentedly munching on a big doughnut.

"Oh, no thanks," said Matty. "I'm not hungry." Both women looked down at the baby, sound asleep in Matty's arms.

Before they could say another word, the guard began calling out the names of the inmates. Matty watched as one by one the women went up to the counter. Her heart resumed its rapid thumping when she heard the name "Billy Taylor."

Handing the baby back to his mother, she walked up to the counter. She took off her shoes, as she had seen the other women do, and placed her keys, watch, jewelry and wallet next to them before walking through the metal detector. Then her hand was stamped with blue iridescent ink. The guard handed her one of the forms she had filled out and pointed her in the direction of the first set of barred doors.

Matty stepped through, and they slammed shut behind her. She had expected to feel nervous but hadn't expected to feel so afraid. She walked through, exited another door as directed and walked briskly across a small courtyard toward another building. Her knees felt weak as she waited for the guard to buzz her in. Finally, she made her way through one more set of bars and into the visiting room.

A guard seated at a desk motioned her over. He took her

form and asked if she planned to leave any money.

"No, I..."

"Have a seat over there." He pointed to a chair at one of the three long tables stretched across the room. They were simple wooden tables with a panel underneath to prevent any intimate contact. No glass separated visitor and prisoner.

It felt good to sit. She pressed her hands against her legs to stop the shaking. *I had no idea about the money,* she thought. *Should I have given him some? How will I know him when they bring him down? Oh, what in the world was I thinking?*

The tables filled with waiting visitors, and one by one the inmates were brought in. The noise level rose as they greeted one another—everyone talking at once. The air became heavy with the scent of perfume and sweaty bodies. Matty watched as couples hugged and exchanged a kiss and children climbed on the tables to reach their daddies.

She saw him standing in the doorway looking around the room with the guard and somehow knew. Their eyes met, and she waved him over to the seat opposite hers.

"You're Billy Taylor?"

He nodded. "I'm Matty Amoruso, Joe's wife. Thank you for agreeing to see me."

The chair seemed much too small for his large frame. His knees banged up against the edge of the table. He didn't say anything—just looked at her with questioning eyes.

From the moment she had first discovered the notebook, Matty had tried to imagine what this moment would be like, meeting this man Joe had come to know. Now that she and Billy sat face-to-face, she didn't know what to say. He looked older than his fifty-five years—his hair almost completely gray, his face lined and worn. His clothes hung loosely, and she wondered if he was ill.

"Joe thought very highly of you, Billy."

"I liked him a lot."

Before she could say another word, he reached across the table and placed his large hand over hers. Her first instinct was to pull back, but she willed herself to sit quietly.

"When Pastor Reed told us Pastor Joe had a heart attack, I felt bad. I'm sorry he died. He was good to me." He spoke quietly. She had to strain to hear.

Matty gently pulled her hand away. "Thank you, Billy. I'm here because I think he would have wanted me to come." She decided to plunge right in. "He talked to you about the murder, didn't he?"

"Yeah, but not just that. He talked about lots of stuff. He cared, you know?"

"You're right. He did care. I believe he wanted to help you."

He shook his head. "There ain't nothin' anyone can do for me."

"Joe thought there was. Do you remember what you told him the last time you saw him?"

"We talked about a bunch of different stuff. Mostly, I guess, he wanted me to try to remember more about the murder."

"And did you? Did you remember something?"

"Why are you askin' about this? I told you there ain't nothin' anyone can do."

She leaned in, so that she wouldn't have to raise her voice to be heard over the din. "Joe mentioned something about a possible lead. Do you know what he meant?"

He sat still for so long she wondered if he had heard her. So many different thoughts raced through her mind: *I shouldn't have brought the murder up so soon. He must think I don't care about him or what he's going through. I didn't even ask how he was doing. Oh, Matty, why can't you ever say the right thing?*

Billy shifted in his seat and then leaned forward a little. "He kept askin' if I remembered seein' anything that day. I told him I thought I remembered seein' someone walkin' over the bridge when I was goin' back home. But I ain't sure if I really do or if I was just tryin' to help Joe."

"Do you know who it might have been?"

"I told you. I ain't even sure I seen anyone." He started to get up, looked over at the guard and sat down hard. He ran his fingers through his hair over and over again. Matty leaned back.

"I understand, Billy." She smiled. "Would you mind telling me what you *do* remember about that afternoon? I'm afraid I don't know the whole story."

Another long pause. He rested his hands on the table and took a deep breath. Then he began:

"I was comin' from the store. I went to get me a Coke.

When I got to the corner by the church, I seen Karen walkin' toward me. I asked her if it would be okay if I walked part way with her. She just sorta shrugged her shoulders, so I thought I could. She didn't talk to me or nothin'—just walked.

"After we crossed the bridge, I said goodbye to her. I had to go to Mr. Martin's farm. I was supposed to help him in the barn. It was gettin' late, and she was in a hurry to get home. She took the shortcut that run behind my daddy's farm. It took her straight to her house.

"When I got to the farm there wasn't no one around. The truck was gone, so I figured he had to go somewhere. I guess I shoulda waited, but I was tired. So I went on home. That's all."

"Did you take the path through the woods?"

"Nah. It's quicker to walk on the road."

"Did anyone see you?"

"There wasn't no one around. It was startin' to get dark. There wasn't even no one drivin' by."

She decided to ask one more time. "Did you see anyone when you got to the corner by the bridge? Try real hard to remember, Billy. I want to help you."

"I'm pretty sure there was someone walkin' across the bridge. It was hard to see, and I was in a hurry to get on home. I just don't see what the point is with all these questions. It ain't gonna change nothin'." He dropped his head into his hands and hunched over the table.

She waited, willing him to remember. He looked up, and

she saw tears fill his eyes.

"I want to thank you, ma'am." The words came slowly. "I know you mean well, just like Joe did. I didn't kill nobody, but it don't help to talk about it. There ain't no way I'm ever gettin' outta this place. Old Mrs. Campbell's gonna make sure of that. It's better to just let it be."

Well, she thought, *I've done all I can.* She looked at him. He was looking at the couple sitting at the next table with such longing and utter hopelessness she had to look away.

She reached out to him, and he turned to face her. "Billy. Please let me help. If there was someone else there that afternoon, it may very well have been the person who murdered Karen Campbell. Can you try to think hard about it? Was there someone there on the bridge?"

He rubbed his large hand over his face and sighed. "Might 'a been. I saw somethin'. It was dusk and I couldn't hardly see. I don't even know if it was a man or a woman."

"Will you try to remember as much as you can? I'm going to see if there's some way I can help you. I'm not sure if I can, but I'm going to try."

She stood to go. He pushed up from his chair and stood towering over her. She felt a little chill of fear, but as she looked up at him, there was something in his eyes that reassured her. She extended her hand. His huge hand closed around it.

The guard was on his way over to the table. Billy nodded and turned away. She watched him shuffle through the door.

Matty opened the door of the waiting room and stepped

out into a perfect spring day. She felt disoriented—trying to reconcile the bright sunshine with the gloom hanging over her, trying to sort through the mix of emotions.

This is what Joe must have felt, she thought. *Pity for a man who has no hope. Anger that no one cared enough to look for the truth. Doubting it all, and yet trusting a gut instinct. Why didn't you write more, Joe? I don't even know where to begin. Is it possible he's innocent, or are we a couple of softhearted fools?*

She climbed into the car and rested her head on the steering wheel. "You always tried to protect me from the hard things, Joe. I'm going to do this for you, but I need you to help me." She smiled at the irony of her own words. "I haven't told another soul—not even Pastor Reed. I think it's the way you would want me to handle it."

She looked up in time to see a guard walking toward her. She rolled down the window and attempted to look composed.

"Are you okay, ma'am?"

"Yes. I'm fine, thanks." Matty gave him what she hoped was a reassuring smile and started the car. He waved her ahead, and she drove carefully out of the parking lot. The massive gray building receded in her rearview mirror as she made the turn onto the highway.

It was early afternoon by the time Matty reached home. She maneuvered the car into the garage and hurried into the house.

Shep greeted her as though she'd been gone for days. She knelt down and caressed his big head. "I'm sorry you were alone for such a long time, pal. Come on, let's go outside."

He bounded out the door and toward his favorite spot near the woods. Matty strolled down toward the old crabapple tree at the far end of property. White blossoms covered the branches, radiant against the brilliant blue of the sky. She stood lost in thoughts of long-ago summer days when she would find Jenny perched among the branches reading a favorite book. A wet nose rubbing against her hand brought her back to the present.

"Hungry? I know I am. Let's go have some lunch. I should weed the flowerbeds. I've been promising myself for days I'd get that done. But I think I'll put it off one more day. I'm just so tired."

~ CHAPTER 10 ~

The next day Matty was on her knees among the tulips and hyacinths when she heard the faint ringing. She got up carefully and then hurried into the house.

"Hello."

"Where were you? I was about to hang up. Are you okay?"

"I'm fine, Willa-Mae. I was outside weeding."

"Oh. Well, I was just callin' to see if you're goin' to the knittin' thing tonight. You didn't come to the last one, and I think it's about time you started gettin' out of the house."

"What time does it start?"

"Seven. I can pick you up."

"No. Why don't you let me drive? I'll pick you up around 6:45."

"It's a deal. I'll see you then."

"Bye, Willa-Mae, and thanks for thinking of me."

"Of course, honey."

Matty walked back outside. She looked around for Shep and found him fast asleep right in the middle of the tulips. "Hey, big guy. Get off my flowers."

Startled, he bounded to his feet and came over to her—tail between his legs, head down. She bent over and rubbed his ears. Immediately his tail began wagging, and he covered her face with doggy kisses.

"Okay, okay. I can never stay mad at you." She tugged her old gardening gloves back on and pulled out the last of the weeds.

"Much better, don't you think?" Shep tilted his head to get a better look at her. His ear flopped over his eye, giving him a rakish look. "It's almost time to get the vegetables planted." She sighed, something she was doing a lot of these days. "I don't know if I'll even bother with a vegetable garden this year, Shep. That was Joe's specialty. He loved working in his garden."

A hot bath helped relieve the stiffness in her knees and back. Supper was a can of soup and a few crackers. *I'm going to have to start eating better,* she thought, *but it's not much fun cooking for one.* Instead of stacking the few dishes in the dishwasher, she washed them by hand. Then she headed upstairs to comb her hair and gather her knitting things.

"Why did I ever agree to this?" she asked the woman reflected in the bathroom mirror. "I'd much rather stay home and curl up with a good book."

Shep looked bereft as he stood watching her slip on a sweater.

"I know. I'm sorry, pal." She stroked his soft fur. "I won't be late."

Willa-Mae was waiting by the gate when she drove up.

"Mercy, that's a big step up. How ya doin' honey?" she slammed the door shut and gave Matty a peck on the cheek.

"I'm fine, just a little sore from all that weeding. I'm getting old, Willa-Mae."

"Aren't we all?"

Matty considered talking to her about the church problem, but decided it would be better left to another time. *I'm just a big, fat chicken,* she thought.

Two cars were parked in the driveway when they arrived at Donna's house.

"Looks like Nancy and Susan are already here." Willa-Mae carefully stepped down from the SUV. "I wonder if Carolyn's comin'. Her mother-in-law hasn't been feelin' well. And Susan is so quiet she may as well not be here. I don't think I've ever heard her say more than two sentences in a row."

Matty gave her a look of disapproval.

"Don't raise your eyebrows at me, Matty Amoruso. You know it's the truth."

Donna came to the door before Matty could reply.

"I saw you pull in. I'm so glad you could make it, Matty."

Nancy got up and hugged both ladies before they made their way into the immaculate living room. Susan, seated in one of the armchairs, looked up and smiled.

"Carolyn won't be coming," said Donna, after they were all seated comfortably. "They took her mother-in-law to the hospital last night. The doctor said it's pneumonia. I brought a hot meal over to their house this afternoon and have called a few others to help until she's out of the hospital."

Susan and Nancy quickly volunteered to help. Willa-Mae looked over at Matty and winked. "Matty and I will bring over a hot meal." Matty smiled, knowing Willa-Mae would insist on taking care of the meal herself.

They pulled out their knitting projects and talked as they worked—careful to avoid any mention of church or music. The time passed quickly.

"Is anyone ready for coffee and pie?" Donna got up from her chair as she spoke.

"I don't know about anybody else, but I am," said Willa-Mae.

Laughing, they set aside their knitting and filed into the dining room. Matty looked around the perfectly decorated room and felt grateful for her own home. It didn't look like anyone lived in this house. Not a single thing out of place. Not one shred of the clutter one expected to find in a home with an active family. She took her seat at the polished table next to Willa-Mae. Nancy poured coffee while Donna went into the kitchen to get the pie.

"I hope you all like rhubarb," she sang out as she set the exquisite pie on the table.

Matty snuck a glance at Willa-Mae who sat up straighter in her chair. "Of course we do," she said a little too loudly.

Susan was the first to compliment Donna. "It's delicious." The others all agreed with varying degrees of enthusiasm.

"I think I'm going to enter it in the baking contest," said Donna. "Phillip says it would win hands down."

"So, Matty," chirped Willa-Mae, "what in the world were you doin' at the state prison?"

Matty nearly choked on her pie. When she could speak, she looked down at her plate and asked, "Who told you that?"

"I saw Bertha in town this afternoon, and she said her husband saw you. He's a maintenance worker over at the prison. So what were you doin' there?"

Matty wanted to throttle her. She couldn't think of a plausible lie, so she tried to tell as little of the truth as possible.

"I went to visit one of the prisoners Joe was counseling."

Nancy gave her a look but didn't say anything. Susan and Donna sat staring at her, forks suspended in midair.

"Well—who was it?" Willa-Mae was not about to let her off the hook that easily.

"Billy Taylor."

"What on earth! Why did you want to go visit him?"

Feeling like a naughty child, Matty snapped back, "Joe thought there might be a chance he didn't murder Karen Campbell. I wanted to talk to him about it. But he didn't have much to say." Her voice dropped as she ran out of steam. The words seem to hang suspended in the air. She wished them unsaid. *Why did I even mention the murder? I'm never going to learn to guard my tongue!*

"Well, what did you expect him to say, Matty? Everyone knows he did it. Imagine goin' to a place like that all by yourself. For the love of—"

"I'm sure there was no danger, Willa-Mae," Nancy came

to her rescue. "Matty was just trying to do something for Joe. Weren't you, Matty?"

"Yes." Tears threatened. "I just wanted to be sure there was nothing to it. It turns out there wasn't, and now I can just put it behind me. I'd appreciate it if we could just keep this between us. Can we talk about something else, please?"

Nancy tried to steer the conversation in another direction, but it had become stiff and strained. Matty excused herself and walked down the hall to the restroom. When she returned, the others were in the kitchen. Only Susan was still seated at the table. She looked at Matty and said, "I think I know why Joe had questions."

Matty looked at her, not understanding what she meant.

"I've never said anything to anyone because we were all convinced Billy Taylor was guilty. But there was something that always bothered me. It's something Karen told me—a secret. We were friends in high school, you know."

Matty nodded and waited.

"Shortly before the murder, she told me one of our teachers was coming on to her."

"One of your teachers?" Matty was shocked. "Did she tell you who it was?"

Susan ducked her head, "I don't want to get anyone into trouble."

"Susan, this could be important. Do you know who it was?"

"Mr. Moran—our math teacher."

"Did she say anything else?" Matty demanded.

Susan squirmed uncomfortably in her seat and looked down the hall that led to the kitchen. "She said he wouldn't leave her alone."

"Did anyone else know about this?"

"I'm not sure," Susan mumbled softly. "Tommy James, maybe."

"Tommy James?"

"Yeah, he was her boyfriend. But I think they broke up right around that time."

Voices drifted down the hall as the others walked toward the dining room.

"I probably shouldn't have said anything."

"It's all right, Susan. It's probably nothing."

~ CHAPTER 11 ~

Matty plumped up her pillow in an attempt to get comfortable. The clock on her night table informed her she'd been tossing and turning for nearly three hours. On the ride home, she had assured Willa-Mae she wouldn't do anything more about Joe's suspicions. As far as Willa-Mae was concerned, Billy Taylor was guilty, and that was the end of it.

But Matty couldn't stop thinking about it. Her conversation with Susan played over and over again in her mind.

Did a silly schoolgirl flirtation get out of hand? Is it possible her teacher followed her after school? Had he waited, knowing she would walk home that way after the meeting at church? Could he have tried to force himself on her and it got out of hand?

In her mind's eye she saw them—the beautiful young girl walking alone through darkening woods, and a shadowy figure stepping out from behind the trees. She envisioned the struggle as his advances were rebuffed—his escalating anger.

Her own heartbeat quickened imagining the girl's mounting fear as he shoved her to the ground.

She willed Karen to fight—to get up and run. Holding her breath, she watched as his hand closed around a rock. He brought it down, crushing her skull.

He couldn't let her get away and tell what he had done, Matty reasoned. It would have cost him his job at the very least. He must have raced down the path, out onto the road and over the bridge to wherever he had hidden his car. Is it possible he was the person Billy Taylor saw crossing the bridge that day?

If it is, what do I do about it? she asked herself. *Should I go to the authorities? I don't have any evidence. What would I say? "A friend told me Karen Campbell's teacher was bothering her"? They would laugh me right out of the police station.*

Well, then, should I tell someone else—ask for help? Somehow I don't think it would be wise. Joe didn't even confide in me. Suppose I talk to Nancy? I think she already suspects I'm up to something. All right—maybe just Nancy. She might know something about the teacher.

"Please help me to do the wise thing, Lord."

The clock flashed 2:48, but Matty didn't notice. She was finally asleep.

❖

The doorbell rang as Matty tossed the last piece of wet

clothing into the dryer. Quickly adding a dryer sheet, she closed the door and hurried downstairs. Stepping outside she looked up to see Laura Schmidt standing on the front porch.

"Laura, I'm down here. I was just putting a load of clothes in the dryer. Come on in."

The younger woman skipped down the steps. "I hope you don't mind my coming over without calling first." She bent down and gave Matty a quick hug. "I took a chance you'd be home."

"I don't mind a bit," said Matty. "Come on in, and I'll make us a cup of tea. Isn't it a beautiful day?"

"It's gorgeous. The weatherman said it's going to get to 75 today."

The two women went inside together. Shep was overjoyed to see company. Perhaps remembering Laura's reluctance, he approached her slowly—tail wagging. She put out a hand and gave him a tentative pat on the head. Taking for approval, he covered the proffered hand with kisses. She drew back, laughing. "He certainly is affectionate."

"Yes, he is. Come on, Shep. Laura doesn't need a bath."

They decided to have their tea outdoors on the flagstone patio.

"This is lovely. Did you do the work yourselves?"

"Joe gets all the credit for this. I'm the idea person. He brings—brought—them to life."

"Well, he did a beautiful job."

For a few minutes they sat quietly. The air was thick with the scent of lilacs. The wind picked up the sound of Willa-

Mae's rooster, causing Shep's ear to perk up.

"Don't even think about it," said Matty. "So, Laura, what brings you here this morning?"

"I was hoping you could help me." She sighed. "Things were so much simpler when I was the assistant pastor's wife. Now that Greg is the pastor, I feel overwhelmed with all of the intangibles nobody warned me about. How did you do it so well, Matty? How were you able to be all things to all people?"

"Oh, Laura, I wasn't; I didn't. Joe was an assistant pastor before we came here, too, and I was every bit as overwhelmed—probably more so. I can't think of anyone less suited to be a pastor's wife than I."

Laura's expression was a mixture of relief and surprise.

"I met Joe when he was in seminary. I was working as church secretary and pianist when he was hired as assistant pastor. I think I fell in love with him the minute he walked into the office. He was so handsome and outgoing."

"Did he feel the same way?" asked Laura.

"He used to tease me by saying it took him awhile, but the truth is it didn't take long," Matty smiled at the memory.

"So did you get married right away? I adore a good love story."

"No. We decided to wait until he finished seminary. My dad had recently passed away, and I had been caring for my mom who was battling cancer. I was twenty-three when we finally got married. We stayed at the church for five more years and then moved here to Miller's Crossing."

"Did your mom come with you?"

"No. She took my Dad's death very hard. The cancer had become very aggressive, and she died shortly after Joe and I were married. I sometimes think she hung on that long to be sure I would be okay."

"So she never saw your daughter."

Matty shook her head, "No. Mom and Dad would have been such wonderful grandparents. I've always felt sad they didn't get the chance, and that Jenny didn't get to have them in her life."

Laura nodded. Neither spoke for a moment. They sat drinking in the beauty all around them. The flower garden was a riot of color set against the deep green of the grass. The woods were lush with new growth, and in the distance, the mountains rose tall and majestic.

Laura broke the silence. "So, when you came to Miller's Crossing, you said you felt inadequate, Matty. What do you mean? Everyone in the church speaks so highly of you. They love you."

"They are a kind, loving group of people—and very understanding. I'm such an introvert, Laura. When Joe asked me to marry him, I told him I was afraid I couldn't be the wife he needed. I'm so much better at following. I dread having to be the leader. I'd rather eat dirt than speak in front of a group of women or lead a Bible study. And as far as dealing with problems within the church, I'm the kind of person who avoids confrontation at all costs. The only place I was comfortable was behind a piano. A pretty poor resume for a pastor's wife."

"What did Joe say?"

"He said I was exactly the wife he needed." Matty paused trying to hold back the tears. "He said he would never ask me to do anything I didn't feel the Lord calling me to do."

Laura smiled tenderly. "He was a wise man."

"Yes. I found I could do things I would never have dreamed possible. I haven't done much speaking, but I've managed to lead a Bible study or two. And I continued with piano, of course, although I haven't touched it in months now."

"What about the confrontation part—when there were issues in the church that had to be dealt with? Did you learn to do that, as well?"

"It was the one thing Joe never asked me to do. On occasion I would sit in the office if he had a meeting, but only if it was a woman by herself. He always wanted someone else in the room with him."

Laura took a deep breath. "I think you must know where this is going."

Matty nodded.

"This business over the worship service is becoming rather divisive. People are beginning to take sides. At first it was just some of the Senior group, but now several other families have joined them. Surely you've noticed that their ranks are growing."

Matty sighed, "I'm so sorry, Laura. What has Greg said about it?"

"He's heartbroken. He's talked to some of them, but they've taken a stand and don't intend to budge. We've tried to make everyone happy by including a couple of hymns in every service, but they're adamant. They want things to go back to the way they were. On the other hand, most of the congregation have embraced the new music and want it to continue.

"I have so many ideas, Matty, but I'm afraid to even try them. We did a children's musical in our old church. It was amazing to watch those kids. They sang and danced. Can you imagine what would happen if we tried that here?"

"Has Greg thought about preaching a series on worship? I have to admit, Laura, it took a little getting used to for me, too. But I've been camped out in the psalms lately, and I'm getting a whole new perspective on worship."

"He's thought about it, but he's afraid it will just stoke the fires. They may feel he's trying to force his ideas on them. Oh, I don't know—but something has to be done. He's beginning to wonder if we made a mistake coming here. We don't want the church to be divided in this way."

"Would you like me to talk to Willa-Mae?" As soon as the words were out of her mouth she wished she could call them back. *What in the world was I thinking?*

"Oh, Matty. Do you think you could? I didn't tell Greg I was coming to see you. I don't think he would approve, but he hasn't been able to get anywhere with her. I know you said you don't like confrontation, but I believe if we could get Willa-Mae to come around, the others would, too. They all seem to follow her lead. "

"I'll try, Laura. I can't guarantee it will do any good. Once Willa-Mae has made her mind up about something it's nearly impossible to get her to change it. Joe was the only one who could charm her—and only on rare occasions. Even Jason can't get her to budge."

Laura reached over and took Matty's hand in hers. "Let's pray about it. Even Willa-Mae is no match for the Lord."

❖

After Laura left, Matty sat alone on the patio for a long time. An aching loneliness rendered her immobile. She doubled over, clutching her stomach.

From somewhere deep inside a guttural cry forced its way to the surface. She gave herself over to it, crying out her pain. When there were no more tears, when she was totally spent, she sat rocking back and forth. Shep, upset by the force of her emotion, tentatively nudged her knee.

"I'm sorry, pal. I sure am a mess." She caressed the soft fur. "I can't do this." Lifting her face to the sky, she whispered, "I can't do this, Lord. I don't want to live this way. Please take me home."

She got up and wearily walked into the house.

She thought of the notebook. She could call Nancy to talk about the teacher, and then she paused, closing her eyes, remembering her promise to talk to Willa-Mae. *Why did I ever agree to do it? And why did I ever start this thing with*

Billy Taylor? What in the world am I supposed to do?

Weighed down by emotion, she trudged up the stairs to the study. Turning her back on the phone, she headed for the couch. Joe's sweater was in the bedroom—she craved its comfort, wanting to feel the soft knit against her cheek, but she didn't have the strength to get it. She cradled her head on her arm and slept.

~ CHAPTER 12 ~

The low rumble of distant thunder wakened her. The curtains rose and fell as the wind gusted through the open windows. She sat up, trying to summon enough energy to get up and close them before it started pouring. Almost before she could form the thought, rain began to fall in torrents. Suddenly energized, she raced around the room, then downstairs to shut the other windows.

By the time she reached the family room, the floor under the windows was soaking wet. She grabbed a couple of towels and knelt to wipe up the mess. Lightning flashed, followed by an ear-shattering clap of thunder. Getting to her feet, she looked around for Shep.

"Shep? Shep, where are you?" Surely she hadn't left him outside? She ran up the stairs faster than she would have believed possible and ran to the back door. The rain coming down in sheets, driven hard by the wind. It was impossible to see more than a blurry outline. "I'm going to have to go look for him, but I'll have to get my raincoat and boots on first. There's no telling where the poor thing is hiding out."

Back down the stairs and into the cellar, she flipped the switch, infusing the dark room with light. It took a few seconds for her eyes to adjust. She hastily searched the room for her boots when a movement by Joe's workbench caught her eye. Matty let out a little yelp and started to run toward the door. Braving one more look in the direction of the workbench, she stopped short.

"Shep! You scared the life out of me. What are you doing there?"

He had backed into the corner as far as he could go, curled into a big furry ball. Another explosion of thunder rocked the ground, and he buried his head in his paws.

Matty went to him. She sat on the hard floor, took his head into her lap and wrapped her body around him. "We're a great pair, aren't we?" she whispered. "Both of us afraid of the storm. Only my storm comes in the form of having to do things I don't think I can possibly do."

She couldn't coax him out of what he considered his safe place, so she sat, her huge dog trembling in her arms, until the storm passed. As she stroked the downy soft fur around his ears over and over, it wasn't lost on her—this mirror image of her own situation. She would have to go through this storm—the loneliness, the pain, the responsibility to do the right thing—but He would be with her.

✤

Matty woke the next morning to a chorus of birdsong. She sat up and groaned, her stiff back reminding her of yesterday's storm. Shep rolled over and looked up at her, his head cocked to one side.

"I'm getting old, Shep." She stretched and swung her legs over the side of the bed. "Come on. I think I'll feel better if I move around. Want to go for a walk?"

He was on his feet in an instant, turning around in excited circles. She grabbed the lamp before his tail knocked it off the table.

"Okay, okay. Calm down. Just let me get dressed, and we'll go."

The sky was awash in color when they stepped outside. Matty stopped and looked, waiting for that magical moment when the sun popped up over the horizon. Shep tugged at the leash, anxious to get moving. "Wait buddy. I need to see this today."

She waited. The color deepened, flooding the horizon. A tiny slip of sun appeared—the sky blazed red and gold. In the blink of an eye it rose—full and pulsing with light. Slowly the colors faded and an ordinary sun hung in a light blue sky.

Matty took a deep breath. Peace settled comfortably in her heart. For now, for this moment, all was well. Her arm nearly came out of its socket as Shep leaped forward, desperate to chase the cat he'd spied ambling across the road.

"Whoa, boy. Willa-Mae's cats are off limits to you. Come on, let's go."

They walked down the road and over the little bridge.

Matty stopped to peer over the rail at the rushing water. The river, swollen from the rain, nearly overflowed its banks. She could have stood there watching for a long time, but Shep wanted to keep moving.

When they reached the corner, she turned left toward the diner. They walked together along the edge of the quiet road. Not another soul was out and about.

Sunlight bounced off the metal roof of the old building. Peeling paint and a few loose boards only succeeded in giving it a bit of character. The calico curtains framing the windows spoke a warm welcome.

"If you're really good, I'll see if Junior will let you in. I'd love a cup of coffee."

Matty opened the door and peeked inside. Fran stood at one of the booths taking orders. Junior manned the grill.

"Hi, Junior."

"Well, if it isn't Miss Matty. How are you, young lady?" He winked and waved the spatula at her.

"Would it be okay if I brought my dog inside? I promise he'll be on his best behavior. I just want to grab a quick cup of coffee."

"Of course it's okay." Fran was rushing over to pull her inside. "You come right on in here. Where's that dog? Oh my, he's a big one. Where'd ya get him?"

Matty bent down and whispered cautionary words in Shep's ear. She wrapped his leash around her hand and led him inside.

"He just showed up on my doorstep and decided to stay."

Matty smiled as she gave Fran a hug. "I didn't expect to see you here, Fran. Has retirement lost its charms?"

Fran chuckled. "Not one bit. Carole wasn't feeling well today, and no one else was available. So here I am. I can still do a fair job of waiting tables when I have to."

Junior gave Matty a quick wink behind his mother's back.

"How are you doing, hon? We haven't seen you here in ages."

"I'm okay, Fran. I'm sorry I haven't come in sooner. I've been busy trying to get things settled." *The truth is,* thought Matty, *I couldn't bear the idea of coming into this place without Joe.*

"Well, I'm glad you came. What can I get you to eat?"

She hadn't intended to eat breakfast, but the aroma of coffee, bacon and freshly baked biscuits was making her stomach rumble. "I didn't plan to stop, Fran. I only have a little bit of change in my pocket."

Junior came out from behind the counter and put an arm around her shoulders. "Your money isn't any good here, sweet thing. You just take a seat, and I'll fix you a breakfast that'll put a little meat on your bones." He looked at the furry face staring up at him and added, "I'll even throw in a little something for your friend here."

Matty sat in the little booth by the back window, the one where she and Joe had shared so many meals. If she closed her eyes, she could see him there—teasing Carole and swapping stories with Junior and the other customers. No one was a stranger to Joe. He had a way of putting people at ease. Matty always admired that, especially because she so often said the wrong thing at the wrong time.

"Here we go, Matty." Fran walked over to the table, balancing a tray in one hand. "Bacon and eggs over medium, home fries and a biscuit. I'll be right back to top off your coffee. Oh, and a little something for...what did you say his name was?"

"Shep."

"For Shep." She set down a plate of sausage and scrambled eggs for the delighted dog.

Matty leaned out into the aisle and called to Junior, "You're going to spoil him."

He waved his spatula a little and called back, "You enjoy—both of you."

Fran came and sat opposite her, a cup of coffee in her hand.

"I think I'll take a little break. Everyone's busy eating right now."

Matty smiled around a mouthful of home fries.

"Oh, boy. I ain't used to being on my feet like this no more, but just between you and me, Matty, I do sometimes miss it. Not the work, mind you. It's the people I miss. And Mike. Oh, I do miss that man."

She looked at Matty and saw her eyes beginning to fill with tears. "Oh, honey. I'm sorry. Here I am going on about myself when your heart is breaking."

Matty reached out to touch Fran's hand. "Please don't apologize, Fran. It's a comfort to talk with someone who understands. You've always been so easy to talk to. Does it ever go away—this loneliness?"

Fran sat quietly for a few moments. "I think it hurts less with time, hon, but you don't ever stop missing them. The good Lord promised to comfort us, and He always keeps His promises. He takes the pain and gives you peace. It just takes a little time."

"There are some days I do feel His peace, Fran, but there are so many more days when I can hardly breathe for the pain."

"I believe that's how it goes, Matty, 'til one day you find the peace is bigger than the pain. When Mike got the cancer, I prayed for a miracle. God didn't see fit to answer that prayer, but..."

"Were you angry at God, Fran?"

"No. I figured He knew what was best. And a lot of good come out of it. Junior came back home in time to patch things up with his Daddy. We had never set eyes on Carole. Mike loved her the minute he saw her. Then when he passed, they said they would stay and help me run the diner. It was like a miracle. That boy swore he would never set foot in this place again. I don't know what I would've done without those two kids. Well, you know the story."

Matty nodded and reached for a napkin to wipe her eyes. Fran put a hand on her arm and reached into her pocket. She handed Matty a small pack of Kleenex and watched her peel open the plastic tab and pull one out. "You never know what customers might need."

Matty pulled out an extra tissue and handed the pack back to Fran. She gave Matty an encouraging smile and winked as she put it back into her apron pocket.

"Excuse me for a minute, Matty. I need to give them fellas a refill."

Matty watched as Fran went from booth to booth with the coffee pot. She stopped long enough to pat a shoulder or exchange a few words.

Fran refilled their cups, then came and sat back down. Looking over her shoulder, she leaned in close and lowered her voice to a whisper, "Whaddaya think of what's going on at church with Willa-Mae and some of the others?"

Oh dear, thought Matty, *here we go.*

"I'm not sure, Fran. I know Pastor Greg's doing his best to meet the needs of everyone."

"Well, I don't think it's right. I know it ain't what we're used to. I can't say I like it all, but it's about time we got outta the rut we was in. Poor Pastor Joe tried so hard to put a little life into the church."

Matty sat still—not knowing what to say—wishing for the millionth time she could be more like Joe.

"Why, we've had more new families coming in the past few months than we've had in years. I don't mean nothing against Pastor Joe, you know that Matty. It wasn't his fault. He did his best, but you just can't change some people."

A couple of farmers walked into the diner and Fran heaved herself out of the booth. "I sure do hope Willa-Mae comes around. I hate to see trouble in church." She trudged off to wait on the newcomers.

Matty sat pushing the last of her breakfast around her plate. Shep looked up at her. He had licked his plate clean.

"Time to get going, boy."

She went to the counter to thank Junior. "That was the best breakfast I've had in...I can't remember when," she said with a smile. "Thanks so much, Junior. You're a terrific chef."

He gave her a little salute with his spatula. "Don't be a stranger, hon."

"I won't."

She gave Fran a quick hug, promising to see her again soon.

When Matty headed outside, she stood on the sidewalk and squinted at the sun. "It's warmed up, Shep." She pulled off her sweater and tied it around her waist. "Come on, pal. Time to go home."

All the way home she mentally rehearsed conversations with Willa-Mae. In every one of them she made a perfectly sensible case for Pastor Greg, which her invisible friend quickly tore to shreds. She dreaded having to face her in real life.

As soon as she walked in the door, she picked up the phone and dialed Willa-Mae's number. "I might as well get this over with," she told Shep. On the fifth ring the answering machine came on. Sighing, she hung up the phone without leaving a message.

"Don't look at me like that." She reached over and rubbed his ears. "I tried. It isn't my fault nobody's home. I'll try again tomorrow."

Matty jumped a little when the phone rang. Praying it wasn't Willa-Mae, she checked Caller ID. "Hi, Nancy."

"Hey, Matty. Feel like a little company? Buddy's gone into town to pick up a part for the tractor, and it's too nice a day to do housework."

"I'd love some company. Come right over."

~ CHAPTER 13 ~

The two friends sat facing each other in the old wicker chairs. Shep slept at their feet. Nancy took a deep breath and smiled.

"If feels good to sit down. We got the hay in last week, and I feel like I've been cooking and washing dishes for ages. Those fellas get mighty hungry."

"Oh, Nancy, you should have called. I would have helped. I feel as though I've been totally selfish for months now—far too self-absorbed. I've got to do better."

Nancy reached over and wrapped her work-worn hand around Matty's. "You take all the time you need, sweetie. You aren't being selfish. You're trying to learn to live again. Besides, it all went really well. We had an abundant harvest. Buddy's hopeful we'll get another cutting. God is good."

Nancy sighed contentedly as she looked around. "Your flower garden is beautiful. You definitely have a green thumb."

They sat without speaking, watching the flowers in Matty's garden gently sway. Yellow primrose and purple lupine mingled with pink peonies. The last of the tulips added a rainbow of colors to the mix. In a shady corner of the garden, Lily of the Valley flourished.

"Well you know I was going for an English Country Garden look. Not sure I've pulled it off, but I do love flowers. Can you smell the lilacs? Everything is so beautiful this year. The bushes around the side of the house were loaded with blooms, but they're fading fast. I hope they'll last just a little longer. I promised Joe I'd bring a bouquet of them next time I visited the cemetery."

"Oh, Matty. I'd do anything to change it. We all miss him so much."

Matty quickly changed the subject. "Nancy, what do you and Buddy think about the problem at church?"

There was no need to explain the "problem." Everyone was well aware of the widening division. "To tell you the truth, Matty, we like what Pastor Greg has done. I understand it's a lot for some folks to take in, but for the most part it has done so much good. For one thing, Buddy's thrilled to death he doesn't have to get all dressed up for church anymore."

"Laura came to see me yesterday. She wants me to try to talk to Willa-Mae. If she comes around, they think most everyone else will follow suit."

Nancy raised her eyebrows.

"I know," Matty said. "I'm dreading it. Jason said she just won't budge on this. She feels very strongly that it's wrong. How am I going to convince her otherwise? You know I'm not good at this sort of thing. Joe was a master. He could get folks to do things they never in a million years thought they'd agree to."

Nancy nodded. "Yes, but even he couldn't get Willa-Mae to budge on what she considered spiritual things. Every time he tried to make a big change, she was there to tell him why it was wrong. Don't you remember the time he had that gospel group come? I thought Willa-Mae would have a fit over the guitars and drums. I felt so bad for those guys. Talk about the church of the living-dead. No one dared even clap along."

Matty laughed in spite of herself. "I do remember. Poor Joe. He certainly got an earful."

"What are you gonna say?"

"I have no idea. I guess I'll appeal to her softer side."

The two women just looked at each other and then laughed until tears rolled down their faces.

"Well, I'd better get my lazy self on home." Nancy began to get up, but Matty put out a restraining hand.

"Wait, Nancy. Before you go there's something I need to ask you. It's about Billy Taylor and Karen Campbell."

Nancy sat down and waited for Matty to explain.

"The other night at Donna's, when you were all in the kitchen, Susan told me she thought she knew why Joe was questioning Billy's guilt."

"What did she say?"

"She said Karen had confided in her that their math teacher was coming on to her—that he wouldn't leave her alone."

Nancy's eyes widened, "The math teacher? Mr. Moran?"

"Yes. Did you know him?"

"He started teaching my senior year of high school. He was fresh out of college."

"Did he seem like the sort of person who would do that?"

Nancy thought for a moment before answering, "Well, truthfully, he did give the girls a bit more attention than the boys. But I never saw anything out of line. Karen was a beautiful girl—very mature for her age. I suppose it's possible. I think he was married by the time Karen would have been in his class."

"Susan said Karen was going with a boy named Tommy James. Did you know him?"

"I know the family. They moved to Petersburg years ago. I don't know whether he's still there or not."

Matty leaned in toward Nancy, "Do you know anyone I can talk to about this? I need to find out if there's any truth to it."

"Matty, what are you getting yourself involved in? This is *murder* we're talking about. You've got to be careful. Why don't you just let sleeping dogs lie?"

Matty smiled, "That makes me think of *Sleeping Murder*, that Agatha Christie book we read last year. Everyone warned Glenda not to try to dig into the past. It's my very favorite."

"This is serious, Matty. You know she nearly got herself killed in that book. If by any chance someone else killed

Karen Campbell, they won't be happy about you snooping around."

"I have to do this—for Joe. And for Billy Taylor. You should have seen him, Nancy. He didn't smile once the whole time I was there. He looks so utterly hopeless and broken. I know I didn't spend much time with him, but Joe thought there was a good chance he wasn't guilty. I came away with the same impression. If he's innocent, how can I just turn my back and pretend I don't know anything? I have to try."

Nancy sat looking into her eyes, then sighed. "Promise me you won't do anything foolish. If you find anything out, you must go to the police."

Matty nodded.

"Mr. Goss was the principal at the time of the murder. In fact, he was principal for as long as I can remember. Of course, he's quite elderly now and retired years ago. Maybe he can help you."

"Of course! I should have thought of him myself. I'm not thinking very clearly lately. He was still principal when Jenny was in school. I was so disappointed he retired right before she started high school."

"We all were. He's one in a million. The kids all knew he wouldn't take any nonsense, but they loved him anyway. He had a special way about him."

"His wife passed away a few years ago, didn't she?"

"Yes. I think she had a massive stroke and died very quickly. His health wasn't good, either. They didn't have any children so he went into the nursing home in Petersburg. He must be in his late eighties by now."

"Do you think he would talk to me?

"He's a kind man. I'm sure he would...as long as he's up to it."

"I wonder," said Matty, "why he wouldn't have said anything during the trial—if it was true about the teacher?"

"You have to remember, Matty, it was an open and shut case as far as the police were concerned. There was no question in anyone's' mind that Billy Taylor crushed Karen Campbell's skull in a fit of rage. Nobody thought otherwise."

"Well, I have to be sure, Nancy. I have to."

"Keep in mind what I said. Be very careful." She got to her feet. "And now I really do have to go."

They walked around the side of the house together, Shep running in circles around them. The smell of lilacs filled the air, and they stopped beside the towering bushes to breathe it in.

"Oh, I nearly forgot. This weekend is Memorial Day. Buddy and I are having a get-together Monday at the farm. Pot-luck and we'll supply the meat and drinks. Can you come?"

Matty hesitated.

"Please come, Matty. It'll do you good. You don't have to stay long if you don't want to."

"I'll see, Nancy. Thank you so much—for everything."

Matty walked her to her car and waved as she drove down the driveway.

"Well, come on, Shep. Let's go inside."

❖

Monday morning Matty stood at the kitchen window watching her frisky dog gallop through the field toward home. The overcast sky cast a pall over everything. She shivered in her thin robe.

Shep, eager for breakfast, made a beeline for the back door. Matty hurried into the pantry to let him in.

"Looks like the weatherman was right this time, fella. I hope the rain will hold off until after Buddy and Nancy's picnic."

She sat at the table cradling a second cup of coffee in her cold hands. *Of course, if it rains,* she thought, *I won't have to worry about going.*

She sighed deeply and looked at Shep. "Finished already?" He sat beside her and looked up into her face. "I know; I have to stop all this sighing. And I really have to stop being such a baby and get myself to that picnic. It doesn't start until three, so I have plenty of time to run to the cemetery before I bake a casserole to take with me."

Thirty minutes later they were in the car, branches of purple and white lilacs heaped on the front seat. It was still early when they arrived. They were all alone except for a young couple walking toward the opposite end of the cemetery. Matty filled a vase she had brought from home with bottled water. She arranged the fragrant flowers in a lavish bouquet and placed it by the headstone.

She had intended to stay a while—to sit and tell Joe about the things pressing on her heart. Seated on the hard bench, she felt chilled right down to her bones. Words wouldn't come, and somehow the idea of talking to him in this place had lost its appeal.

"Come on, boy. Let's go home." A few drops hit the windshield as she pulled out of the long drive and turned onto the main road.

By the time they reached home, the sky had brightened, and the rain had stopped. Matty rushed inside and began working on her casserole. Going through the familiar motions, she felt her spirit lifting. *It'll be good to see everyone,* she told herself.

A little after three o'clock, Matty carried her casserole out to the car. The sky was still overcast, but every now and then a little beam of sunlight broke through the clouds. Cars lined both sides of the road in front of the farm. She drove slowly looking for a spot to park.

A piercing whistle startled her as she drove past the farmhouse. She turned to see Buddy waving his arms in the air and running toward the car.

"Saved you a spot in the driveway, Matty. Back up and pull on in."

Buddy took the casserole from her and led the way to the picnic tables lined up outside the barn. Nancy had covered them with cheerful red-and-white checkered tablecloths. Mason jars filled with apple blossoms stood in the center of each one. The longest table was reserved for the food.

Donna stood behind the table, a checkered apron tied around her slim waist.

"Hi, Matty. So glad you could make it. Just set the casserole down right here, Buddy. Oh—that looks delicious. I brought my lasagna. Everyone seems to really like it. Plus I've been up since dawn baking cookies. I promised the kids I'd bring the ice cream maker, too, so I'll have to get busy with that while you folks are eating all this wonderful food. Oh! There's Phillip. I need him to get the ice cream stuff out of the car." She turned to go and then called over her shoulder, "I hope you're doing okay, Matty."

"I'm fine, Donna."

Buddy gave Matty a mischievous wink. "She makes me tired just listening to her."

Matty placed her casserole between a crock pot filled with beans and a huge bowl of macaroni and cheese. She looked at the dishes piled high with biscuits, the brightly colored bowls of every kind of salad imaginable from potato to fruit, and mouthwatering desserts. She made a mental note to be sure to get some of Carolyn's peach cobbler. The aromatic fragrance of smoked barbeque made her mouth water.

Buddy put his arm around her shoulders. "We won't go hungry! Come on down to the field. The baseball game is just gettin' started."

Together, they walked through the freshly cut grass and down to the field. Everyone greeted her as though they hadn't seen her in years. She felt warmed from the inside out as she took a seat next to Nancy.

She yelled and cheered for both sides and chatted with the women about everything from recipes to world affairs. After the game, they gathered around the food tables and joined hands while Pastor Greg said grace.

Matty got in line and filled her plate with the delicious food. She even went back for seconds on the peach cobbler. There was a moment, as families grouped together around the tables, when she ached to hear Joe's voice and feel his arm around her. This time, instead of trying to push the feeling down, she let it come. She looked around at the people who were like family to her and took her place beside Willa-Mae and Jason.

They had just finished clearing the tables and were getting ready to make s'mores on the big campfire when the wind picked up and the first drops of rain began to fall. It increased steadily, sending everyone scrambling to gather up their dishes and kids and make a mad dash for their vehicles.

Matty was giving Nancy a quick hug when she heard someone calling her name. She turned and saw Susan running toward her. "Would you mind giving me a lift home, Matty? I rode here with Carolyn and Josh, but they had to leave early."

"No, of course not. Climb in. Thank you again, Nancy. I had such a good time."

"I'm so glad you came. Talk to you soon."

It was pouring now, and Nancy ran onto the porch. She turned and waved as Matty backed out of the driveway.

Matty switched on the headlights and windshield wipers

before turning her attention to Susan. "Is Carolyn's mother-in-law all right?"

"Oh, yes. She's in the nursing home in Centerville now. They had to leave because Josh got a call from work. The alarm went off in the building, and he's on call."

They drove in silence for a little while. Matty had a feeling there was something Susan wanted to say. She seemed fidgety. *I wonder if she's thought of something else about the murder?*

The rain let up a little as Matty pulled up in front of Susan's home. The windows of the small house were dark. A light over the front door did little to dispel the darkness. She looked at Susan and felt a twinge of pity for her.

"It's been a little lonely since Mama passed away. I've been thinking about possibly renting out a room or something."

Matty waited for her to continue.

"I've been feeling a little funny about what I told you the other day. I don't want to make any trouble or anything."

"Please don't worry, Susan. As I told you, I'm sure there's nothing to it. Don't give it another thought."

"Well, there was something else that's been bothering me. I'm not sure I should say anything, but..."

Matty leaned toward her. "What is it, Susan?"

"It's about Karen. Everyone says what a sweet, beautiful girl she was, but that isn't quite true."

"What do you mean?"

"I mean she was kind of self-centered, and she used

people. Karen sorta thought she was entitled to special treatment—like she was better than everyone else. I don't really know how to explain it."

"I thought she was popular. Did she treat everyone that way?"

"Oh she was popular, especially with the guys. She was rich and beautiful, and everyone wanted to be her friend. She only used certain people when it suited her purposes."

"Were you one of those people?"

"No...not really. I've always been shy, and the boys weren't exactly crazy about me. I felt lucky to be part of Karen's crowd. We were friends from the time we were little kids. I understood why she acted like that. Her mother really spoiled her, and she was used to getting her own way. "

Matty was having difficulty making sense of it all.

"Was there someone in particular Karen treated badly?"

Susan chewed on her lower lip. "Yeah...Donna."

"Donna Johnson?"

Susan shrugged her shoulders. "She was friends with Karen, too. It was sort of surprising, you know?"

"Why? Was there something wrong with Donna?"

"Not wrong, exactly...but you know...she lived in the trailer park. And her father was a terrible drunk."

Matty brushed at an invisible piece of lint on her jeans and tried not to look shocked.

"She just didn't fit in, Matty. She bought her clothes at the Salvation Army store and tried to fix them up so they'd look new—but it was obvious. Sometimes she smelled like she hadn't had a shower in days. She just wasn't one of us. But she was really, really smart—so I think that's why Karen befriended her."

"What do you mean?"

"I think you know what I mean. Donna would sometimes write a paper for Karen or help her with her homework— stuff like that. I think she knew Karen was using her, but she wanted to be part of our group so bad she didn't care." Susan looked down at her pocketbook and rubbed her hand across the damp surface. "Another thing. Everyone knew Donna had a crush on Karen's boyfriend, Tommy James. When he and Karen broke up, Donna got real chummy with him."

"Why are you telling me this, Susan?"

"I don't know. I just wanted you to know what she was like, I guess. I'd better let you go. It's getting late. Thanks so much for the ride."

Matty watched as Susan ran through the puddles to the small porch. She waited until a light came on in the house before pulling away. *I wonder what that was all about. I haven't heard Susan talk that much in all the time I've known her.*

~ CHAPTER 14 ~

Matty shivered as she walked through the house pulling down blinds to shut out the storm. After a brief run outside, Shep curled up on the rug in front of the empty fireplace. It felt chilly enough for a fire, but the thought of having to clean out all the ashes again made her decide against it.

"I'm just too lazy, Shep." He got up and ambled over to her, leaning his head on her thigh.

"You too, huh? Let's call it a night and go on upstairs. A hot bath, a cup of tea and a good book sound mighty inviting to me."

He turned and began climbing the stairs. Matty watched him go and shook her head. *You'd think he understood every word I said,* she thought. Smiling, she followed her canny dog.

The light from the upstairs answering machine was flashing when she stepped into the bedroom. She pushed the button, and Jenny's voice filled the quiet room.

"Hi, Mom. It's me. Just called to see how you were doing.

Give me a call when you get home."

Matty dialed the familiar number. While she waited for Jenny to pick up, she climbed onto the bed and settled in for a nice long chat.

"Hello."

"Hi, Jenny. I just got home. Is everything all right?"

"Everything's fine, Mom." She hesitated for a moment. "Dad's voice is still on the answering machine."

Matty felt her face flush, "I'm so sorry, Jenny. I'll have to change it."

"No, Mom. Please don't. Don't ever change it. It was so good to hear his voice."

Matty fought back the onrush of emotions. "I won't, honey."

They sat quietly. Matty listened to the rain beating against the bedroom windows. When they were finally able to talk, Jenny filled Matty in on all the family news.

"The kids are on a camping trip with the youth group this weekend. The house is so quiet I can hardly stand it. Pete hired a new deputy. The population on the Island always explodes in the summer, and he finally admitted he can't do it all by himself."

Matty sat back and listened, only able to squeeze in a word here and there. She smiled thinking of all the times she had sat on the end of Jenny's bed while her daughter poured out her heart. She was as thankful then as she was now that they could talk so easily.

"We want you to come for a visit, Mom. When do you

think you can come?"

"Oh, honey, I have so much to do here. I think I'm going to plant a few things in the vegetable garden after all, and I'm helping out with the big Fourth of July celebration at church. Why don't we plan something for September? I'll come just before the kids have to go back to school."

"All right, Mom. I wish we could come to you, but Pete just can't get away in the summer and both of the kids are going to be working. Joey's starting a little lawn business, and Anna has a babysitting job."

"I'm okay. I really am. Shep is great company, and honestly, I'm doing better."

"I love you, Mom."

"Love you, too, honey. Love to Pete and the kids."

"And Mom?"

"Yes?"

"Please think about getting a cell phone. You really ought to have one—especially when you're driving somewhere by yourself."

"I'll think about it. Bye, Jenny."

"Bye, Mom."

Shep watched as she hung up the phone, looking as though he had something to say.

"Okay, okay. I didn't tell her about Billy Taylor. I don't want her to worry."

He continued to stare at her with such intensity she felt uncomfortable.

"I promise to talk to Pete if I think there's really anything to all of this. So stop looking at me like that."

He came over to her, and she stroked his head.

❖

The weatherman promised the clouds would break up by mid-morning and the day would be clear and sunny. Matty turned off the radio and pulled the phone book out of the kitchen drawer. She had been making excuses for a couple of weeks, but it was time to get this done.

She punched in the number and to her surprise a real person answered the phone. Evidently the Shady Oaks Nursing Home hadn't quite made it into the 21st century. The courteous receptionist said it would be perfectly fine to come and visit Mr. Goss. He got very few visitors, poor man.

She drove with the windows rolled down. The weatherman had been right—it was a perfect June morning. She popped her favorite CD into the player. Strains of Mozart's Symphony No. 40 filled the air. A lavish bouquet of lilacs rested on the passenger seat.

Forty-five minutes later, Matty turned into the entrance. Towering oaks bordered the long drive, their branches forming a canopy overhead. She wondered what it must have been like to draw up to this mansion in a chauffeured limousine and mount the steps to the graceful porch. In her mind's eye she saw the magnificent chandelier in the front hall and the butler waiting to take hats and shawls from the arriving guests.

She drove around the circular drive that ran in front of the house and found a space in the parking area. The wind carried a fine mist from the fountain in the center of the drive, showering her lightly as she walked toward the building.

Before climbing the steps, Matty stopped to admire the flower garden. It looked like the English Country gardens she had seen in magazines—a riot of color and blooms all jostling one another for space. She breathed in the rich perfume and sighed. "Absolutely beautiful."

"It is. Isn't it?"

Startled, Matty looked up to see a middle-aged woman standing at the top of the steps.

"Are you here to visit someone?"

"Yes. I called earlier. My name is Matty Amoruso. I'm here to see Mr. Goss." Matty climbed the steps as she spoke.

The woman extended her hand. "Doris Anderson. I'm the administrator here at Shady Oaks. Is Mr. Goss expecting you?"

"No...at least I don't think so." Matty felt distinctly frumpy next to this beautifully tailored woman.

"Are you family?"

"No. Just a friend. That is, I knew him when he was the principal at Centerville High School. We live in Miller's Crossing, but all of our town's kids were bussed to school in Centerville."

"I see. Well, I'm sure he'll be glad to see you, Mrs. Amoruso. He rarely, if ever, has visitors. No family, you see, and his wife passed away years ago."

"How is he doing?"

"His health is declining a bit, but he's quite lucid. I think you'll find him good company."

She led the way through the massive front doors and into the entrance hall. An ornate desk stood at the end of the hall; otherwise it looked very much as it must have looked when it was a residence. Long hallways branched off in either direction. Matty followed the straight back of the administrator down the hallway to the left.

There were rooms on either side of the wide, carpeted hallway. Most were empty, and Matty tried to peek inside. Here, the similarity to the old days ended. With the exception of the beautiful old windows, high ceilings, and decorative crown molding, the rooms looked like those she had seen in other nursing homes. The furnishings consisted of a single bed, small bedside table, dresser and upholstered armchair. Some were filled with treasures too precious to leave behind, others nearly devoid of any personal touches.

"Most of the residents are watching a movie in the family room right now. Mr. Goss doesn't like movies." She smiled thinly.

They stopped at the last door. Ms. Anderson tapped lightly before going in.

The corner room appeared to be a little larger than the others. Sunlight poured in through the two large windows. Mr. Goss had pulled his wheelchair up to the one overlooking the flower garden and sat looking out.

"Mr. Goss, we have a visitor. Mrs. Amoruso has come to see you. Isn't that lovely?" She spoke in a sing-song voice and Matty cringed inwardly. *I thought you said he was "quite lucid," you silly woman.*

He continued to gaze out the window.

She turned abruptly and gave Matty a knowing look. "Sometimes we just aren't in the mood for chit chat. I'll leave you two alone. Enjoy your visit."

Matty stood just inside the room, not quite knowing what to do.

"I'm sure you don't remember me, Mr. Goss, but you were the principal in Centerville when my daughter was little. I'm afraid we didn't get to know you because you retired just before she started high school."

He didn't move or even twitch.

"If you don't feel up to company today, I'll just leave these here for you and go on home. Perhaps I can come another day...when you're feeling better." She placed the bouquet on the table by his bed and turned to go.

"Please don't go, Mrs. Amoruso."

She stopped and turned to face him.

"I don't mean to be rude. It's just that sometimes that woman irritates the daylights out of me."

Matty raised her eyebrows and looked at him. He smiled, and she gave him a conspiratorial wink.

"Are those for me?" He pointed at the lilacs. "They're beautiful."

"Yes. I picked them this morning. If I can find a vase, I'll put them in water for you."

"You'll find one in the closet. There's a rather fidgety woman who comes here to do good deeds once a week, and occasionally she brings flowers."

Matty filled the vase at the tiny bathroom sink. She arranged the flowers and placed the vase on the table.

"Would you mind bringing them here so I can smell them?"

She walked over to him and held the vase out in front of her. He took a deep breath and smiled. "I used to have a lovely rose garden. After I retired, I spent many happy hours tending my roses. They were my wife's favorite flower."

He ran his hand through what little hair he had left and motioned for Matty to sit in the armchair. He turned his wheelchair toward her and smiled, revealing a matching set of dimples.

Matty looked at his gentle features. The years had etched deep grooves along his forehead. Fine lines crisscrossed his cheeks. Only his eyes remained untouched by time. Keen intelligence peered out from behind the clouded pupils. She felt drawn to him, as though she had known him for a very long time.

"Now what can I do for you, young lady? I have a feeling you haven't come here to do good deeds."

Matty felt a familiar wave of guilt sweep over her. Why didn't she come to do "good deeds"? She had gotten so busy with her own plans and pet projects, she had never given a thought to the lonely lives hidden in plain sight.

"I'm sorry, my dear. I didn't mean that the way it sounded. It's just we don't get many visitors dropping in to say hello."

A wistful smile played at the corners of her mouth, and she reached out to touch his arm. "You're right. I did come to ask you something."

He leaned back and adjusted the nine-patch quilt on his lap. When he didn't say anything, Matty plunged ahead. "My husband was the pastor of Miller's Crossing Baptist Church. He passed away several months ago..."

"I'm so sorry to hear that."

Matty hurried on, not wanting to risk the tears more sympathetic words would undoubtedly bring. "Last August he retired from the ministry. I say retired, but the truth is he immediately began doing some of the things he had never had the time to do. A pastor friend had a regular Bible study at the state prison, and Joe began going with him once a month. Apparently, on one of those visits he met Billy Taylor."

Mr. Goss sat a little straighter in his wheelchair and nodded.

"Joe had a knack for being able to read people," she added.

"A blessing in his line of work."

Matty smiled. "Yes. After meeting with Billy several times, he became convinced he wasn't guilty of murdering Karen Campbell."

"Did he tell you why?"

"The truth is, he never talked to me about it. I found a little notebook when I was sorting through his papers. He had written down his impressions of Billy without going into the facts of the murder. But the final entry was different. He wrote about a lead—something he thought might help to prove Billy was indeed innocent."

"What was this lead?"

"He didn't say. He must have written the note shortly before he died."

"How can I help, Mrs. Amoruso?"

"Matty. Please call me Matty."

"Is that your given name?"

She smiled and said, "No. My given name is Martha."

"A lovely name. I'm sorry—you were going to tell me how I can help."

"I'm not sure you can. After reading his notes, I felt I had to do something. I visited Billy in prison myself, and I came away with the same feeling. Of course, I know they say everyone in prison claims to be innocent, but Billy is different somehow. He seems hopelessly resigned to spending the rest of his life in that awful place."

"Did he say he was innocent?"

"Yes, but he doesn't believe there is any chance for parole."

Mr. Goss made a slight face. "I understand Beatrice Campbell attends every parole hearing."

"She's convinced Billy did it."

They sat looking out the window. A robin landed

gracefully on the edge of the birdbath someone had placed in the center of the garden. They watched as he cautiously stepped into the water and dipped his little body below the surface. He finished his bath with a flutter of his wings, sending rainbow colored drops of water into the air. With one hop he was back on the rim. He sat for a little while, then spread his wings and soared to the top of the nearest oak.

Mr. Goss turned to Matty. "Did Billy say anything to you about this lead?"

Matty moved forward a little in her chair. "He said he thought he saw someone crossing the bridge when he was on his way home the day of the murder. It was dusk, and he couldn't tell whether it was a man or a woman."

"Or whether or not anyone was really there?"

Matty nodded and leaned back into the comfortable chair.

"I still don't understand how I can help you, Martha."

She hadn't been called Martha since she was a little girl, but coming from him, it felt right. "Someone told me something about Karen Campbell and one of her teachers—a Mr. Moran."

The look on his face spoke volumes. Matty's heart rate quickened.

"Is it true, Mr. Goss? Was Mr. Moran bothering Karen?"

"If by bothering you mean sexually harassing, I don't think so."

Matty couldn't help feeling a little disappointed.

"But there was something. I surprised the two of them in Mr. Moran's classroom one afternoon after school. There was nothing indecent going on. She was sitting on his desk. He was seated in his chair. They were laughing and talking. Innocent enough, but I could tell immediately there was an attraction. At least, on his part. I'm not sure about Karen. She may have been quite innocent."

"But you don't think so."

"I'm not sure. In any case, I had a long, very serious talk with Mr. Moran. He assured me it would never happen again, and I assured him he would be fired if there was even a hint of anything happening again."

"And was there?"

"No. Karen was killed very shortly afterwards. The following year Mr. Moran took a teaching job in another state—Pennsylvania, I believe."

"What did you think of Billy Taylor, Mr. Goss?"

"I had great hopes for Billy, Martha. He had so much stacked against him, and yet he did remarkably well." He smiled and shook his head. "He was never going to be a great success in the eyes of the world, but I thought he had every chance for a productive life. We were working to find him a job on one of the local farms."

"What about his father's farm?"

"Zach Taylor let the family farm go to ruin. He spent his nights drinking and his days sleeping it off. He lost his job and had to sell whatever he could just to get by. Before things got so bad, Billy tried to keep the farm going—but it was hopeless."

Matty felt pity for the lonely boy Billy Taylor had been

and anger at a father who cared so little for his own son. She looked into Mr. Goss' eyes and saw her own feelings reflected there.

"Did Billy ever get into trouble?"

"There were the usual teenage problems. One time he had a scuffle with some boys who were making comments about his father. I tried to make time to visit with him every so often after that. I discovered his love of farming and began to steer him in that direction. He began doing some odd jobs on some of the local farms. He had a natural affinity for the work. Yes, I had great hopes for Billy."

"So you must have been shocked when he was arrested."

"I couldn't..."

A gentle tapping on the door brought the conversation to an abrupt halt.

"Lunchtime, Mr. Goss. Want me to take you down to the dining room or do you want a tray in here?" A young woman with bright red curls stuck her head around the door. "It's spaghetti and a salad."

"Thank you, Tiffany. I think I'll have a tray in my room."

"Alrighty. I'll be back in a few."

Matty picked up her purse and got up to leave.

"I'm sorry I couldn't be more help, Martha."

Matty smiled and leaned over to kiss him on the cheek. "You've been a big help. I've enjoyed spending time with you. Would it be okay if I came again?"

"I should like that very much."

She turned before opening the door and said, "No

questions next time—just a nice visit."

He had already turned to face the window.

Matty closed the door behind her. She turned to walk down the long, carpeted hall and collided with a woman coming out of the adjacent room. The tray she was carrying flew out of her hands and cookies scattered in every direction.

"Oh, I'm so sorry. I didn't see you...Donna? What are you doing here?"

"Matty! Well, hi, Matty. Not your fault. I wasn't looking where I was going. I come to Shady Oaks once a week to do a little volunteer work."

"I didn't know that. I thought you did volunteer work at the nursing home in Centerville."

"Oh, I do, but there are so few people who volunteer to come to this particular nursing home, and I know how these dear folks appreciate a little company."

Matty fought down the familiar feeling of annoyance Donna inevitably aroused in her. She had the uncomfortable feeling it came more from a sense of guilt than anything else. "I don't know how you find the time, Donna. You do so much. I'm sure the people here are very grateful." She tried to make eye contact with her, but Donna was looking down at the mess on the floor.

"Here, let me help you clean this up."

They got down on their hands and knees and began picking up the mess. "Do you know someone here, Matty?"

"Um, I...Joe had an old friend here he used to visit occasionally. I thought I should come and explain to him why

Joe wouldn't be coming anymore." She got to her feet and brushed her hands off on her slacks. "I'm sorry to rush, Donna, but I have an appointment back in Centerville. I'll see you next Tuesday—or I guess in church Sunday. Bye."

She could feel Donna's eyes boring into her back as she practically ran down the length of the hallway and out the massive front doors, muttering under her breath the whole way. "Matty Amoruso, what on earth is the matter with you? Forgive me, Lord. I didn't mean to lie. It's just...it didn't seem like a good idea to tell Donna why I was visiting. Doesn't the woman ever stay home? Talk about doing good deeds. She never stops. Oh dear...sorry again, Lord."

She stepped up into the SUV and rested her head on the steering wheel. "Some detective you are, old girl."

~ CHAPTER 15 ~

Matty picked up the phone and dialed Nancy's number as soon as she walked in the door. Sidestepping her exuberant pet, she waited for her to pick up.

"Hi, Nancy. I have something I need to tell you. Do you feel like taking a little walk? If I don't get Shep outdoors right this minute, I think he'll have a fit."

They agreed to meet at the corner. Matty took off her sweater and grabbed Shep's leash off the hook by the door. She clipped it to his collar, and they took off down the road.

Joe loved this stretch of road, and they had walked this way countless times. He enjoyed getting out in the fresh air after a day spent in the office or studying at home. Dozens of little violets poked their heads through the long grass growing on the side of the road. A memory filled her mind of the summer afternoon Joe had presented her with a little purple bouquet. She brushed away the tears before Nancy could see them.

"Hi, Matty. Isn't it a gorgeous day?" She looked closely at

her friend, put an arm around her shoulders and drew her close.

"Oh, how I miss him, Nancy."

They walked slowly up the little hill toward open farmland, neither speaking for some time. At the top of the hill they walked toward the neat stone wall surrounding the Martin farm and sat down.

"This is where Billy Taylor said he was the day Karen was murdered."

Nancy gave her a puzzled look.

"When I asked him about the day of the murder, he said he was supposed to do some work for Mr. Martin. The farm was deserted when he got here, so he just walked on home. That's when he saw, or thinks he saw, someone walking over the bridge."

"He told you that?"

"Yes. It's what he told Joe, too. I believe it's the lead he wrote about."

"Wait a minute, Matty. What lead? And what notebook? Tell me everything, please."

Matty knew her face was bright red. "Well, that's pretty much everything. I found a notebook in Joe's file cabinet—a sort of journal detailing his impressions of Billy Taylor. The last entry mentioned a lead Joe thought might prove Billy's innocence."

Nancy shook her head. "I don't like this. You could be getting yourself involved in something very dangerous. You should go to the police if you think you have any information that would clear Billy Taylor—especially if there's a murderer walking around loose."

"What would I say? I don't have any real evidence. I promise not to do anything foolish. I just want to see if there's anything to all this. I'd like to try to talk to Mr. Moran."

"And say what? 'By the way Mr. Moran, I was just wondering if you murdered Karen Campbell?'"

Matty smiled in spite of herself. "No. Of course not."

"Well, what then?"

"I'm not exactly sure. I could pretend I'm writing a story about the murder and ask if he would mind if I asked a few questions. I won't make it obvious or anything."

"If he's the real murderer, you won't have to. He'll get suspicious right away."

"Well, I have to do something. I've tried to ignore it, but I can't. I can't let an innocent man sit in prison."

"Do you even know where Mr. Moran lives—or if he's even alive?"

"No. That's where you come in."

"Me?"

"I thought you could help me find him on the Internet, or whatever it is you do on the computer. You're so knowledgeable, and I don't know a thing about computers. You could use Joe's old laptop and find him. I know you could."

Nancy sighed. "I guess I could do that. But if we do find him, you must go to the police with the information."

"If we find him, I'll call and ask a few innocent questions.

There may be nothing to it at all. I don't want to make trouble for him if he's totally innocent." Matty stood and looked down at her friend.

"Okay, Matty. I'll help you. But we're going to be very careful about this. I don't want you getting yourself hurt." She got up, and they started walking toward Matty's house.

"Thanks, Nancy. I promise I won't do anything foolish. If I have any doubts at all, I'm going to call Pete and ask him what I should do."

Nancy laughed. "I can tell you exactly what Pete is going to tell you to do."

"Yeah, I know."

When they arrived at Matty's house, the two friends sat side by side at Joe's massive desk in front of the laptop.

"Mr. Goss said he thought the Morans moved to Pennsylvania. We could start there, couldn't we, Nancy?"

"Did he say where in Pennsylvania?"

"No. Does that make it harder?"

Nancy chuckled. "I know. Let's try to Google his name and see what comes up. He's a teacher. So if we can narrow down the city, we can look at the school directories."

Matty didn't have a clue about "Googling." She watched, fascinated, as Nancy typed his name and dozens of items showed up on the search page. Nancy clicked on several without success.

"Let's just try this one that lists all the James Morans in Pennsylvania."

"Look, Nancy. There's a James Moran in Lancaster. Try

that one."

Matty felt her heart racing as they waited for the information to pop up.

Nancy looked at the screen. "It says he's sixty-seven years old. I think that's about the right age. This could be him. I don't know if he had any kids, but this lists a couple anyway. These things aren't a hundred percent accurate. Let's try looking at the Lancaster High School website. I should have thought of that first. Of course, he certainly could have retired by now."

Minutes later they sat with their heads together scrolling through the school directory. Nancy pointed at the screen "There it is. James Moran. Unfortunately they don't list teachers' phone numbers—just email addresses."

"Well, since we're pretty sure that's him, why don't we just try calling information and get the phone number that way?"

"That will only work if he has a land line. There's no directory for cell phones."

"But it's worth a try. If we can't get it that way, we'll just have to think of something else. Would you do it? I'm so nervous my legs are shaking."

She sat watching as Nancy dialed information and asked for the number of James Moran in Lancaster, Pennsylvania. Her heart was thumping so loudly in her ears she could hardly hear. Nancy reached over to get the pad and pen and began writing. She hung up the phone and turned to Matty.

"We're in luck. Here it is!"

They both whooped. "You'd think we just won the lottery or something," said Nancy. "I hope it's the right James Moran."

"Me, too." She gave Nancy a hopeful look.

"You started this, Matty. You have to make the call."

Matty took a deep breath. *I hope I don't say all the wrong things,* she thought. Then she dialed the number. The phone rang four times before a woman answered.

"Hello."

"Hello. Is this Mrs. Moran?"

"Yes. Who is this?"

"Mrs. Moran, my name is—" Nancy slapped her on the arm and whispered, "Make up a name." Hoping they didn't have Caller ID, she winced and blurted out, "Cynthia Jones. I'm a freelance writer, and I'm doing a story on murders in small towns."

"I don't understand how I can help you?"

"Did you and your husband live in Miller's Crossing at the time of the Campbell murder?"

"Why, yes, we did."

Matty put her hand over the receiver and nodded at Nancy.

"Well, I'm including that one in my piece. I wondered if I might interview your husband. I believe he was one of Karen Campbell's teachers. Is that right?"

"Yes he was. I'm sure he'd be glad to help. Is this going to be a book or something?"

Matty's eyes widened, and she made a face at Nancy. "I'm

hoping so, Mrs. Moran. Could I speak with your husband?"

"Unfortunately he isn't here right now. In fact, he's out of the country for a couple of weeks. He's taking a group of students to Europe. It's their senior trip."

"Well, why don't I call you back in a couple of weeks. I'd like to interview both of you, and it will take a little time."

"That would be fine. Thank you so much.'

"Good-bye, Mrs. Moran."

"Good-bye, Ms...Jones, was it?"

Matty grimaced. "Yes. Yes, Ms. Jones. Talk with you soon."

She hung up the phone and grabbed Nancy's hands. "He's out of the country and won't be back for a couple of weeks. I think it'll work. She sounded thrilled with the idea of a little notoriety. I think I have the makings of a good detective after all."

"Matty, this isn't a game. It's serious business. Remember your promise. Mr. Moran may not be nearly as thrilled as his wife with the idea of a little notoriety." She got up and walked over to the stairs. "I'd better get myself home. Buddy will be wondering where I've gotten off to."

Matty walked to the end of the driveway with her. "Thanks, Nancy. Tell Buddy hi."

"I will. See you soon."

Shep walked beside her, but she hardly noticed. The excitement of the past hour was beginning to give way to doubt. *What will I say to Mr. Moran if he agrees to talk to me? If he's guilty, will I be putting myself in danger? I really must be careful, but I don't want to talk to Pete yet. He and Jenny will worry.* She shivered despite the warm breeze.

When she looked up, she was surprised to find she was safe and sound in her own front yard. The wind ruffled the branches of the trees and formed tiny dust devils in the unpaved driveway. Huge cumulus clouds raced across a sky so blue it almost hurt her eyes. Reluctant to go inside, she got her gardening gloves out of the garage and headed to the backyard.

Joe had fenced in an area for a vegetable garden shortly after they moved into the house. The white paint was peeling in places and she mentally added "scrape and paint fence" to her to-do list. Only a small portion of the area was planted. It was all she could manage this year: a few tomato plants, some squash and lettuce, a row of carrots. She knelt between the rows and began pulling weeds. She breathed in the pungent aroma of soil and plants—and prayed.

❖

The Fourth of July celebration was now only a few days away. Everyone at church was involved in one way or another. Matty had volunteered to sell hot dogs. It felt like a fairly safe job. Several of the farmers had worked together to mow the big field across the street from the church, and a few of the tents were already set up in anticipation of the big event.

Matty sat out on the patio enjoying her second cup of

coffee. Shep was on the trail of something exciting in the far field. She watched as he sniffed the ground and then took off running. He'd run for a while, come to a sudden stop and look around in confusion. Not a thing in sight except the tall grass waving in the wind.

Well, he's definitely not a hunter.

The problems at church between Willa-Mae and Pastor Greg were never far from her thoughts. Nearly a month had passed since she promised Laura she would talk to Willa-Mae. Procrastination, hoping and praying it would resolve itself, hadn't done a bit of good. Things had only gotten worse. Everything felt stiff and strained last Sunday.

"It can't go on like this much longer." Speaking the words out loud, she got up and began walking toward the house. "Come on, Shep. Time to go inside." For once he came as soon as he heard his name.

"You must be hungry." She rubbed his ears and got a moist lick on her hand in return. "Okay, okay. Let's go on in. I have a phone call to make. I can't put it off any longer."

~ CHAPTER 16 ~

Matty meandered along the quiet road toward Willa-Mae's. She inhaled the fragrance of the roses she carried—a sort of peace offering. They hadn't exchanged angry words, but they had tiptoed around the subject for so long the friendship felt strained.

Her legs began to feel weak as she approached the house. *This is ridiculous,* she thought. *I've known Willa-Mae for over thirty years. Why should I be afraid to talk to her? But I am afraid. Please, Lord, help me do this right. Give me the words and give me wisdom—please.*

Willa-Mae opened the door before Matty had a chance to knock. "It's been a long time, Matty. Come on inside."

She took the proffered bouquet and led the way into the kitchen. "Come on and sit a spell. I have a feelin' we're gonna need a cup of coffee."

Matty sat looking at the familiar room while Willa-Mae bustled around filling the coffee pot and getting mugs out of the cabinet. The homemade calico curtains stirred in the breeze coming through the open bay window. Willa-Mae wore the matching calico apron she'd sewn with the leftover fabric.

For the thousandth time Matty read the words Willa-Mae had embroidered on the framed picture hanging over the table: "You don't have to thank us or laugh at our jokes. Sit deep and come often, you're one of the folks." She could have cried over the whole foolish mess but was determined to do this well. She waited while an uncharacteristically quiet Willa-Mae poured the coffee and took the seat across from her. It seemed foolish to try and make small talk. They both knew why she had come.

"Willa-Mae, I want to talk to you about church. I don't want there to be any misunderstandings or hurtful words. I simply want to talk things through if we can." Deep lines framed the corners of Willa-Mae's mouth. Matty's heart sank.

"I know we don't see eye to eye on this, Matty. Frankly I'm havin' a hard time understandin' how you can go along with Pastor Greg." The words were laced with such anger that Matty was taken aback. All hope for a happy resolution to the problem flew right out the bay window. She had grossly underestimated the depth of Willa-Mae's feelings.

"Willa-Mae. Why must we choose up sides in this? Surely there is a way we can work this out so everyone is reasonably happy. I know Pastor Greg has prayed about all—"

The kitchen chair overturned and clattered to the floor as Willa-Mae jumped to her feet. "Prayed about it! *Prayed* about it?" Her voice grew louder as she paced back and forth between the table and the back door. "Who is he praying to? I tell you this is an abomination, Matty, and for the life of me I

163

can't figure out why God allows it to go on. That kind of music does not belong in His house. All those drums are doin' is drummin' up the demons from hell. I swear, if I closed my eyes I would think I was in some honky-tonk. It isn't right, Matty, and I'm ashamed of you for not takin' a stand against it."

Matty sat in stunned silence.

"And that's not the worst of it. I got to my deaconess meetin' early the other evenin' and there she was—just as big as brass—teachin' those innocent little children a dance. I could hardly believe my eyes. It's wrong, Matty, and God will not put up with it for long."

She reached down, lifted the old wooden chair up off the floor and sank onto the cushioned seat. She cupped her flushed cheeks in her hands and looked into Matty's eyes. "Listen to me, Matty. You know I love you like a sister, but you are wrong in this. Trust me, I know what can happen when you defy God."

"What do you mean, Willa-Mae?"

"Never you mind. You just trust me on this one. I know what I'm talkin' about."

"But there are so many verses..."

"Stop it, Matty. I know what you're gonna say...about David dancin' before the Lord and all. That was different. It was a different time. The church is supposed to be a place of reverence where we worship a holy God. No. It can't go on, I tell you. We have a church business meetin' comin' up right after this Fourth of July shindig. We'll settle it then."

"Willa-Mae, please can't—"

"I don't want to hear another word about it, Matty. You and I will always be friends, but on this we will never agree. I ask you to search your heart. You'll see I'm right, and then maybe you'll stand with us."

There were tears standing in Willa-Mae's eyes, but the firm set of her jaw spoke volumes. Matty got up and came around the table. Putting her arm around her friend's shoulder, she laid her cheek against her head and whispered, "I promise to pray about it, Willa-Mae."

Willa-Mae patted her hand and got to her feet. She pulled her handkerchief out of her apron pocket, the one with the pink crocheted edging, and dabbed at her eyes. "I think I'll just go have a little rest, if you don't mind."

Matty watched her walk away. Her friend seemed to have aged in the past few months. The once ramrod straight back curved; the lively footstep had slowed to a weary shuffle. She waited until she heard Willa-Mae shut the bedroom door before leaving the house. She felt so discouraged.

Halfway down the sidewalk she saw Jason trudging up the hill from the barn. He waved and called to her.

"Matty, I didn't know you were here. I had a few chores to do down in the barn. Where's Willa-Mae?"

"She said she wanted to take a little rest. Oh, Jason, I really made a mess of things."

"What are you talking about, Matty? Here, don't cry. Tell me what's wrong."

Matty swiped at the tears and tried to compose herself.

"Oh, it's all this church stuff. I just wanted to try to make her see things from Pastor Greg's point of view. I thought I could somehow make everything right. Instead, I made it all worse. I always say the wrong thing."

"Listen to me, Matty. This is not your fault. Willa-Mae feels very strongly about obeying what she believes the Lord has said."

"She said something about knowing what happens when you 'defy God.' What did she mean, Jason?"

A sad smile flitted across his face. "It's Willa-Mae's story to tell, Matty."

"I'm afraid of what will happen to our church if we can't somehow resolve this, Jason. She said she's going to settle it at the next business meeting. We could see our church split wide open, and it would impact so many lives. Can't you get her to at least meet Pastor Greg halfway?"

He shook his head. "I've tried, honey, but you see what she's like. I'm afraid if I push her too hard something might happen to her. Let's you and me keep praying about it. We know God's in the miracle-working business."

"Have you talked to Pastor Greg, Jason?"

"I have." He smiled and cupped her chin in his work-worn hand. "He's a bit on the stubborn side too, you know, Matty. But he does believe he's doing what the Lord sent him here to do. I believe it will all work out."

"Oh, I hope you're right." Standing on tiptoe, she kissed his scruffy cheek. "You're a good man, Jason Miller."

❖

Her legs felt like lead as she trudged up the driveway. She longed for the comfort of the old couch but stopped long enough to let Shep outside for a quick run. In just a few minutes he appeared at the back door whining to get inside. He seemed to have an uncanny ability to sense her moods. He came to her and leaned against her legs. She bent down and hugged his neck.

With one foot on the top of the steps leading to the study, she stopped. "Matty Amoruso, stop this." She spoke the words out loud. "You can't curl up in a ball and go to sleep every time things don't go the way you planned. This isn't the way Joe would have wanted you to act."

She turned so quickly she nearly knocked her poor dog down the stairs. "Oh, I'm sorry, pal. Come on, let's do something constructive."

Pulling the telephone book down off the shelf in the little kitchen closet, Matty thumbed to the "J's." There is was, Thomas James. Her hand shook as she punched in the number. It rang several times, and in spite of her good intentions, she felt a sense of relief. She started to hang up when she heard a man's voice on the other end. "Hello. Hello? Is anybody there?"

Matty put the phone to her ear. "Yes, is this Mr. James?"

"It is. Who's calling?"

Matty took a deep breath, "My name is Cynthia Jones, Mr. James. I'm a freelance writer, and I'm writing a story on small town murders."

"I don't understand how I can help you, Ms. Jones."

"Yes, of course. First, may I ask if you're the Thomas James who was a classmate of Karen Campbell?"

"Yes. I went to school with Karen."

"Your name came up in my research. If I'm correct, you and Karen were going together at the time of the murder."

"That's not entirely correct, Ms. Jones." Matty wished she had thought of a more original name. "We broke up shortly before Karen was murdered. I really don't see how I can be of help."

"I don't mean to pry, Mr. James. I'm simply trying to get an accurate picture of what happened. I've interviewed several other people who knew Karen at the time. One of them insinuated she was having a problem with one of her teachers."

"I don't understand."

"Apparently Karen told one of her friends, and I'm quoting here, 'one of her teachers was coming on to her and wouldn't leave her alone.' Did Karen talk to you about her concerns?"

He took so long to answer Matty thought he had hung up. "Look, Ms. Jones. It all happened such a long time ago. They got the guy who murdered Karen. Why dig it all up again?"

"I understand how you feel, Mr. James. I'm not trying to stir up trouble. I'm attempting to tell the whole story as truthfully and factually as I can."

"The facts are Karen and I were going to get back

together. It was just one of those teenage misunderstandings. I thought at one time something might be going on with one of our teachers, but Karen never said a word about it to me. Billy Taylor murdered Karen—that's a fact."

"I'm sorry if I've overstepped, Mr. James—"

"I really have nothing more to say to you, Ms. Jones. Good luck with your story."

Matty could feel the blood rushing to her face. She let out a breath and carefully hung up the phone.

"That went well." She sat shaking her head, trying to get her heart rate back to normal. "I need to talk to someone. "

Nancy picked up on the first ring.

"Oh Nancy, I'm so glad you're home."

"I just walked in the door. What's wrong, Matty?"

"I called Tommy James. You know, Karen Campbell's boyfriend."

"Oh dear. Did something go wrong? You sound upset."

"Not wrong, exactly. He wasn't particularly friendly, but I did get a little more information."

"I wish you would let this thing go. I'm afraid you're getting in over your head."

"It's all right, Nancy. He told me he and Karen had broken up but that they were going to get back together. He didn't say so, but they must have talked or something. Anyway, he said he suspected something might be going on with one of her teachers, but Karen never spoke to him about it."

"Did he say which teacher?"

"No, he got a little angry and hung up after that."

Nancy's sigh carried over the phone. "What do you plan to do now?"

"I'm not sure. I guess I need to wait and talk to Mr. Moran."

"I don't see how that will help, Matty. He's never going to admit he was interested in Karen. What do you hope to accomplish?"

"Oh, I don't know...maybe I should go visit Billy Taylor again and see if he remembers anything more about the person he thinks he saw walking across the bridge. If I mention Mr. Moran, it may jog his memory."

"Or he could lie about it. Please give this up. At the very least tell someone in authority what you're doing."

"I promise not to take any chances. So far I really have nothing to tell. Unless Billy remembers who he saw, I don't have any way of proving he didn't do it. Don't worry. I'll be very careful."

Matty sat looking out the window for a long time after she hung up.

~ CHAPTER 17 ~

It's a perfect day for a parade." Nancy smiled and gave Matty's hand a little squeeze. The sun shone down from a cloudless blue sky. She inhaled the fresh, clear air. "I think I can hear the band tuning up. It ought to start soon."

"I think we have the best seats in the house," said Buddy. He stretched his long legs out in front of him and leaned back in his lawn chair. "Even you should be able to see, Matty." She reached over and slapped his arm. "Ouch! I just meant you're such a petite lady and so very charming..."

"All right, you two. Stop fussing before I make you both go sit in the truck. Look! Here comes the Grand Marshall."

They sat cheering and waving their little flags as the homemade floats made their way down Main Street. Buddy gave a piercing wolf whistle when the Cadillac convertible drove by with Miss Washington County perched on the back. He was rewarded with another slap on the arm, this time from his wife.

They called out to the local kids decked out in their Little League uniforms and nearly jumped out of their seats when the fire trucks blasted their horns. Last of all came the horseback riders, their sequined shirts sparkling in the sunlight.

Nancy got up, folded up her chair and handed it to Buddy. "It's always the same, and I love it more every year."

They walked behind the crowds of people headed to the parking lot. "I've got to hurry and get my things together for the celebration. Are you entering the contest, Matty?"

"No. I think Willa-Mae has that all sewn up." She laughed at the look on Nancy's face. "Well, at least in *her* mind she has. Are you entering?"

"Yeah. I baked an apple pie. At the very least, it'll help the kids raise more money."

Buddy slung the chairs into the bed of the truck and opened the passenger door. Bowing deeply from the waist he said, "After you, my dears." He was quicker this time and ducked before Nancy could give him another playful slap.

During the short ride home they talked about the parade and their plans for the rest of the day. They carefully avoided all discussion of what was probably uppermost in all of their minds—the church "problem." They shared an unspoken hope there wouldn't be any trouble. Buddy idled the truck in Matty's driveway and jumped out to give her a hand down. "Do you want to ride to the celebration with us?"

"No thanks, Buddy. I'll take my car. I may get brave and let Shep come. I'm working in the hot dog booth, and I could keep him there with me. I hate to leave him home alone all day."

"That dog's spoiled; that's what he is," chided Buddy.

Nancy leaned out the window and waved as the huge truck rolled down the driveway. "See you in a little while."

Shep spun around in circles when Matty walked in the door. His tail banged against the little coat rack, nearly tipping it over. She reached down and tried to grab him around the neck. He licked her cheek and ran to the door. "Yes, yes. I know you need to get outside."

She stood in the shade of the big maple tree and watched as he galloped through the field. Peeling off her sweater she gazed up. It might very well be as hot as the weatherman had predicted. They rarely enjoyed a summer day in the low nineties.

Shep returned to her, his tongue nearly touching the ground. "Come on, boy. Let's get you a nice cold drink of water." Together they ambled toward the house. Matty's heart lifted at the sight of her flower garden. The hydrangeas were in bloom, a beautiful splash of blue against the white house. Before they went inside, she buried her face in a huge pink rose, inhaling its exquisite fragrance.

✣

"I'm a Yankee Doodle Dandy. A Yankee Doodle do or die." Matty heard the music before she pulled the SUV into the parking area. The warm breeze ruffled the red, white and blue bunting on the fronts of the concession stands and carried the aroma of grilling meat across the field.

A good-sized crowd had already gathered, and Matty waved to friends as she made her way to the hot dog stand. Shep, overwhelmed by all the sights and sounds, pulled hard on his leash. When he spotted a couple of little boys walking toward him, he nearly pulled Matty off her feet trying to get to them. She held tight and bent down in an effort to calm him. He wriggled and whined as the two little boys approached, gripping their huge puffs of cotton candy. Matty tightened her grip on Shep's collar, hoping he wouldn't make their sugary treats disappear in two big gulps. To her surprise he sat still while the older boy reached out a sticky hand to pet his furry face.

"What's his name?" he asked.

"His name is Shep. What's your name?"

"Josh. He's nice." He giggled when Shep licked his cheek, wiping clean the sticky mess. "He likes me."

The younger boy drew back as Shep attempted to clean up his face, too. Matty reached out a hand and took his small, syrupy one in hers. "What's your name, honey?"

"Ben." His little lip trembled slightly as he eyed the big dog.

"It's all right, Ben. Shep won't hurt you. He just wants to give you a kiss. But if you don't want him to, he won't mind. I think he'd like to be your friend. Would you like to pet him?"

He looked at her with enormous blue eyes and gave a tentative nod. She placed his hand carefully on Shep's head. The big dog sat quietly, somehow sensing this little guy needed to be treated gently. It didn't take long before Ben moved closer, gently patting the downy head and touching the floppy ear, flipping it up to watch it fall back down.

"He's always been scared of dogs. I can't believe you got him to do that."

Matty looked up to see a young woman standing behind the boys. She got to her feet, keeping an eye on the little group. She extended her hand to the woman. "I'm Matty Amoruso, and this is Shep."

"Ellen. Nice to meet you. Actually, I knew who you was. I went to your church once or twice...that was years ago. I'm sorry to hear about your husband. He was a real good man."

"Thank you, Ellen. I hope you'll visit the church again sometime. There's a new pastor now, and he's doing some exciting things. I think you might like it. And the boys might enjoy Sunday School."

"Well, my husband don't care much for church. I'll see. Maybe he'll let me bring the boys." She looked down at the ground. "Come on, boys. We gotta get going. Your Daddy'll be home soon and wanting his dinner."

The boys gave Shep one last hug. "I wish we had a dog, Mama."

"You know your Daddy don't like dogs, Josh. Come on, now. We gotta go. Say thank you to Mrs. Amoruso."

They smiled up at her and said, "Thank you, Mrs. Amoruso." Shep whined and tried to follow them as they walked away. They hadn't gotten far when Ben turned and waggled his little hand at them. A wave of sadness swept over Matty. She stood watching until they were lost in the crowd.

"We'd better get going, boy. We're late." She hurried to the hot dog stand. Donna, face red and beaded with perspiration, greeted her.

"Hi, Matty. I'm so glad you could come and help. I made us some patriotic aprons. They're over there in the corner. Just help yourself to one, and I'll put you to work."

"Hi, Donna. I'm sorry I didn't get here sooner. It looks like you've been hard at work. I hope you don't mind my bringing Shep along. He won't be a bother. I promise. I just didn't want to leave him home alone all day."

"Oh, no bother at all, Matty," Donna replied with a somewhat pained expression. "We'll just have to make sure he doesn't eat all the profits!"

Not quite knowing what to say, Matty busied herself getting things ready. Across the way, a group of men were putting the finishing touches on the dunking booth. Pastor Greg, who had gamely volunteered to take the first shift, was dressed in red and white striped shorts and a blue T-shirt. Someone had evidently given him an old-fashioned bathing cap, and he wore it perched on top of his head.

"Wasn't Susan supposed to help sell hot dogs with us?"

Donna paused for a moment and looked at Matty. "Yes, she was. She called this morning and said she wasn't feeling well. Just between you and me, I think she's too shy to be around so many people. You know how Susan is."

Matty didn't say anything. She caught sight of Willa-Mae walking toward the huge tent at the end of the field. Jason came behind her, carrying a huge pie plate with both hands. She called out to them, but they didn't hear her over the noise of the music. At least she hoped that's what it was.

Within a few minutes a line formed outside their little stand, and Matty spent the next couple of hours fixing hot dogs and pouring drinks. Every now and then a huge roar went up from the crowd standing around the dunking booth, and Pastor Greg would disappear from sight, sending water cascading over the sides.

"Matty, would you mind shutting things down by yourself? It's time for me to get over to the big tent for the baking contest. Besides, we don't have anything left to sell except a little bit of soda."

"Not at all, Donna. I'll clean up and then head over there myself. It should be fun."

"I'm so excited, Matty. I think my rhubarb pie has a really good chance to win. I'll see you over there."

"Well, Shep, this ought to be interesting." She filled a bowl with water and set it down for him. "You've been such a good boy. Just be patient a little longer, and I'll let you stretch your legs a little."

By the time Matty and Shep reached the tent, the judging was almost over. The ribbons for the cookies and cakes had been awarded, and the judges were making their way to the table with the pies. Pastor Greg stood behind the table all dried off and looking more refreshed than anyone else. He had the honor of being head judge. It was just the sort of thing Joe dreaded. She could almost hear him saying, "Poor guy. Why is it the preacher is the one who gets stuck in these no-win situations?"

She walked up to the front row and slipped into the empty seat next to Jason. Shep lay down at her feet. Jason turned and gave her a little smile. His raised eyebrows spoke all the things he couldn't say. Willa-Mae sat forward in her seat, eyes glued to the table where the pies were displayed.

The three judges went about their work, tasting each pie in turn. When they finished, they gathered in a little huddle for what seemed like an eternity. Then they returned to the table and took another taste of two of the pies. Another huddle and they were ready to announce the winners. Pastor Greg stepped forward and cleared his throat dramatically.

"The third prize ribbon goes to the baker of this delicious cherry pie. Will the lady please stand?" There was a smattering of applause as an elderly lady in the back row stood.

"We had a difficult time deciding on the second and first place winners. Both pies are outstanding, and coincidentally, both are rhubarb pies. However, there can only be one winner, so we had to make a decision. The red ribbon goes to the one who baked this amazing rhubarb pie. Will you please stand?"

Willa-Mae inhaled and reached for Jason's hand. Deliberately she rose from her chair and faced the judges as the crowd applauded. The look she gave Pastor Greg would have slain a lesser man.

"The winner of the blue ribbon is this one." He held aloft

the dish containing Donna's rhubarb pie. She squealed and jumped out of her chair as the crowd hooted and hollered.

"Congratulations to all the winners," Pastor Greg shouted. "Now we'll have the judging for the grand champion."

Willa-Mae turned to Jason, barely acknowledging Matty's presence. "Let's go, Jason. I'm tired. I need to get on home."

"Of course, Darlin'." He took her hand, and they headed toward the exit. Matty grabbed Shep's leash and went after them.

"Willa-Mae, please stay. There's still the softball game, and then they're going to shoot off fireworks when it gets dark."

"I have no desire to stay, Matty. I think we know what's goin' on here, and it seems awful petty to me."

"Surely you don't think Pastor Greg deliberately chose Donna's pie over yours? How could he possibly have known which pie was which? Please don't do this, Willa-Mae."

"I have nothin' more to say, Matty. Good-bye now." She let go of Jason's hand and strode toward the parking lot.

"Oh, Jason, I feel awful about this."

"Now, Matty. It isn't your fault. You've got to stop taking responsibility for everything that goes wrong. We'll work this out."

For the first time that day Matty looked closely at him. He looked tired beyond words and so pale. She reached up and gave him a hug.

"Jason. You comin'?"

He turned and walked slowly toward Willa-Mae.

❖

A cheer went up from the crowd as the last of the fireworks exploded into a shower of swirling colors. They watched, fascinated, until the last spark flickered out. For a minute or two no one moved. Then they began to gather up blankets, folding chairs and empty picnic baskets. Sleepy little ones were hoisted onto strong shoulders as families began making their way to the parking lot.

Matty looked over at Buddy and Nancy. They sat close together on the old quilt, Nancy's head resting on his shoulder. A wave of longing swept over her. She felt tears starting and quickly turned the other way.

"Well, ladies, the show's over. Time to get this weary old body home to bed."

Buddy extended a hand to each of them and helped them up off the ground. They gathered up their things and began walking toward the parking lot.

Nancy looked closely at Matty and put her free arm around her waist. She didn't say a word, just walked by her side.

"Well, I'm glad I took Shep home before the fireworks started. Can you imagine how he would have reacted to all that noise?" She tried hard to sound upbeat. "He may look fierce, but he's just a big baby at heart. I sure hope everything's all right with Willa-Mae and Jason. She was so upset, and Jason looked completely worn out. If it wasn't so late, I'd call and check up on them. I think I'll go over in the morning."

Afraid of breaking down, she couldn't seem to stop talking. She couldn't wait to get home and curl up in Joe's old chair.

Nancy handed the quilt and picnic basket to Buddy and wrapped her in a hug.

"I'm sure she'll see things differently in the morning. Would you like us to follow you home?"

"No, no. I'm fine. You go on. You'll have to be up bright and early tomorrow morning."

Buddy opened the car door for her, and she climbed inside. She sat for a minute watching them walk to his pickup before starting the car and heading home.

~ CHAPTER 18 ~

Matty's hands shook so badly she couldn't dial the number. Over and over again she tried to call for help and repeatedly the number failed to connect. Above the pounding of blood in her ears, she heard the scream of sirens and a dog barking.

She forced her eyes open and sat up. A dream. It was just a dream. She took a deep breath trying to control the rapid beating of her heart. Shep stood at the window barking. A light flashed into the darkness—a strobe winking on and off. She felt confused, trying to reconcile the dream with what was happening around her.

"Shep, what is it?" She walked over to the window and put her arm around his neck. The barking changed to an anxious whine, his whole body quivering. She could just see the Miller's house from here. The light was coming from that direction.

The phone rang, startling her and setting Shep off again. She ran to answer it—at the same time trying to calm her agitated dog.

"Matty—please help me."

"Willa-Mae? Is that you?"

"Matty, it's Jason. Oh, Lord, please don't take him. Can you come, Matty? They're takin' him to the hospital in Centerville...I can't ride in the ambulance..." she sobbed into the phone.

"I'll be right there, Willa-Mae."

She hung up and raced to the closet, grabbing whatever came to hand. She hurried over to the bed and got dressed. Her legs felt like Jell-O and for a minute she couldn't move. Covering her face with her hands, she whispered a desperate prayer for help.

She pulled up in front of the house with no memory of having driven there. The EMTs were loading Jason into the ambulance. Willa-Mae stood in the driveway, pale and shaken. Matty put her arm around her, and they stood watching as the ambulance pulled away.

"Hurry, Matty." Willa-Mae whirled around and started marching to the SUV in her nightgown. "I've got to be there with him."

"Let's go inside for a minute and get you dressed, Willa-Mae. Jason's in good hands."

Speaking softly, she led her friend down the hall to the bedroom. "Sit for a minute while I get your things together." Matty gathered up the clothes Willa-Mae had been wearing the day before from the rocking chair and brought them over to her friend. Silently, she helped her dress.

"Do you want anything before we go, Willa-Mae...a drink

of water?"

Willa-Mae looked at her with vacant eyes and shook her head. "I need to get to Jason, Matty. Please hurry."

They had just reached the front door when Matty remembered the glasses.

"Willa-Mae. We forgot your glasses." She raced back into the bedroom and grabbed them off the night table.

Willa-Mae was waiting for her by the car. Matty helped her up into the front seat then ran around to the driver's side and hopped in. Before starting the car, she gently placed the glasses on Willa-Mae's face. Neither woman spoke until they reached the city limits.

"I couldn't wake him up. Oh, Matty, he can't die. He just can't die."

"He won't die, Willa-Mae. They'll take good care of him."

"You can't know that, Matty. It's all my fault. Oh, God, it's all my fault."

Matty reached over and grabbed her friend's hand. It was icy cold, and she gently rubbed her thumb over the gnarled fingers, trying to bring some warmth and comfort.

Light was just beginning to peek over the edge of the horizon. Matty glanced at the clock—5:20. She noticed lights in some of the houses bordering the quiet street and thought about the people inside going about their usual morning routine unaware of the tragedy driving past their front doors. Did they wonder about the person in the ambulance speeding past, or had they grown immune to the sights and sounds of pain and suffering?

They reached the emergency room entrance just as the techs were walking out of the huge double doors with the empty stretcher. Matty parked quickly and helped Willa-Mae out of the SUV. She slipped her arm through her friend's, and together they walked into the E.R.

Matty felt light-headed as they walked through the doors. Images of that awful day flashed through her mind—running down the hall behind the stretcher; waiting outside, pacing the hallway and praying frantically for a miracle; seeing the doctor walk toward her; knowing Joe was gone. *I can't do this,* she thought. It took every ounce of strength she possessed to keep moving forward when all she wanted to do was turn and run.

The silence in the E.R. was unsettling. They made their way to the nurses' station where two nurses were sitting at their computers. Matty jumped when Willa-Mae's voice cut through the silence.

"Where is he? Where's Jason? I need to be with him? Where did they take him?"

One of the nurses stood and came around the divider.

"Are you looking for Mr. Miller, ma'am?"

"Yes. Please, where is he? I..."

She swayed and leaned heavily into Matty.

"They've taken him back into a room. The doctor is with him now, and they'll be running some tests. Please sit down here for a moment. I'll need you to give us some information. Then I'll take you back so you can see your husband and talk to the doctor. He'll have some questions for you, too."

"Oh, God. Please, I just want to see him."

Matty led her to a seat, and together they managed to answer most of the nurse's questions. Just as they were getting up to go see Jason, the double doors whooshed open and Pastor Greg walked in.

☘

Pastor Greg handed Matty a cup of coffee and took the seat next to her in the empty waiting room. At Willa-Mae's request, he had prayed with her before she went to see Jason. When he finished, she took his hand and whispered her thanks.

"How did you know Jason was in the emergency room?" asked Matty.

"I was sitting in my study and heard the ambulance drive past the house. When it came back so quickly, I knew it had to be someone close by, so I called the hospital. They told me they were bringing Jason in. Ministerial privilege, I guess." He smiled. "Do you know any details?"

Matty held the Styrofoam cup in two hands and pressed her arms close to her body. The waiting room was cold, and she hadn't taken time to grab a sweater.

"Willa-Mae said they got up very early this morning because Jason wanted to check on the calf. He complained of a bad headache that got worse quickly. The pain was so bad he said he felt sick to his stomach. She found him passed out on the bathroom floor."

The waiting room doors swung open, and Willa-Mae shambled toward them. Pastor Greg was on his feet, guiding her to a seat beside Matty. She looked pale and drawn.

"They're takin' him for a CT scan. Oh, Matty, I know he's gonna die, and it's all my fault."

Matty put a comforting arm around her, but this time she shrugged it off. "The doctor asked if he'd been under a lot of stress lately. Stress? Of course he's been under stress, and it's all because of me and my stubborn ways." She looked over at Pastor Greg, and for the first time that awful morning, she began to cry. Matty moved closer and rubbed her friend's back. Willa-Mae looked at her and began fumbling in her skirt pocket. "Can you believe I don't have a handkerchief, honey?"

Before Matty could move, Pastor Greg got up and walked over to the little table by the door where someone had placed a box of tissues. He pulled a couple out and brought them to Willa-Mae. She took them and patted his hand.

The minutes dragged. Other people began coming into the waiting room: a mother carrying a little one bundled up against the chill; an elderly man in a wheelchair, bleeding profusely from a head wound. Every time the inner door opened, they looked up expectantly. After what felt like an eternity, a doctor came in, looked around, and walked over to them. Pastor Greg got up and gave him his chair. He sat on the edge of the seat and leaned in to speak to Willa-Mae.

"Mrs. Miller, my name is Dr. Sanders. I've just looked at your husband's scan." He went on to explain the results.

The CT scan showed bleeding in Jason's brain, the result of a ruptured aneurysm. In order to prevent further bleeding he would have to perform a procedure called surgical clipping. He explained that he would make an opening in Jason's skull in order to reach the aneurysm. Then he would place a surgical clip at its base to prevent any more bleeding.

The surgery would have to be done immediately. There was a risk of stroke or brain damage if they waited. The surgery itself was not without risk, and there was the chance that brain damage had already occurred. Since Jason had not regained consciousness, Willa-Mae would have to give permission for the procedure.

He reached over and took Willa-Mae's hand. "He's still with us, and that's a good sign. We need to take care of this as quickly as possible."

Willa-Mae just looked at him, as though she couldn't quite take it all in. Then she nodded.

"The nurse will bring you the papers to sign. The surgery will take anywhere from three to five hours, depending on what we find. I'll come talk to you when it's over. Do you have any questions for me?"

Willa-Mae sat twisting her wedding band round and round her finger. She opened her mouth but couldn't seem to form the words.

"There are risks with every surgery, Mrs. Miller, but I am going to do my very best for your husband. "

She nodded and asked, "Will he have brain damage?"

"We won't know until he wakes up." He gave her hand a

gentle squeeze and stood up. "Now...I must go. I'll come and talk to you as soon as it's over."

Pastor Greg put a restraining hand on his arm. "We'll be praying for you, Doctor."

The doctor smiled. "I would very much appreciate that, Pastor."

❖

Matty got up to walk around the surgical waiting room. *This kind of waiting is more tiring than running a marathon,* she thought. She looked at Willa-Mae, who had hardly moved a muscle in the last three hours. After signing the necessary paperwork, she hadn't spoken a word—just took her seat and stared into space.

Pastor Greg had gone home to keep an important appointment and to rearrange his schedule. He returned within a couple of hours with coffee and buttered rolls, but neither he nor Matty could get Willa-Mae to take a thing. She just shook her head, eyes focused on the door.

"I've called the intercessors. Everyone is praying for him, Willa-Mae." She turned to look at him for a brief moment. "I've also asked the hospital to tell folks not to visit just yet."

The small waiting room began to fill with family members waiting for news of loved ones. The noise and laughter provided a welcome relief from the suffocating silence.

At varying intervals the phone on the little table by the door rang—the O.R. nurse calling to inform family members that their loved one was out of surgery and the doctor would be in soon to speak to them. One by one, doctors came to give a report to the waiting families.

Another hour passed. Matty had to fight to keep her eyes open. She was just about to take the short walk to the ladies room when the phone rang. She jumped up to answer it. Jason was out of surgery.

"The doctor will be here soon, Willa-Mae."

❖

The knot in Matty's stomach tightened as they sat waiting. The minute hand on the old wall clock seemed to stand still. Pastor Greg asked Willa-Mae if she would rather see the doctor alone. She spoke for the first time, her voice barely audible over the incessant noise of the television. "No. I think I'd like for you and Matty to stay."

The sound of footsteps coming down the hall caused Matty's heart to race. "Please, Lord," she whispered.

Dr. Sanders walked to Willa-Mae and sat down beside her. He was dressed in green scrubs and deep lines creased the corners of his eyes.

"It went well, Mrs. Miller—even better than I had hoped. It was a fairly good-sized aneurysm. We sealed it off with surgical clips, and the bleeding has stopped. Fortunately, we found no secondary bleeding. We'll keep him here for the next couple of weeks to be sure that doesn't occur. Right now they're taking him to the ICU where we'll monitor him closely for the next few days."

"Is he gonna be okay, doctor? Is there any brain damage? Is he out of danger now? Oh, Lord, please let him be all right. Can I see him?"

"We won't know anything until he regains consciousness. The nurses are getting him settled. I'll have someone come and get you when they're finished. For now, I think it best for only two people to be in his room at a time. You may stay overnight if you want to, Mrs. Miller, but keep in mind that this is going to be a long recovery. You'll need to get your rest. It looks to me like you have good friends to support you. You'd be wise to allow them to do just that."

"Thank you, doctor."

~ CHAPTER 19 ~

It was after three o'clock in the afternoon when Matty pulled the car into the garage. She said a little prayer of thanks when Shep came running to meet her. Not knowing how long she would be gone, she had taken a chance and left him outside. He looked up at her with big, sad eyes.

"I know, buddy. I'm so sorry."

The minute they were inside, he went to his food dish. Matty reached for the canned food and gave him a little extra helping—hoping to bribe her way back into his good graces.

Now that she was home, she didn't quite know what to do with herself. She had stayed long enough for a short visit in ICU, taking turns with Pastor Greg. Jason was still unconscious, so they tried to persuade Willa-Mae to go home for just a little while, but she wouldn't hear of it. They left her standing at Jason's bedside.

"I'm going to call Donna Johnson and have her organize the ladies. Then I'll get some of the men to take care of the chores," Pastor Greg had said as they walked toward the parking lot. "I'll go over myself now and see to things."

"I'm going to come back and stay with Willa-Mae as soon as I can," Matty replied. "I'll try and get her to take a little break. And she needs to eat something."

"Why don't you let me take the night shift, Matty? You get some rest and then you can relieve me in the morning."

It had been on the tip of her tongue to argue with him, but something stopped her. Willa-Mae's reaction to seeing him in the E.R. had surprised her.

"All right, Pastor. Call me if you need me to come. Otherwise, I'll see you first thing tomorrow morning. I'm praying Jason will be awake by then."

The sharp whistle brought her back to the present. She made herself a cup of tea and took it outside to the patio. She had missed the best part of this beautiful day. Cupping her hands around the mug, she sat looking out past the fields to the mountains.

She thought about Willa-Mae and her insistence that it was all her fault. "Oh, Lord," she whispered into the stillness, "why do we do this to ourselves? We heap blame and guilt on hearts already burdened with sorrow. Please help her, and please let Jason recover from this with no complications."

Her thoughts turned to prison cells and a man who might possibly be innocent. *How can he bear it,* she wondered? *All those years...and for something he may not have done.* "Lord, please give me grace and strength to do this. Help me find the truth, for Billy and Karen. And Joe."

She finished the last of her tea and walked into the house. Mr. Moran's phone number was on a small piece of paper in the little basket by the telephone. She dialed the number. It rang several times before someone picked up.

"Hello?"

"Hello. Is this Mrs. Moran?"

"Yes. Who is this?"

"It's Cynthia Jones, Mrs. Moran. I spoke to you a couple of weeks ago about an article I'm writing about the Campbell murder."

"Oh yes, I remember. What did you want?"

"Well, you said your husband would be back from his trip in a couple of weeks. I was hoping to talk to him."

"I told him about your article, and he said he doesn't care to be involved. He doesn't have any information that would help you. It was a terrible tragedy, and he doesn't think it's helpful to dig it all up again."

"But if I could just speak to him—"

"He said he doesn't want to talk to you. Please don't call here again, whatever your name is."

She hung up the phone before Matty had a chance to say another word.

"Is it because you don't have any information, Mr. Moran, or are you hiding something? And what was that comment about my name? Did my real name show up on caller ID?"

Shep tilted his head to one side and looked up at her. "I guess I'd better be more careful from here on out, buddy. I can't believe I'm doing this. I'm the last person in the world to be visiting prisons and trying to solve a mystery. But I think when Jason is better—please Lord, let him get better—I should take another trip to the prison. I can't ignore the fact that Joe thought Billy was innocent."

❖

Matty walked into the ICU unit, stopping for a moment to talk to the nurse seated in front of a wall of monitors. The news on Jason wasn't good. He still hadn't regained consciousness.

The small window set in the door to Jason's room framed Willa-Mae seated in the chair pulled close to his bed. To Matty's eyes she looked somehow shrunken—so different from the tall, straight-backed, take-charge woman she had always known. She clutched a wadded-up tissue in her hand. Her eyes never left her husband's motionless face.

Matty pushed open the heavy door and went to Willa-Mae's side. Squatting down beside her, she took the worn hand in her own and removed the tissue. She looked up into the older woman's face. "I stopped by your house to check on things. I thought you might like to have this." She gently pressed a clean handkerchief into her hand. Without shifting her gaze, Willa-Mae gave Matty's hand a slight squeeze.

"Willa-Mae, please let me take you home for just a little while. The nurses will call us if there's any change. You need to take care of yourself so you'll be strong when Jason wakes up."

Slowly, Willa-Mae turned her head. The pain reflected in her eyes caused Matty's heart to catch. "This is all my fault,

Matty."

"You mustn't think that, Willa-Mae. This is no one's fault..."

Willa-Mae pulled her hand free of Matty's. "You wouldn't say that if you knew the whole story."

Matty felt a gentle touch on her shoulder and turned to see one of the nurses standing next to her. She gave them a little smile and leaned in to speak to them: "I'm going to ask you to leave the room for just a little while, ladies. The doctor has ordered a CT scan. Then we'll need to change the bedding and make Mr. Miller more comfortable. It may take a while. Why don't you have a cup of coffee in the waiting room? I'll come and get you as soon as we're done."

Reluctantly Willa-Mae struggled up from her chair, and together they walked to the small waiting room. Magazines were scattered across the small table along with empty coffee cups. The coffee in the coffeemaker smelled as though it had been sitting since early morning.

"Why don't we go outside for a few minutes, Willa-Mae. The fresh air will do you good. I'll tell the nurse at the desk where we're going, and she'll come and get us as soon as they're done with Jason."

Matty tried not to register surprise when Willa-Mae nodded in agreement. Before she could change her mind, Matty walked to the desk to talk to the nurse. Then she tucked her hand under Willa-Mae's arm and led her to the elevator.

A cool breeze greeted them as they stepped out into the

sunshine. Matty took a deep breath of the fresh air and gently guided Willa-Mae along the path to the little park behind the hospital. A gift from a generous donor, it provided a peaceful haven for patients and visitors.

They followed the path past luxuriant flowerbeds and around the sculptured fountain to a little bench at the far end of the park. They had the place all to themselves—birdsong and cascading water the only sounds to break the silence.

"I thought I would find Pastor Greg here this morning, Willa-Mae."

"Oh, he was here all night. His wife called just before you came. There was some sorta problem at the church he had to take care of. Said he'd come back later today. I told him he didn't need to do that—not after the way I've treated him. He just smiled. Oh, Matty, what have I done? God's punishin' me..." She began to weep.

Matty put her arm around her friend and drew her close. Willa-Mae's head rested on her shoulder.

"Willa-Mae, why do you think God is punishing you? I don't believe—"

"You don't know, Matty. You just don't know." Her back stiffened, effectively shrugging off Matty's arm. "But *I* know." Her words came quickly and softly. Matty had to lean in to hear.

"My mother and daddy were God-fearin' people. Daddy was a deacon in the church—had been for years—and Mother...she was a saint. They were in their forties when I was born. Mother didn't think she would be able to have children, so they were real happy when I came along. Mother thought the sun rose and set on me. And Daddy...I guess he loved me too, but he didn't tolerate any nonsense—from me or Mother. I learned early on that God and Daddy expected me to obey the rules, and if I didn't, there would be hell to pay—sorry, honey, but that's the way it was. You know me, Matty. It wasn't easy, but I tried my best for Mother's sake."

A hint of a smile played around her lips and for a moment Matty caught a glimpse of the old Willa-Mae.

"I did okay 'til I got in my teens. Asked Jesus into my heart when I was just a little girl. But all those rules like to drove me crazy. I wanted to do the things my friends were doin', but Daddy wouldn't hear of it. They weren't bad kids. They all went to church, too. But they could date and go to dances and the movies. Those things were strictly forbidden in my house.

"I began to sneak out whenever I could. I was so mad at Daddy I even started goin' around with a crowd I knew he would never approve of. When I was in my senior year of high school, a new boy came to our school. Oh, he was everything I'd ever dreamed of, Matty. Good lookin', lots of fun and a little on the wild side. I fell like a ton o' bricks. I couldn't believe it when he actually asked me out. 'Course, I had to tell him he couldn't come to my house on account of my overbearin' father.

"I told every lie in the book so I could get to see him. He told me he loved me, and I was head over heels in love with him. We talked about gettin' married someday. I knew he drank too much, and he sure never went to church. But I figured I'd get all that stuff sorted out after we were married.

"One month before graduation I found out I was pregnant. I was scared and happy all at the same time. I knew Daddy would probably kill us both when he found out, but I didn't care. All I could think about was gettin' married and havin' his baby.

"Imagine my surprise when my true love told me he had no intention of gettin' married and sure didn't 'want no baby.'" Tears trickled down her weathered cheeks. "He told me to get rid of it. I never had a word from him again, and I was too proud to chase after him.

"I knew I could never get rid of the baby, but I didn't know what to do. I was terrified to tell Daddy. Somehow I made it through graduation. I knew I wouldn't be goin' to college in the fall, the way I'd planned. I didn't even have a job. I had no choice but to tell Mother and Daddy. I prayed to God to forgive me and to please let Daddy not be too angry. I wanted my baby, Matty. I really did. Even though I knew the shame of it all.

"I tried to put it off as long as I could, but pretty soon I got to where even the baggy shirts I was wearin' didn't work. Daddy made a few comments about how much weight I seemed to be puttin' on. I could tell he didn't think things were quite right.

"I thought about runnin' away, but I didn't have any idea where to go. So one evenin' I told them. I had never seen Daddy like that. He didn't yell—just seemed to turn to stone right before my eyes. He told me God would punish me for this terrible thing I had done. Mother just sat on the sofa cryin'.

"He paced up and down the livin' room for the longest time. I could hardly stand it. I just wanted him to say somethin'. I kept prayin' God would soften his heart toward me. Finally, he stopped and looked at me with such cold, hard eyes. He said they would send me to a home he knew of in another part of the state where I could have the baby. Then it would be put up for adoption. I cried and begged him to please let me keep my baby. I said I would go away, and they would never have to see me again.

"But I was only seventeen. There was nothin' I could do. Things were a lot different in those days. I was a disgrace to myself and my family.

"Daddy told folks I had changed my mind about goin' to college. Said I was goin' to live with an aunt who was real sick and help her out while I prayed about what I wanted to do. Oh, Matty—all I wanted to do was have my baby.

"He didn't waste any time. Before I knew it we were on our way to a home for unwed mothers in San Antonio, Texas. While he was there, he made all the arrangements for the adoption. I never even saw my baby. One of the nurses told me it was a little boy."

"What about your mother, Willa-Mae? Couldn't she have persuaded your father..."

Willa-Mae laughed—a harsh sound so unlike her throaty chuckle. "I heard them arguin' that night—well I should say I heard Daddy yellin' and mother cryin'. I kept hopin' she could help me somehow, Matty, but I shoulda known better. The next day she helped me pack my things. Never said one word about the baby. Not even when I kissed her goodbye. I don't know which of 'em I hated more in that moment."

"What did you do after you had the baby?"

"I vowed I would never go home again. The people at the home were real nice. They let me stay until I could find work. They even helped me find a room to rent. I got a job at the Air Force Base working in the PX, and then I met Jason."

The tears threatened again as Matty sat waiting. Willa-Mae put the damp handkerchief to her eyes.

"I couldn't believe someone like him would want to have anything to do with me. When he asked me out, I nearly fell over."

"And of course you said yes."

"Of course I did not! I had also vowed not to have anything to do with men ever again. I wasn't about to let a uniform turn my head. Not this girl. I told him thanks, but no thanks."

"Willa-Mae, you didn't!"

"I sure did. But he was a persistent son of a gun. Seemed like every time I turned around, there he was. So I finally said yes, just so he'd quit botherin' me. I figured once he got to know me I'd never hear from him again."

"But it didn't turn out that way." Matty couldn't hide the smile that threatened to split her face.

"No. For some reason, nothin' I said discouraged him. Not

even when I told him about the baby. He never said a word, just sat there holdin' my hand. I never met anyone like him. He was so kind and gentle with me."

Matty swiped at her eyes and inched a little closer to her friend. "Did you get married right away, Willa-Mae?"

"We did. Jason had two more years to serve, and then he planned to come back here to the family farm. He said he always thought he wanted a career in the military, to get away from the farm and see more of the world. But his Daddy's health was failin', and they needed help. You know Jason. He gave up his dream to go back home."

"Did he have regrets?"

"I don't think so. Leastwise he never said so. He told me once that he had everything he ever wanted right here—with me and all."

"I'm sure that's true, Willa-Mae. Jason is a very contented man."

"I could never give him children, Matty. The one thing he wanted so bad, and I couldn't give it to him. I believe it was my punishment for what I'd done. I accepted that, but I felt awful for him. He would have been a wonderful daddy."

"Oh Willa-Mae, I wish I could make you understand. These difficult things aren't a punishment from God. He's forgiven you, and He loves you. He isn't like your earthly father. He covers you with His grace."

"I know He's good, Matty, but He doesn't tolerate sin. That's why I got so upset over the goin's on at church. I just knew there would be somethin' terrible happen if Pastor Greg didn't change his ways. But now that it's too late, I see I was wrong. He's a good man tryin' to do the Lord's work as best he can. We've done a lot of talkin' over the past couple a days. I should have given him a chance. Now God is punishin' me for my wicked tongue and judgin' ways and for gettin' so many others all stirred up. The church is in a mess because of me. That's why this has happened to Jason. It's all my fault."

Matty reached over to take her hand, but Willa-Mae stood and began walking back toward the hospital.

"I need to get back in there. They must be done with all that nonsense by now."

"Wait. I'll come with you."

"No, honey. You go on home. I want to be alone with Jason for a while. I'll be fine. You go on now."

Matty watched the older woman walk slowly toward the entrance. She seemed to have aged ten years overnight. She sat for a few more minutes thinking back over the conversation. *How can I make her understand that You don't work that way, Lord? Please help her see who You really are.*

~ CHAPTER 20 ~

Matty drove slowly through the quiet streets. She tried to picture the teenaged Willa-Mae. On the one hand she couldn't reconcile the image of the rebellious girl with her straight-laced friend. On the other hand, Willa-Mae had lost none of her feisty spirit. She had learned to channel it in another direction, but there were still times it got her into a bit of a spot.

Matty smiled to herself, remembering the time her friend had confronted the Centerville City Council when she heard they planned to level the old city hall. Willa-Mae had sailed into their monthly meeting with a group of supporters following in her wake. Then she proceeded to deliver a spirited defense of the historic building only to discover, when they could get her to calm down, that they were just planning to make some much needed structural repairs to the foundation.

She thought about Jason and prayed he would recover. It didn't look hopeful. The longer he remained in a coma, the bleaker the outlook. "Why must life be so difficult, Lord?"

She came to a stop at the town's only traffic light. As she waited for the light to change, the image of a dark prison cell filled her mind. She almost wished she had never found the notebook.

"Why does this have to be my responsibility? I can't do this—not any of it. Why did you leave me, Joe..." The blast of a horn sounded behind her, and she looked up to see the light had turned green. Flustered, she gunned the engine and nearly lost control of the big car. Fighting back tears, she gripped the steering wheel and drove home as quickly as she dared.

Shep, faithful Shep, greeted her with his usual enthusiasm. Rubbing her face against his, she felt a deep gratitude for this sweet blessing. She couldn't imagine how she would have managed without him. Together they climbed the stairs and walked into the kitchen. The house felt so empty, and the day she had planned to spend in the hospital with Willa-Mae stretched out before her in long, lonely hours. She filled the little copper teakettle with water and placed it on the stove. Two minutes later she walked over and turned it off.

Roaming from room to room trying to decide what to do she picked up the phone and dialed Nancy's number. Just as she was about to hang up she heard Nancy's breathless, "Hello."

"Oh, Nancy, I'm so sorry to bother you. Are you busy?"

"No, Matty. I'm not busy at all. I was just coming in from the barn when I heard the phone. What's up? Is there any news on Jason?"

"No, I'm afraid not. I was there this morning, and he still hasn't woken up. They were just taking him for some tests when I got there. Willa-Mae is so upset. She didn't want me to stay. Said she wanted to be alone with him. I wish there was something I could do to help. I was just calling to see if you might like to come have a cup of tea with me, but if you're busy I'll understand."

"I told you I'm not busy." Matty could almost "hear" the smile on her friend's face. "I do need to jump into the shower first, though. I wouldn't want to bring the lovely fragrance of the barn into your nice clean kitchen."

Matty laughed. "You can come any way you want, any time you want. You know that."

"I do. But frankly, I can't stand the smell of myself right now. So give me thirty minutes or so, and I'll be there. In fact, I'll bring some cinnamon buns. Made 'em fresh this morning."

After a quick good-bye, Matty began getting things together for tea. She was just coming out of the pantry when the doorbell rang. She ran down the hall and unlocked the door.

"Wow, that was fast. I thought—" Matty stopped mid-sentence as she opened the door and saw Donna standing there with a large picnic basket slung over her arm and a rather disgruntled look on her face. She stepped inside before Matty had a chance to say another word.

"Pastor Greg asked me to organize meals and whatever

else Willa-Mae needed," she huffed as she made her way to the kitchen. "I left a message on her answering machine saying I would be bringing her dinner. I specifically said I would come in the morning so I would catch her before she left for the hospital. I hope she doesn't think I forgot or something."

"Here, let me take that, Donna. Why don't you sit down for a minute."

Looking slightly mollified, Donna took a seat at the table. "I worked so hard on that, Matty. All the things I know Willa-Mae loves. I even baked her a rhubarb pie. You know I like to do whatever I can to help. I even offered to sit with Jason, but I never heard a word back."

"I'm sure Willa-Mae will appreciate everything you've done, Donna. I'll bring the food over to her house later and leave her a note telling her it's from you. She's been staying at the hospital night and day ever since Jason went in. The doctor felt it would be better if Jason didn't have any visitors right now. I'm sure when he's feeling a little better you'll be able to visit him."

"Well I've lined up meals for however long she needs them," Donna replied. "Susan and I plan to do a bit of housecleaning for her before Jason comes home from the hospital. Do you know when that will be?"

"I'm afraid we don't know that yet, Donna. He's still in a coma, and—"

"Still in a coma!" Donna interrupted. "I didn't know. Oh, my. Do you think he'll make it, Matty? Whatever will Willa-

Mae do?"

"We're praying he'll pull through. He's a strong man. I think he has a very good chance."

Matty breathed a silent prayer that the woman would leave. She didn't want her here when Nancy arrived. She was looking forward to a nice long chat with her friend. Just as quickly she felt guilty for thinking such a thing and heard herself inviting Donna to stay for tea.

"Oh that sounds lovely, Matty, but I really couldn't. I have a million things to do. I'm organizing a little outing for the folks at the nursing home. I have a meeting with the director in a little while."

Of course you do was Matty's uncharitable thought. "Oh, I'm so sorry. We'll do it another time then, Donna."

She walked her to the door and hurried back into the kitchen to make tea. A few minutes later she heard a tap on the back door, and Nancy walked in.

"I come bearing cinnamon buns," she called out.

Matty took the dish from her and gave her a hug. "I'm so glad to see you."

"Was that Donna I saw driving down the road?"

"Yes. She had come to do her good deed for the day. Oh, I'm sorry, Nancy. She didn't know Willa-Mae was staying at the hospital with Jason. That was mean of me. There's just something about that woman that sets my teeth on edge. I know she means well, and she does more in a week than I've done in a lifetime."

Nancy put an arm around her shoulders. "Don't feel bad.

She has the same effect on me. I think it's the way she goes about doing those good deeds. I wish she would relax. I get worn out just watching her."

The kettle gave a shrill whistle, and Matty ran to turn off the gas. "Have a seat, Nancy. Tea's almost ready."

While the tea steeped, Matty lit a couple of candles and brought them to the table. "It must be getting cloudy out. It's kind of dark in here. We'll have a little ambiance with our tea."

Nancy smiled, "It looked like rain when I drove in. Now come and sit, old friend, and tell me what's troubling you."

"I never could fool you." Matty poured the tea and sat facing her friend. "It's nothing and everything. I thought I had worked through all the so-called stages of grief, but grief doesn't seem to want to be pinned down to a set of rules. I go from peaceful to angry, to desperately sad, to lonely and empty and all the way back again. Sometimes all within the space of a few hours." Matty folded her napkin over and over, pressing it into a tight little square. "I miss Joe."

Nancy sat quietly. Listening.

"I think this thing with Jason has stirred up all those things I thought I had dealt with. And then there's this business with Billy Taylor."

"I wish you would just let that go, or at the very least talk to someone in authority. You shouldn't be meddling in this."

Matty tucked the napkin under her plate and dropped her hands into her lap. "I can't let it go. What if he's innocent? And I'm seeing enough other possible suspects to believe he is. I can't turn my back on him. As far as talking to someone goes, I don't have anything to go on other than a few sentences in Joe's notebook and some thirty-six-year-old gossip courtesy of Susan Martin."

"Well, what do you plan to do?"

"I want to go visit Billy again. I'm going to try to get him to remember that day a bit more clearly. He says he saw someone walking across the bridge that evening. Maybe he can at least tell me if it was a man or a woman."

"Do you suspect someone?"

Matty looked a little sheepish. "Well, I called the Morans again, you know, the math teacher. His wife said he didn't want to talk to me. She hung up on me before I could say much."

"Is that all?"

"Well, no. As she was hanging up the phone she said, 'Please don't call here again, whatever your name is.'"

"So she didn't buy the Cynthia Jones routine. You have got to be careful." Nancy leaned across the table punctuating the words with her finger. "This isn't a game. We're talking about murder here."

"I know, Nancy. I will. I promise."

They both jumped a little when the phone began ringing. Matty rushed to answer it. She listened for a minute then turned to Nancy, her face pale and pinched.

"That was Willa-Mae. She said to come quickly. Oh, Nancy, I can't bear it if Jason dies."

Nancy immediately got to her feet. "Come on. I'm going to

drive you there."

❖

Neither woman spoke as they bounced and rattled their way down the old country lane. Nancy gripped the steering wheel and drove as fast as she dared. Matty sat staring out the window. Images of Joe lying lifeless on the basement floor, the ambulance speeding through the streets and the empty hospital corridor all flashed through her mind. She was desperate to get to Willa-Mae and yearned for the safety of her own home at the same time.

Nancy stopped the pickup in front of the entrance to the hospital.

"You go on in, Matty. I'll park and meet you up there."

Matty hung back for just a moment, not wanting to do this on her own. Taking a deep breath, she stepped down, shoved the door closed behind her and rushed through the open doors. She waited for the elevator, her heart feeling like it would beat right out of her chest. She closed her eyes and whispered a prayer—the only words she could find—"Jesus, help us." The elevator door swished open, and she stepped out.

She expected to see chaos when she reached the ICU. Expected to see nurses running in and out of Jason's room with mysterious machines and tense faces. Expected to see doctors gathered around Jason's bed. Instead, the entire area was quiet. The tapping of her shoes against the tile floor echoed down the empty hallway. She walked hesitantly toward Jason's room and opened the door.

Willa-Mae sat in her usual spot, holding Jason's hand. She looked up as Matty walked toward her. The sweetest smile played across her face, and her eyes glistened.

"He's awake, Matty," she whispered. "Oh, thank You, Jesus. He's awake."

Matty went to her. She got down on her knees and wrapped her arms around her friend's waist. Willa-Mae's arms closed around her.

"Oh, Willa-Mae. I'm so very sorry." Nancy stood at the foot of the bed, looking at her two friends.

"Oh, no, Nancy. It's all right." Matty slowly rose to her feet. "Jason's awake. He's still with us."

The three friends hugged each other and cried and tried to be quiet all at the same time.

"Oh, Willa-Mae," whispered Matty, trying to pull herself together. "You scared us to death. We thought...well, you know. You sounded so urgent on the phone."

"I'm sorry, honey. I didn't mean to scare you. I wanted you to be surprised and happy. I didn't think. Nancy, I'm sorry. I deserve a kick in the pants. I was just so happy." She looked down at Jason and gently covered his hand with hers. Matty and Nancy watched as he slowly opened his eyes.

"Look who's here, darlin'."

In spite of tubes and machinery that beeped and flashed all around him, he smiled and then wearily closed his eyes.

Willa-Mae motioned for them to follow her outside. There

was no one in the waiting room, so they sat together in the worn plastic chairs and talked.

"It was like a miracle, girls. The nurses kept pesterin' me to go home last night, but somethin' told me I should stay. Right when the sun started to peep up out of the treetops, I felt a squeeze on my hand. I nearly fell on the floor. I squeezed Jason's hand, and I felt it again. So I started to talk to him. I asked him to come back to me. And he opened his eyes. I could hardly believe it. I wanted to jump up and start runnin' around that stupid room. Instead, I ran out there and got the nurse.

"She saw him open his eyes, too. And she called the doctor—and, oh, girls—he said he thinks Jason is goin' to make it. Oh, thank You, Jesus!"

Matty and Nancy smiled tentative smiles, neither wanting to ask what was uppermost on their minds.

"I know what you're thinkin'. The doctor didn't make any promises. He said we won't know for a little while yet if there's permanent brain damage. They have to watch him real careful to be sure he doesn't have another bleed. He might have some disabilities and need rehab or a dozen other problems—but I don't care. All that matters is he's not gonna die. Thank You, Jesus."

"Yes, Willa-Mae, that's all that matters," Nancy said. "You know we'll help you in any way we can."

Matty felt too overwhelmed to speak. She sat not even trying to hide the tears. Willa-Mae reached over and dabbed Matty's eyes with her own crocheted handkerchief, then squeezed her hand. "I'd give anything if it could have been the same for Joe, honey. You know I would. I don't know why God should be so good to me."

"He loves you, Willa-Mae. He loves me, too. I'm so thankful Jason is going to be all right."

"Well, I got to get back in there with him." Willa-Mae stood up to go. "I called Pastor Greg, too. He'll be here soon."

"I'll come and sit with Jason tonight so you can go home and get some sleep."

"Never you mind, Matty. Pastor Greg and I have got this thing. I'll be fine. You come see me tomorrow."

The three women hugged goodbye. Matty and Nancy turned when they reached the elevator, but Willa-Mae had already walked back to Jason's room.

~ CHAPTER 21 ~

The ride back to Miller's Crossing was quiet, neither woman willing to put her thoughts into words. Jason hadn't regained consciousness after the surgery as quickly as they had hoped. Every hour that had gone by over these long days had left them wondering what he would be like if he woke up. They knew the list of complications was long and frightening, and the possibility of permanent brain damage all too real.

The tension in the truck was palpable. The air felt heavy and stale. Matty rolled down her window and inhaled the fresh air. She looked over at Nancy and saw her shoulders shaking. She reached over to comfort her friend and realized she wasn't crying at all. Instead, she was trying to keep from laughing out loud.

"What's so funny?"

"I'm sorry, Matty. It's just—you know I'm as concerned about Jason as you are, but..."

The laughter bubbled over, and Matty hung on to the door handle willing Nancy to get herself under control before they ran off the road.

"Nancy, be careful. What is it?" Matty looked over at her friend, and then she began to laugh. "I don't even know why I'm laughing."

"Oh, Matty," Nancy gasped, trying to get out the words, "'Pastor Greg and I have got this thing?' Since when are Willa-Mae and Pastor Greg best buds? I almost fell over when she said that."

"I know. It's like a miracle—a silver lining in this awful tragedy. Pastor Greg isn't the heathen Willa-Mae thought he was. Do you know he's been with her from the moment they brought Jason to the hospital? Believe it or not, she admitted right out loud that she was mistaken."

"Well, that *is* a miracle. I don't remember Willa-Mae ever admitting she was wrong about anything. I hope things will settle down at church now."

"I'm hopeful. Do you want to come in for a few minutes?"

Nancy brought the truck to a stop in the driveway. "I don't think so. I really should get home. I told Buddy I'd only be gone for a little while. He must wonder what on earth's become of me. Give me a call when you know anything more about Jason."

"I will. Thanks for everything. See you soon."

She stood for a moment watching the truck rattle its way down the road, then turned and went inside.

❖

Matty inhaled deeply as she set the large pitcher filled with

Queen Elizabeth roses on Willa-Mae's old farm table. Their sweet fragrance filled the room, and the polished surface reflected the beautiful pink of the blooms. Matty stood back and nodded, satisfied.

She walked from room to room, opening windows, fluffing pillows and rearranging things she'd already organized the previous day. The freshly washed curtains billowed in the early August breeze.

A strawberry-rhubarb pie sat cooling on the countertop next to a casserole all ready to pop in the oven. The freezer was filled with enough meals to last for weeks. The youth group from church spent last Saturday weeding the garden and cutting the grass. It seemed every single person in the community had done their part to welcome Jason. After weeks of rest and rehab, he was finally coming home.

It was decided, or rather "gently requested" by Willa-Mae, that they not have a big crowd at the house when he arrived. He would need to rest. There would be plenty of time to visit in the coming days. Matty would be there to get the house ready and then quietly leave them to get settled in.

For what seemed like the hundredth time, Matty walked to the window and looked down the road. Not a soul in sight. She thought back over the past few weeks, to the miracle God had done in both Jason's and Willa-Mae's lives.

The doctors had prepared Willa-Mae for the worst. God had other plans. Almost from the moment he woke up, Jason was clearly going to do much better than anyone dared to hope. They monitored him closely for fear of another bleed.

There was none.

They moved him out of ICU, and within days he was sitting up in bed and taking tentative steps with his walker—Willa-Mae bringing up the rear. The thing everyone had feared most was not to be: Jason showed no sign of brain damage. His astounded doctors merely shook their heads when discussing it among themselves. All except Dr. Sanders. The day Jason opened his eyes, he came and took Willa-Mae's hands in his. "I've been praying for your husband, Mrs. Miller. I believe God is going to do a miracle in his life."

And so He had.

Lost in thought, Matty didn't see the car until they were turning into the long driveway. She ran to the door and rushed out to meet them. Pastor Greg helped Willa-Mae from the car and then quickly went to the trunk to get Jason's walker. Before he had a chance to get to him, Jason opened the car door and beamed up at Matty.

She had visited him often over the past few weeks, but seeing him now in his own surroundings she thought he looked better than ever. He had lost weight, but the familiar smile made him look years younger.

"Oh Jason, it's so good to have you home. You look wonderful." She gently put her arms around him and gave him a long hug.

"It's good to be home, honey." She leaned in to catch his words as he murmured, "I'm so thankful—to the good Lord and to everyone who has been so kind."

Willa-Mae hustled around the car and took his arm. "Come on, darlin'. Let's get you out of the hot sun." She grabbed Matty with her other hand. "Come on in for a minute, Matty. I wanna talk to you."

Pastor Greg went ahead and held the door. The others moved up the path at the pace of the walker, stopping every now and then for Jason to look around his beloved farm. He admired the flowers and the garden and gazed out across the fields. The old barn cat wound herself around his ankles, and he smiled down at her.

Willa-Mae sprang into action the minute they got inside.

"Let's get you to bed, darlin'. I know you must be plumb tuckered out. Pastor Greg, will you just put his things in the bedroom—first door on your right down the hall. Here, let me help you with your walker. Do you want a nice cold drink of water? Or how about some sweet tea?"

Jason chuckled. "Just let me sit right here in the living room for a little while, hon. I'm fine. It's so good to be home. He pulled an old handkerchief out of his pocket and wiped his eyes. Matty felt her own eyes beginning to get misty. She looked at Pastor Greg and Willa-Mae and saw that they, too, were having trouble holding back the tears.

"Well, a fine bunch we are," said Willa-Mae a little too loudly. "This is the happiest day in the world, and we're all sittin' here bawlin'. I'm gonna get us all a glass of sweet tea." And she marched off into the kitchen.

"She's something, isn't she?" Jason smiled his sweet smile. "She never left my side for a minute. I love her to death."

Later, after they got Jason settled down for a nap and Pastor Greg had gone home, the two women went outside to sit on the front porch. Matty set her glass of tea on the rail and rocked back and forth in the old rocker, waiting for Willa-Mae to tell her what was on her mind.

She watched as a huge bumblebee hovered over the rose bush. The only sounds were the birdsong and the wind rustling the leaves of the trees. The old barn cat climbed up on the porch and sat at Willa-Mae's feet. She reached down to pick her up, and Matty saw the tears. She sat quietly. Waiting.

"Matty. I've wasted so many years believin' a lie."

Matty reached over and put her hand on Willa-Mae's arm.

"I hated the way my Daddy treated Mother and me, but somewhere deep down inside I thought he was right. And I thought God was just like he was—demandin' and judgmental and real short on love when it came to people who didn't obey. Oh, I believed He loved me all right, 'cept I had to earn that love, and if I messed up, well, then He was just gonna have to punish me so I'd learn my lesson and behave."

She took out an old flowered handkerchief and crumpled it in her fist.

"I believed everything bad that happened was God's way of punishin' me. I was so wrong." She lifted her glasses and pressed the handkerchief to her eyes. "I didn't understand His love. I didn't know He loved me no matter what I did. Oh, I heard it often enough in Sunday school and church, but it never got down into my heart. I couldn't imagine He felt that way about me. I thought I had done too many wrong things to deserve to be loved that way.

"I didn't deserve for Jason to get better. Not after the way I've been behavin' in church. But he did, and it was a flat-out miracle. He wasn't supposed to get well. None of the doctors believed he would. But God answered my prayer. Oh, Matty, I've been such an old fool."

Matty got up and put her arms around her friend. Willa-Mae rested her head on Matty's shoulder and wept for a long time.

"Oh, Willa-Mae..."

"You don't have to say a word, Matty." Wiping away tears with her soggy handkerchief, Willa-Mae leaned back and cupped Matty's face in her hands. "Me and Pastor Greg had some long talks while we were sittin' by Jason's bedside. He's a fine young man. He never did preach at me. Mostly he listened. And He lived God's love right there in front of me.

"I'm not sayin' we'll always see eye to eye on everything, but I believe his heart is right before the Lord. I guess I'll just have to learn to bite my tongue every now and then. And who knows? Pastor Greg might just think I'm on the right track once in a while, too." She gave Matty a wobbly smile.

"I love you, Willa-Mae."

"I love you too, honey. And you don't have to worry about church anymore. I asked Pastor Greg to forgive me for causin' so much trouble. I plan to stand up in church when Jason is all better and tell everyone what an old fool I am."

"You are not—"

"Hush, now. We both know the trouble I've stirred up. I got all het up over music and clothes and petty things, and all the while I was the worst offender of all. No, I got to make this right. Now you run along home. You've been with us two old folks for days and days. We're gonna be just fine."

Matty stood to go and gave Willa-Mae a hand up. She drew Matty into her arms and kissed her cheek. "Thank you for everything, honey."

"You're more than welcome. You're like family, Willa-Mae. I'll call you later to see how things are going, but you call me right away if you need anything at all."

"I told you we're fine, and we are. I'm fixin' to take a little rest and then we'll have a little somethin' to eat. Go on now."

Matty turned when she reached the end of the driveway. Willa-Mae gave her a little wave.

❖

Matty came in from the garden and waited a minute for her eyes to adjust to the comparative darkness. It was another scorcher, the sun bright in a dazzling blue sky. She deposited the bounty on the counter by the sink and, after filling Shep's bowl with cold water, got a cold drink for herself.

She turned on the ceiling fan and sat at the kitchen table to cool off. They didn't often need air conditioning, but this past week made her consider buying one. Joe had installed an attic fan years ago. Thankfully, it drew in enough air to make the nights bearable.

She thought back over the past few days. Jason was doing better than anyone had dared hope. The church continued to support them in every possible way, everyone coming together to do their part. Willa-Mae's freezer was overflowing with casseroles and desserts. The kids from the youth group were doing the mowing and weeding, and some of the men were taking turns tending the livestock. Someone even donated an air conditioning unit for their bedroom so they could sleep comfortably. The whole incident had done much to bring the little church family back together.

Nancy was busy helping Buddy on the farm. This was a busy time of year for them. Aside from her visits next-door, Matty and Shep had been on their own. The day often dragged; she longed for Joe all the time, feeling it like a chronic ache.

She tried to occupy her mind with other things. The pantry was spotless, and all the shelves were lined with new shelf paper. There wasn't a single weed in the flowerbeds or the garden. Even the garage looked clean and tidy.

Most mornings she brought her coffee and Bible out to the patio and watched the sun rise over the mountains. Evenings were the most difficult. The quiet house seemed to close in around her.

The phone rang just as she was about to get up and put her glass in the dishwasher.

"Matty, it's Nancy. Come on over and have supper with

us. I made way too much fried chicken, and you need to come help us eat it. I won't take no for an answer."

Matty laughed. "In that case, I'll be over as soon as I take a shower. I've been working out in the garden. My word, it's hot outside."

"Don't I know it! We decided to call it quits a little early today. We got a lot of the sweet corn in, and Buddy will take it to the market in the morning. It did really well this year. I'm glad we decided to plant it. We'll have a few ears for supper. See you in a little bit."

It was just what Matty needed, good company and delicious food. Their old farmhouse, with its worn wooden floors, wavy glass windows and rickety front porch, spoke peace to her.

After supper Buddy took off to go bowling with a group from church. Matty and Nancy worked together to clear the table and wash the dishes. Then they took their iced tea outside and sat on the porch. The sun had slipped down behind the tree line, coloring the gathering clouds a beautiful shade of pink. The heat had eased a bit, but the air still felt heavy. Nothing stirred.

"The weatherman is predicting a thunderstorm tonight. Hopefully that will break the heat."

"That would be nice, although Shep is not a big fan of thunder and lightning."

They sat rocking in companionable silence.

"Will you be going to visit Jenny soon?"

"I thought I'd wait until the beginning of September.

She's been after me to come, but I have a few things I want to get taken care of before I go."

"Do those few things include Billy Taylor?"

"Oh, Nancy. I know how you feel about it. I just want to give it a little more time. I managed to push it to the back of my mind while we were so involved with Jason and Willa-Mae, but I need to be sure one way or the other if I possibly can. Just imagine how it would be if you were imprisoned all those years for something you didn't do."

"I do understand, but I think you should...well, you know how I feel. Please be very, very careful."

"I promise I will. Now I need to get home and take Shep for a little walk. It's beginning to feel like it'll rain."

"Yeah. The wind is picking up. Come inside for a minute, and let me give you a few of those brownies to take home with you."

"Just what I need."

"You do. You're looking far too thin. Are you eating regularly?"

"Yes, ma'am. I'm eating regularly."

Nancy gave her a playful smack on the shoulder. "Don't be a smarty pants. You know I'm just looking out for your well-being."

Matty laughed. "Yes, I know. And those brownies are just what the doctor ordered."

Shep greeted her as he always did, as though she had been gone for ages. She grabbed his leash and clipped it to his collar. The clouds were beginning to gather, and it smelled like rain. They turned right at the end of the drive and hurried past Jason and Willa-Mae's. The lamp in the living room window made the house look cozy and inviting.

Right across the way stood the old Taylor place. Far from cozy and inviting, the house looked desolate. No light spilled from the shattered windows. Overgrown bushes and weeds populated the front yard. Matty shivered in spite of the heat. She had always loved old, abandoned houses—imagining the life they had once contained. But this house held no happy memories. She tugged on the leash and turned for home.

A distant flash of lightning caught her eye as they approached the house. Matty decided to fix a quick cup of tea and get ready for bed even though it was still early. She hoped she could shut out enough of the storm to make Shep feel safe.

She was tucked into bed with her big dog beside her before the worst of the storm hit. She never allowed him onto the bed but told herself this was an exception. Shep burrowed his head against her side and quivered at every roll of thunder and flash of lightning.

Matty picked up her mystery book and hoped to lose herself in the story, but images of the Taylor farm kept intruding. The rain beat against the windows, and she thought of Billy in his tiny prison cell. What was he thinking about on this stormy night? Was he feeling the desperation she would have felt if she had been wrongly accused and imprisoned?

"I can't turn my back on him, Lord," she whispered. "I'm

going to go see him tomorrow, before I lose my nerve. Maybe he'll be able to remember more about the person he saw."

The light on her bedside table flickered and then went out. Sighing she put the book aside and scrunched down under the covers. The storm raged outside. She put her arm around Shep and drifted off to sleep.

~ CHAPTER 22 ~

Matty stood in line waiting. Dozens of conversations swirled around her. Children climbed onto the laps of daddies they rarely got to touch. Some of the women sat silently, others laughed just a little too loudly.

A part of her wanted to turn around and run away from it all, but that wasn't an option. *I have to see this thing through—for Joe.* Following the example of the women in line ahead of her, she handed an envelope with Billy's name printed on the outside to the guard. *I'm glad I remembered to bring him some money.* The guard pointed to one of the chairs pulled up to the long table. She took a seat, eyes riveted to the doorway.

The minutes dragged by, and she wondered if he had refused to come and see her. Surely the guard would have told her if that was the case. She was just about to walk over and ask if Billy was coming when he appeared in the doorway.

She could hardly believe her eyes. He looked like he had shrunk since her last visit—thin and fragile. He shuffled toward her, and she saw the terrible bruising on his face.

"Whadda you want? I don't mean to be rude, ma'am, but I don't know why you bother comin' here. I told you before there ain't nothin' anyone can do."

"Please sit down, Billy. I won't stay long. I just wanted to talk to you a little bit more." She felt tears welling and bent her head. "What happened to you, Billy?"

The chair scraped across the concrete floor, and she lifted her head. Up close, his face looked even worse. Both eyes were black and blue. His nose looked broken. Bruises in various shades covered his jaw. He looked at her, and she felt a frisson of fear. She had never seen such empty eyes.

She repeated the question, her voice barely above a whisper. "Billy. What happened?" She thought he hadn't heard. He sat for a long time staring into space, then turned to look at her.

"It's just business as usual, ma'am. Just business as usual."

Matty didn't know what to say. Any words of sympathy would sound sanctimonious. Instead, she decided to get right to the point.

"I wanted to ask you if you'd thought any more about the person you saw crossing the bridge—to see if you remembered anything else that might help us find out who it was." Her words trailed off. She thought how pointless it all seemed and wished she hadn't come. She jumped a little when he finally spoke.

"Whadda you think you're gonna do? I told you there ain't

no way old lady Campbell is gonna sit by and watch me walk outta this place. Don't make me your Sunday School do-gooder project. You can't help me. Ain't nobody can help me."

"Did you feel that way about Joe?" She tried to keep the rising anger out of her voice. Did he really think she came to this horrible place because she wanted to do a good deed? Maybe everyone was right. Maybe he really was guilty.

Again a long silence. Then, "No. He was different. He cared about me."

Matty caught the eye of the man sitting next to Billy and lowered her voice to almost a whisper. He had to bend down to hear her, and she looked into his wounded eyes.

"Well, I care about you too, Billy. But I'll be honest with you. I'm doing this out of love for my husband. He believed in you, and I promised myself I would do my best to finish what he started. How can I do that, though, if you won't cooperate?"

She saw his eyes begin to fill and looked away. In spite of his attitude there was something about this man that touched her deeply.

"I'm sorry, Mrs. Amoruso. I don't mean to be ornery. It's just hard to believe anyone would care about me like that. I been thinkin' about it like you asked. It was just startin' to go to dark when I was walkin' back home that day. But I did see someone."

"Think hard, Billy. Was it a man or a woman—or maybe a teenager?"

"I can't be sure."

"Do you think it could have been someone you knew?"

He shook his head. "I don't know." Suddenly his whole demeanor changed. He sat up straight and perched on the end of his chair. "I remember white shoes. It was real dusky-like, but those shoes stood out. Maybe it was a lady."

Catching his excitement, Matty put her hand over his without thinking. "Or could it have been a man or a teenager wearing sneakers?"

"I guess it coulda been."

For the first time there was a glimmer of hope in his eyes. Matty prayed silently for the right words. *Don't let me give him false hope, Lord, but please let this be the beginning of the end of this terrible nightmare for him.*

He looked at her with such expectation she could hardly bear it.

"Do you think it was the one who done it? Do you think we can find out who it is after all this time?"

"I honestly don't know, Billy. I think it gives us something to work with. Now we're certain you saw someone. There can't have been many people who would have been on the bridge that time of day. It definitely gives us something to go on."

He slumped back into his chair.

"I don't want you to get yourself in no trouble, Mrs. Amoruso. I thank you for wantin' to help me, but I'm afraid you're gonna get hurt tryin'. Maybe it's best to let this thing lie."

She looked down at the scarred wooden table. Her hand

still covered his, and she gave it a squeeze. "I'll be careful, Billy. If I find something important, I'll go to the police and let them take over. It'll be all right."

He got up to go. "I'll be prayin' for you, Mrs. Amoruso."

Slightly taken aback she answered, "Thank you, Billy. I'll be praying for you, too."

❖

Matty replayed the conversation over and over again in her mind all the way home. Her emotions swung wildly between hope and doubt. Was it possible they had found the real killer? Or was it merely a figment of Billy's imagination? Had she pushed him too hard and forced him to remember something that never happened? Or, worse yet, was he simply making it up?

She thought about stopping at Nancy's but decided against it. Shep needed to get outside, and besides, she felt nervous about sharing this new information. She tapped on the steering wheel. "Nancy will pressure me to go to the authorities, and I'm not ready to do that yet. If there isn't anything to it, they'll just get upset with me. Then if I do find something important, they won't even bother listening." She turned down her drive, still sorting it through out loud. "I don't want anything to happen to Billy, either. He must have taken a terrible beating. No. I think I'll just keep this between you and me, Lord." She gazed briefly into the heavens and smiled.

The light on the downstairs answering machine was blinking when she walked into the house. *I really should break down and get a cell phone,* she thought. *It's time, as Jenny says, to step into the twenty-first century. I just don't want to have to learn one more thing.*

The computer had been difficult enough. Joe had patiently tried to teach her the basics. It had been agonizing. She still only used it sparingly—e-mail and an occasional Skype with the kids, although she hated seeing her own face on the screen. She much preferred the phone.

She pushed the button, and Willa-Mae's shrill voice filled the room. "Where are you, Matty? Is everythin' alright? I suppose you've just gone shoppin' or visitin' or somethin'. Anyway...Jason is havin' a real good day. Come on over, and have supper with us. Same time, same station!"

Matty smiled and shook her head. "Come on, Shep. Let's get you outside before you burst. I'll call Willa-Mae when we get back."

A little before five-thirty Matty left the house and walked up to Jason and Willa-Mae's. Last night's storm had cleared the air and lowered the temperature. Everything looked fresh and new. Matty stopped in the driveway before going up to the porch. She inhaled the fragrance of freshly-cut grass.

"Well, are you gonna stand there all day or are you comin' in?"

Willa-Mae stood holding the screen door open, one hand on her hip and a mock scowl on her face.

"I'm coming in, boss." I was just admiring your yard.

Everything looks so nice."

"It does, doesn't it? A couple of the boys from church came by this afternoon. They cut the grass and weeded the flower beds. Honestly, folks are bein' so kind, I hardly know what to do. I sent them home with chocolate chip cookies right out of the oven, but it doesn't seem nearly enough."

"Willa-Mae, we all want to do for you what you and Jason have done for so many others. It's your turn to receive right now. Don't try to deprive folks of the blessing. I think I've heard you say that yourself a time or two."

"Well! If you're gonna throw my own words back at me..." She put her arm around Matty and led her inside just as Jason was walking down the hall.

"Oh, my, Jason. Look at you! You aren't even using your walker." He walked gingerly toward her and held out his arms. Matty stepped into the embrace. He held her for a long moment before letting her go.

Willa-Mae took off her glasses and swiped at her eyes with her embroidered handkerchief. "Isn't it amazin'? He'll be out there in the barn before I know it. I'm havin' to keep him tied down as it is."

Jason smiled at them. "Come on, you two. No more tears. It smells like supper's about ready, and I'm starving."

"I'm sorry," said Matty. "I'm like a leaky faucet these days."

She offered to help but was told in no uncertain terms to act like a guest and sit. Willa-Mae had set the table with her good china. The blue floral pattern looked lovely against the snowy white tablecloth. A beautiful bouquet of roses in a cut-glass vase held pride of place in the center of the table.

"Everything looks so beautiful, Willa-Mae. You didn't have to do all of this for me."

"Nonsense. What's the sense of having all these nice things if I never use them? And besides, we happen to think you're pretty special." Willa-Mae went back and forth carrying a platter of fried chicken, mashed potatoes and a squash casserole to the table before taking her seat.

Jason said grace in his own quiet way, thanking God for all He had done. Matty furtively wiped her eyes before looking up and caught Willa-Mae doing the same thing.

"Oh, for heaven's sake. Look at us. We're like a bunch of babies. Jason, take a piece of chicken and pass the plate. Oh my goodness, I forgot my biscuits!" She hopped up from the table faster than any seventy-one-year-old woman had a right to do and ran to the oven.

"Whew! Just in time. Another minute and they would've started to burn. Okay, everyone. Dig in."

Matty looked at her two friends and sighed contentedly. It was just like old times. She thought of all the meals she and Joe had eaten at this table. This time, instead of grief, there was a deep sense of gratitude for the times they'd shared. She got up to help clear the table, but Willa-Mae stopped her.

"Let's leave this mess be for now and take our coffee out on the front porch. It's cooler out there than in this kitchen."

Jason cautiously raised himself out of his chair. "I think I'll go have a little lie down if you girls don't mind."

"Are you okay, darlin?" Willa-Mae rushed over to take his arm.

"Now, Willa-Mae. I'm fine. I just tire more quickly than I used to. You and Matty go on and have a little visit."

She insisted on walking with him into the bedroom and helping him into bed before she would go. Matty carried out their coffee cups and sat in one of the old rockers. As she settled into the back-and-forth rhythm, her thoughts returned to Billy. Who could he have seen on the bridge that day?

She wasn't sure exactly what time of year the murder took place, but she seemed to remember it was late fall. If so, it would be unlikely a woman would be wearing white shoes. Of course, they could have been sneakers. In that case it could have been anyone. But weren't platform shoes the big thing in the '70s? Or could the white shoes have been part of a uniform?

Think, Matty. Who wears white shoes? Nurses. Nurses wear white shoes. But there isn't a hospital within walking distance of Miller's Crossing. I doubt it was a nurse. What kind of work do we have here in Miller's Crossing that might require white shoes?

"Well, he fell asleep before I walked outta the room." Willa-Mae picked up her coffee and sat in the rocker next to Matty. "He does get tired out real quick, but he looks good. Doesn't he, Matty?"

Matty reached over and patted her arm. "He looks wonderful, Willa-Mae. It's hard to believe he was so ill just a short time ago. He's a walking miracle."

"He is that. Thank You, Jesus. I was just sayin' the same thing to Fran."

"Fran from the diner?"

"That's right, honey. Only Fran I know. She came to the house with a casserole and peach cobbler the other day. At the rate everyone's been feedin' us, I'll weigh two hundred pounds before the end of the summer."

"How's everything at the diner?" Something tickled the back of Matty's mind but she couldn't seem to grab hold of it.

"Oh, fine. She's thrilled to death with the way the kids are handlin' everything. She sorta hinted around about church stuff, so I came right out and told her I was sorry for the way I had acted. She was real relieved. Pretty soon I've got to get to church and tell all the others."

Matty finished her coffee and got up. "Let me help you with the dishes, Willa-Mae. I need to get home soon and check on Shep. He's been alone almost all day."

"No, no. You go on. I'll take care of it. By the way, where were you? I never did ask."

"Oh, I drove into Centerville to do some shopping. All the summer stuff is on sale, and I need a couple of shirts."

Matty gave Willa-Mae a quick hug and scurried down the steps. Surely the lie was written right across her readable face, and Willa-Mae would spot it in a second.

"Thanks for the delicious supper. I'll see you soon."

✣

A soft breeze drifted in through the open bedroom window. Matty rolled over, plumped up her pillow and yawned. As tired as she was, she couldn't fall asleep. Her mind swirled with the days' events—an endless cycle of play-rewind-play.

She tried praying, but her mind refused to cooperate. Images of Billy and a stranger wearing white shoes floated in and around her conversations with Billy and Jason and Willa-Mae. There was something Willa-Mae said that seemed important, but she couldn't think what it could be.

Matty closed her eyes and tried to relax her body. She'd done a yoga tape years ago where the instructor ended the session by having her relax her whole body little by little until even the muscles of her face loosened. Matty tried to do it herself. She began with her feet and worked her way up. Her hands relaxed, and she could feel herself drifting off. Suddenly, there it was. The thing that had been eluding her: Willa-Mae mentioning her talk with Fran.

The diner. A waitress. A waitress would wear white shoes. Could it have been a waitress from the diner Billy saw?

She sat up and immediately Shep stood. "It's okay, boy. Lie down and go back to sleep." She rubbed his ears. If the woman lived close by, it would make perfect sense. She could have been on her way to work.

Is it possible this person knew Karen and had something against her...something that had been building for a long time...something so intense she would have spotted Karen taking the path, followed her, and taken the opportunity to...to kill her? What would warrant such a thing?

No one ever mentioned bad blood between Karen and a waitress. Although Matty thought back to the strange conversation with Susan the night of Nancy's get together. If she was telling the truth, Karen could be manipulative. Could she have used this girl in a way that was so devastating she wanted revenge?

Matty lay down and closed her eyes. *It all sounds like a bad movie,* she thought. She yawned again and rolled over onto her side. *Still, I think I'll go talk to Fran. See if she remembers who worked at the diner thirty-six years ago.* A faint light was already peeking in the window before she finally drifted off to sleep.

~ CHAPTER 23 ~

It no longer startled her to wake up to a pair of clear brown eyes only inches from her own. She reached out and rubbed Shep's head.

"Well, good morning to you, too, silly boy." He licked her nose and walked to the bedroom door.

"In a hurry this morning, aren't you?" She looked at the clock on her bedside table. "Oh my word. No wonder you're antsy. It's nearly ten o'clock. I can't believe it. Just hold your horses a minute, and I'll let you out. You poor thing."

She threw on her robe and, without bothering to find her slippers, hurried down the stairs. Shep turned circles while she unlocked the door. Almost before it opened he shot out into the yard. She watched him for a few minutes before closing the door.

"Goodness, gracious, Matty. Look at you. The morning is half gone, and here you stand in your nightgown and robe."

She heard Shep whining at the back door. "I'm coming." That was fast. *He must be starving.* She filled his bowl before letting him in and watched as he practically inhaled the entire contents. Feeling a tad guilty, she went to the pantry and got out a couple of doggie treats. "Here you go, boy. I promise to do better from now on. You should have dragged me out of bed." She rubbed his droopy ear and laughed.

"Here's an idea. After breakfast I'll call Fran, and if she's home, we'll take a ride over and visit with her for a little while." Shep seemed to approve the plan, so she put on the coffee and went upstairs to get dressed.

Fran answered on the first ring. "Good Mornin'!"

"Hi, Fran. It's Matty."

"Yeah, Matty. What can I do for you?"

"I wondered if I might come over for a little while. That is, if you aren't busy."

"Why, I'm never busy, sweetie. I've taken retirement serious." Her deep laugh made Matty grin.

"Would fifteen minutes be too soon? Oh, and would it be all right if I bring Shep?"

"Fifteen minutes ain't too soon, and of course you can bring him. I'll put the coffee on right now."

Matty hung up and turned to look at her furry companion. "She says you can come, but you have to be on your best behavior." He tilted his head and looked into her eyes as if to say, "Aren't I always?"

"Okay, let's go." Together they went downstairs and into the garage.

Matty pulled the car around Fran's driveway and parked in front of the little house. When Junior and Carole came home to help run the diner, they moved into the big house

241

and renovated the garage out back for Fran.

The smell of fresh coffee greeted Matty when she walked into Fran's little kitchen. The tiny table was set for two with brightly colored mugs, cake plates and cloth napkins. A dish of blueberry muffins sat alongside a cut-glass vase filled with white and yellow daylilies.

"Oh, Fran, you shouldn't have gone to so much trouble."

"It ain't no trouble at all. I don't get enough chances to use my pretty things anymore. Folks just don't visit the way they used to. I can remember the days when neighbors would just pop in for a little visit. We'd sit out on the porch or at the kitchen table and swap stories. Nowadays folks punch a few words into a phone and call that a visit."

Matty smiled and gave her hug. "I miss those days too, Fran. Jenny is after me to get a cell phone. So far I've resisted, but I think I may eventually have to give in."

"Well, I'm glad you came over." She glanced down at Shep. "You, too, Shep. The both of you sit yourselves down now and get comfortable."

They chatted over coffee and muffins, sharing all the latest bits of news, chief among them Jason's illness and Willa-Mae's change of heart.

"I'm real thankful she decided to give Pastor Greg a chance," Fran said. "I sure did hate to see any kind of bad feelings in our little church. It only leads to heartache." She helped herself to another muffin and pushed the plate toward Matty. "I believe most folks will follow Willa-Mae's lead in this. She's a good woman. It ain't easy to admit when you're wrong."

Matty took another muffin and voiced her agreement. Fran got up and refilled their cups.

During the drive over, Matty rehearsed several "mental" conversations with Fran. She wanted to find a way to ask about a possible waitress without mentioning the murder or Billy Taylor. She also hoped she wouldn't have to lie—not too much, anyway.

To her amazement, her visit to the prison hadn't become the talk of the village. She thought it must have been a combination of the problems at church, Jason's surgery and the women honoring her request not to talk about it. Unfortunately, it was also true that no one believed Billy Taylor could possibly be innocent.

"Do you ever miss working at the diner, Fran?"

"The only thing I miss is seeing the folks. It can get a little lonely here." She smiled. "But then I just take myself down to the diner, order lunch and have me a nice visit. I sure don't miss being on my feet all day. It wears a body down, that's for sure."

"Did you have someone else help wait tables when you and Jack were running things?"

"Not at first. But once we started doing pretty good we was able to hire someone to work the supper crowd so I could take a break and be home with Junior."

"It must have been a relief to get some time off. Did you hire someone from the village?"

"Yeah. Crystal Hoyt. I remember it clear as day 'cause it

was right around the time of the murder. 'Til they arrested Billy, we was worried about her walking home by herself. She lived up to the trailer park and had to go right by that path. Her no-good husband should've picked her up in his fancy hot rod, but he was too busy getting drunk and having a good time to think about that poor girl. That old trailer falling down around them, but he had his car. It was a disgrace."

Matty hoped her facial expression didn't betray the increasingly rapid beating of her heart. "I think I know who she is. Does she still live there?"

"She does. I ain't seen her in years. Nobody sees much of her. A little while after the murder, that miserable excuse of a husband left her for some sassy young thing. She quit the diner 'cause she needed to earn more money. Got a job as a janitor at the hospital. Worked nights."

"How old is Crystal?"

"Let me think. She must be in her fifties by now. Why all the questions, Matty?"

"Oh, no special reason. I was just wondering how you managed things when you started the diner." *Please don't let my face turn red, Lord, and forgive me for this.*

Fran tilted her head and opened her mouth as if to say something, but must have decided to let her thought pass unspoken.

Matty couldn't think of another thing to say. She reached down to pet Shep, hoping for inspiration or a graceful way to get up and leave. Fran came to her rescue.

"He's a good dog, Matty. He must be good company for

you."

"Oh, he is. I never thought I wanted a dog, but he's been such a blessing. I don't know what I'd do without him." Sensing he was the topic of conversation, Shep got up and put his head in Matty's lap. "I think I'd better get going, Fran. I think he needs to get outside for a while."

"Of course he does." She got up and walked over to the dog. She stroked his head, looked into Matty's eyes and said, "Thanks for coming, Matty. You take care of yourself. You hear me?"

Fran stood outside waving as they pulled out of the driveway.

"Well, I didn't handle that very well, big fella. She knows something's up. But I don't think she knows exactly what."

She looked at him in her rearview mirror. "I know I shouldn't have lied, but I don't want her to get involved in this. And I don't want her to worry." He stared back at her with big, innocent eyes. "Don't look at me like that. I won't tell any more lies. Promise."

The sun shone from a brilliant blue sky, and the pleasant breeze blowing through the windows carried the scent of late summer. She drove past cornfields, the stalks standing tall, ready for harvest. Little roadside stands stood unattended, baskets of squash, tomatoes, green beans and corn lining the tables next to the handmade cash boxes. The honor system on display—one of the many things she loved about this place.

After pulling into the garage, Matty headed out to her own garden. She picked a few tomatoes and some zucchini before going into the house, Shep running circles around her feet. "Okay, okay. You're right. It's too nice to stay inside. Let's go for a walk."

She stacked the vegetables in the downstairs sink, clipped the leash to Shep's collar, and together they set off down the driveway. Instead of turning left at the end of the driveway, they turned right heading in the direction of the trailer park. Lost in thought, she passed Jason and Willa-Mae's without even looking. Was it possible the waitress, Crystal, was the murderer? What reason would she have had?

Let's see. Suppose Crystal's husband was having a fling with Karen. According to Susan, she was beautiful, manipulative, and the guys were crazy about her. If there had been an affair or even just a flirtation, and Crystal found out about it, she may have confronted Karen. Fran certainly hadn't had anything positive to say about Crystal's husband.

Suppose she was walking to work and saw Karen take the path behind the Taylor farm. She may have followed her with the intention of telling her to stay away from her husband. The argument escalated and in a moment of blind rage, Crystal reached down, picked up a rock and hit Karen in the head. Then, realizing what she had done, she raced back down the path and out onto the road.

If she had gotten as far as the bridge, she wouldn't have seen Billy coming down the road. But he would have seen her. Matty could see it clearly in her imagination...the dusky light making it difficult for Billy to see, at the same time causing the white shoes to stand out.

At the intersection of Miller Lane and Green Mountain Road she paused for a moment, undecided about continuing on past the trailer park. Shep pulled at the leash, eager to keep moving. They crossed the road and walked past the entrance to the park.

Matty rarely came this way. She usually headed in the other direction toward church and the diner. She was surprised to see there were some fairly new looking trailers with little bits of lawn out front and flowers in pots by the steps. A dog, tied to a post by the nearest trailer, began barking as they walked by. Shep strained at the leash while Matty pulled hard in the opposite direction.

Once past the entrance, she stopped and looked back. The trailers along the back of the park were in a sorry state. The grounds were littered with all sorts of debris—old carriages, rusted lawn mowers, filthy plastic toys. Nothing seemed to make its way to the trash. Once no longer useful, items were simply discarded and forgotten.

She crossed to the other side of the road and picked up her pace, hoping to get by the park before the dog noticed them. They had just about made it when she heard a small voice call to her, "Hey, I know you. His name is Shep."

Standing just inside the entrance were two small boys. The younger of the two huddled behind his big brother, their little bare feet covered with dirt. "We seen you at the Fourth of July fair. Remember?"

"Of course I do." The trailer dog spotted Shep and started barking again. He strained at the short rope tied to a scraggly tree. Shep responded in kind. Matty could barely hear herself think.

Slowly the boys walked to edge of the road and crossed over to where Matty struggled to hold her delinquent dog still. When he spotted the boys, he immediately settled down, his long tail fanning the air.

Josh reached out to pet him. "Don't pay that ol' dog no mind. He don't know no better. We don't like him. Mama says he'll bite us if we get too close. Your dog is nice. We like him. Don't we, Ben?" Ben nodded and stuck a filthy thumb in his mouth.

Matty had to restrain herself from gathering him up in her arms. "Do you live here, Josh?"

"Yes, ma'am. Right over there. He pointed to one of the dilapidated trailers."

"Is your Mama home?"

"Yes, ma'am. She's sleepin'. We ain't supposed to bother her when she's sleepin'."

"Where's your Daddy?"

"He's workin'. He works down at the slate quarry. Can we pat your dog?" He shuffled his little toes in the dirt.

"Of course you can." She squatted down, drew Shep close and made him sit while Josh ran his hand over the soft head. Ben hung back, his thumb still firmly in his mouth.

Matty reach out to him. "Come here, Ben. Shep won't hurt you." She took his free hand and placed it on Shep's back. He smiled at her around his thumb and gently patted the big dog. Shep sat still.

"Josh! Ben! What in blazes are you doing over there? You know you ain't supposed to cross that road. Get back here." Both boys jumped at the sound of the shrill, angry voice. Ben stepped behind his big brother and grabbed hold of his shirt with his free hand.

Matty stood quickly as the young woman approached. "I'm so sorry, Mrs.—I'm sorry I don't remember your last name." She was tripping over her words in a vain attempt to appease the younger woman.

"Name's Ellen."

"Ellen. I'm so sorry. I shouldn't have let the boys cross. We were just trying to get away from that other dog. It's my fault. I apologize."

"There ain't no need to keep saying you're sorry. It's okay. But these two know they ain't allowed to cross the road. Get on home the two of you! Your Daddy'll be home soon. If he sees you here he'll tan your hides."

The boys petted Shep one more time and ran across the road. When they reached the other side, little Ben turned and waved a tiny hand at her. The door to the trailer hung open. They climbed the rickety wooden steps and went inside. Even from where she was standing, Matty could see the chaotic mess. Dirty dishes filled the sink and spilled over onto the counter. The floor was littered with toys and dirty clothes.

Ellen looked her right in the eye, daring her to comment.

"I apologize again, Ellen. It was thoughtless of me. Those two boys of yours are so sweet. I hope I didn't get them in trouble."

"Nah. It'll be fine. I wouldn't want their Daddy to know, though." A barely perceptible smile played across her face. "I need to get going. Bye, Mrs. Amoruso."

"Good-bye, Ellen." She started down the road, then stopped and called out, "If I can ever be of any help to you, Ellen, please let me know."

"I thank you, ma'am, but we're just fine." Ellen didn't look back as she strode toward the trailer.

~ CHAPTER 24 ~

Shep circled his blanket by the empty fireplace and plopped down with a contented exhale. He was sound asleep before Matty reached the staircase. She roamed from room to room feeling at loose ends. There were clothes waiting to be ironed, but she didn't feel like dragging out the ironing board. The vegetables needed washing, but she didn't have the energy to go back downstairs to get them.

Instead, she climbed the back stairs to Joe's study and sank down onto the old couch. Images of two barefoot boys collided with visions of a violent confrontation between two young women and a man waiting in a dark prison cell. Warm sunshine streamed through the windows, but she felt chilled. As she pulled the old afghan up over her shoulders, an overwhelming sense of grief pressed in on her. She wept because of evil and sorrow and injustice, because she was lonely and empty and ached with longing for her husband.

She longed to lose herself in sleep, but it wouldn't come. It remained just out of reach, like the words of a prayer. She lay still and whispered Jesus' name. The silence of the old house closed in around her. Then, something soothing filled the space, and like a living force, peace settled over her. Her wrists tingled, as though someone were touching her hands— taking them in His own. She didn't move, willing Him to stay close.

Gradually Matty opened her eyes and sat up, the palpable sense of His presence all around her. No words; only peace, deep peace surrounding the sorrow. She had no idea how long she had lain there, but the sun had made its way to the other side of the room. Sunlight played across the shiny surface of Joe's old desk. *How strange it looks,* she thought, *so neat and clean. I was always after the poor man to straighten up his mess. Now I would give anything to see the little bits of paper and opened books strewn all over that pristine surface. Oh, my darling Joe.*

Calmer now and wide awake, she got up and went to her bedroom. She picked up the little notebook. "I wish you'd had more time with Billy," she spoke aloud, "or at least written something more substantial for me to go on. I don't know what to do. Should I try to talk to this Crystal Hoyt? Is it foolish to try to do this on my own? Help me out here, Joe."

She flipped through the pages of written notes. Not daring to hope for anything more, she had almost reached the end when she saw some numbers scrawled across the bottom of the next to the last page. Seven numbers hurriedly written. It was Joe's writing. She was certain of that.

"It must be a phone number." She stood staring at it for a moment, as if it would somehow become a bit clearer. Then, heart pounding, she reached for the phone on the desk and punched in the numbers.

"Hello."

"Hello. Who am I speaking to, please?"

"Who you lookin' for?"

"I was trying to reach Crystal Hoyt." The words came without thought.

"This here's Crystal. What do you want?"

She could barely hold the phone, her hand was shaking so badly. "Crystal, my name is Matty Amoruso. I live just down the street from you. I had something I wanted to discuss with you. Would it be all right if I came by and talked to you sometime? Or you could come here to my house, whichever you prefer."

"I got to leave for work in a little while, and I sleep durin' the day. Why don't you tell me what it is you want?"

"It isn't anything serious, but I think it would be better if I talked to you in person. I can wait for a time that's convenient for you." *But please don't let that be too long,* she thought.

"Well, I suppose you could come by tomorrow afternoon around six o'clock. I should be up by then."

"That would be fine, Crystal. Thank you so much. Can you tell me which trailer is yours?"

"It's the one clear down on the end by the road. There'll be an old green pickup parked out front of it."

"I'll see you tomorrow, then."

Matty put down the phone and plopped onto the bed. Her

legs felt too weak to stand, and her heart was still racing.

"Matty Amoruso, if you ever did find the bad guy, or girl, you'd probably faint dead away." She heard Shep coming up the stairs. "Hey there, buddy. Did you have a good nap?" He came to her, and she took his face in her hands. "You'll never guess what just happened. It's almost like a little miracle." He cocked his head, curious, as if he were truly interested in what she had to say.

"What are the odds I would discover Crystal Hoyt worked as a waitress at the diner when Karen was murdered and then find her phone number in Joe's notebook? I think we may be onto something, Shep." He wagged his tail.

"But we'll have to be very careful. I'm not sure how to go about asking Crystal about that day. I don't suppose I can just come out and ask her if she killed Karen. Probably not a good idea. Maybe I can use the old 'writing an article about the murder' ruse. I'll say I know she worked at the diner and wondered if she saw anything out of the ordinary that day. Or I can just ask her to give me her memories of that time. If she's guilty, I may be able to tell."

Shep sat very still giving her his undivided attention.

"I know. I can ask her if she knew Karen and what she thought of her. And I promise, if I get even an inkling she might be guilty, I'll go right straight to the police."

She got up and headed for the stairs, Shep right at her heels.

"Come on. I'm hungry. Let's get something to eat."

❖

It threatened rain all the next day. Dark clouds hung heavily in the sky, and the humid air felt electric. Late in the afternoon the wind picked up, swishing down the chimney and bending the tree branches low.

The storm clouds would release their burden at any moment, so Matty decided to take the car to Crystal's. Remembering the dog at the entrance to the trailer park, she opted to leave Shep home, though part of her longed to have him along for company on this particular visit.

Huge raindrops spattered the windshield as she turned into the trailer park. She drove slowly down the dirt lane, toward the back of the park. The green pickup was parked in front of a rusted-out old trailer. A piece of heavy plastic covered the opening where one of the windows had broken. Some of the siding was loose and had come away completely in a couple of places. Crystal had made no effort to make the much-needed repairs, but the grounds were neat and free of the debris littering so many of the other small yards.

It was raining hard now. She made a run for the door and was startled when it opened before she could even knock.

"Come on in before you drown."

Matty stepped inside. She wiped her feet on the little mat and stood awkwardly facing Crystal. She extended her hand and introduced herself.

Crystal ignored the proffered hand. "I know who you are. You're the Pastor's wife. Sorry for your loss."

Matty thanked her. She stood awkwardly on the worn mat and tried not to look too closely at her surroundings.

"Well, I suppose you better come and sit down."

Matty followed her into the tiny living room, feeling a little put off by the greeting.

"Can I get you somethin' to drink? I got some tea out there in the kitchen."

Feeling like a heel, Matty nodded, "Yes, that would be lovely. Can I help you?"

"No, you stay put. I'll be right back."

Matty sat back in the armchair and took advantage of the opportunity to look around. A crocheted afghan and matching pillows gave warmth and color to the room. The rug was threadbare in places and the furniture old and worn, but everything was spotlessly clean. A black-and-white portrait of an elderly couple was the only decorative piece in the room.

Crystal came back carrying two mugs of hot tea. "I didn't know if you took cream and sugar. I can get it if you want." She placed a mug on the little end table beside Matty.

"No, this is just fine. Thank you, Crystal. Is that a picture of your mother and father?"

Crystal looked up at the wall as she sat down. "Yeah. They both passed years ago. They was the only family I had."

She looked far older than her years. Deep lines crisscrossed her cheeks. Her graying hair was pulled back into a thin ponytail. The eyes were the most telling—old eyes, filled with what Matty recognized as a deep sorrow and something else.

Crystal took a sip of her tea and said, "Now what is it you wanted to talk to me about, Mrs. Amoruso?" She spoke so softly, Matty had a hard time hearing her over the clatter of rain on the metal roof.

"Well, I'm not sure you'll even be able to help me, but I wanted to ask you a few questions about Karen Campbell's murder. And please. Call me Matty."

Crystal put her mug down and looked at Matty with steely eyes. "That was a long time ago, Mrs. Amoruso. Why are you askin' questions about it now?"

"Oh, well. Someone down at the newspaper asked me if I would write an article about different crimes that have taken place in the county. I've written a few little articles now and then, and the editor thought it would make an interesting story."

"What is it you wanna know?"

"I know you were working at the diner at the time, and I wondered if you remembered much about that day. I believe you used to walk right by the old Taylor farm on your way to work. Is that right?"

"Yeah, that's right. What about it?"

"Did you notice anything out of the ordinary that day? You must have been on your way to work right around the time of the murder." Matty squirmed inwardly. This conversation was veering far from the well-rehearsed one she had had in mind.

"I went over all that with the police when it happened. I didn't see nothin' or nobody. Not even the one who done it—

Billy Taylor." Her voice rose a bit when she mentioned Billy's name.

"I see. Of course I researched all of that, but I wondered if it was possible you remembered something after all these years. That sometimes happens, you know."

"Well, it ain't happened to me. It's just like I told the police back then. Ain't nothin' changed."

"Did you know Karen Campbell?" Matty rubbed her legs to keep them from shaking.

"I knew who she was, a course. But she didn't exactly go around with the likes of me. No, Karen was much too high and mighty for that."

Matty felt decidedly uncomfortable. She picked up her mug, trying to think what to say next.

"Well, if you ain't got no more questions, I got to get ready for work." She stood and began walking toward the door.

"No. No more questions." *Although I was wondering if perhaps you were the one who murdered Karen*, she thought. "I'm sorry if I upset you in any way, Crystal. That certainly wasn't my intention."

She turned and stared into Matty's eyes. "I find it's smarter to let some things just lie, Mrs. Amoruso."

She opened the door, and Matty stepped out into the rain.

❖

On the short drive to the house, a dozen different thoughts swirled through Matty's mind. She felt as though a thick fog was surrounding her and something significant was hidden just out of her sight—something that would make everything fall into place. For the life of her, she couldn't make out what it was.

Who had a real and compelling motive to kill Karen? Did someone deliberately plot her death or strike out at her in a moment of fury? Or was Matty so blinded by her love and loyalty to Joe that she couldn't see Billy for who he was—a murderer?

Was there more to the business with Karen's teacher, Mr. Moran? Did he try to force himself on her, and when she rejected him, did things get out of control? And what about her old boyfriend, Tommy James? What if he believed Karen was having an affair with Mr. Moran? It's possible he could have waited for her on the path. Maybe they argued, and he got so angry he struck her. He claimed he and Karen were getting back together, but what if that wasn't the truth?

Then there's Donna. Susan told Matty that Karen took advantage of her—using her to help with schoolwork in exchange for a distorted form of friendship. Matty imagined the younger Donna, the girl from the wrong side of the tracks, desperate to be part of the popular crowd. Had Karen used her one too many times? Susan had also made it clear that Donna had a crush on Karen's boyfriend. Was she upset that they were getting back together?

And why did Susan feel compelled to share all of this information with me, Matty wondered. *Does she know something more she isn't telling me? Could she be trying to divert attention away from herself?*

Crystal was so defensive. She admitted she walked to work that way. She must have been the one Billy saw. That places her on the scene. There was enough time after Billy and Karen went their separate ways for someone else to have committed the murder. Was that someone Crystal? I didn't know the police had questioned her. But wouldn't they have arrested her if there was the least suspicion? Or was Billy an easier target?

She sat in the car for a few minutes before going into the house, rain dripping from the bumpers onto the garage floor, trying to make sense of everything she knew. "Well, I don't think I'm any closer to knowing who killed Karen," she said out loud, "but it's possible it wasn't Billy Taylor. I can't shake the feeling that the answer is staring me right in the face. I just can't see it."

~ CHAPTER 25 ~

A clear blue sky greeted Matty the next morning when she stepped outside to get the mail. Yesterday's rain had washed everything clean. A clear, fresh wind blew through the trees, showering her as she walked under the branches. Shep pranced along beside her.

Navigating her way around puddles, Matty crossed the road. She hadn't bothered to get the previous day's mail, so the little box was nearly full. Everything was damp because the old mailbox didn't close as tightly as it once did. She flipped through sales circulars, a couple of magazines and several envelopes as she walked back across the road.

"Just bills," she informed her furry friend. "Oh, wait. What's this? It looks like an actual letter. What a nice surprise. Hardly anyone writes letters these days."

By now they had reached the house. Matty hurried inside. *Hmmm. There's no return address. I wonder who could be writing to me?* Whoever had sent it had typed Matty's name and address on the envelope. She hurried upstairs and took the letter opener out of her little desk.

Her heart began to thump when she saw the cut-out letters pasted across the page:

LET SLEEPING DOGS LIE MRS. AMORUSO. THEY ARE LIABLE TO HURT YOU IF THEY GET RILED UP!

The horrible letter fell to the floor as Matty dropped onto her chair. She closed her eyes and covered her face with her hands. Shep, sensing something wrong, came and rested his head in her lap. Keeping one hand tight to her face, she reached down and began stroking the silky head.

"Oh, Shep. What am I going to do?" She got up suddenly, raced back downstairs and locked the door, then hurried back upstairs to check the locks on all the other doors. Not until she was sure everything was secure did she walk back to her desk. Careful to pick it up by the corner this time, she placed the letter on her desk and read the vile message over and over.

"Who could have done this?" Trying hard to keep calm and think clearly, she went back over yesterday's events. Had anyone strange gone by the house? Did the letter come in the mail or had someone dropped it off—and if so, when? Yesterday? This morning?

She'd been indoors most of the day yesterday—except for her visit to Crystal. Someone could have put it in the mailbox then. Or during the night. Even early this morning.

She thought back over her list of "suspects" and realized it could have been any one of them. Even Crystal would have had time to drop it off on her way to or from work. She couldn't even eliminate Billy from the list—he could have mailed it from prison. "Why in the world would he do that?" she wondered out loud. "Think, Matty. Who would do this? There's got to be something I'm overlooking. Something I've seen or done that's gotten someone else's attention. Someone who has something to hide."

She picked up the envelope and looked for the postmark. That should tell her something. Turning it over, she saw that any hope of reading it had been washed away by the rain that had made its way into the mailbox. She couldn't even be certain there had ever been one.

Shep looked at her with what seemed to be genuine concern. "What do I do, pal? I think this has finally gotten to the point where I have to go to the police."

The phone rang, and her heart began to pound again. She felt lightheaded and had to brace her hand against the wall as she walked toward the phone.

"Hey, honey. Whatcha doin'?"

Matty thought she might faint with relief when she heard the familiar voice. "Oh, hi, Willa-Mae. Nothing at all. Did you need something?"

"Well, matter of fact, I did need just a little favor. Would you mind comin' over to stay with Jason while I get my hair done? I won't be long, but I just don't like leavin' him alone. He says he'll be fine, and I'm sure he will. But you know how it is, Matty. I would just die if somethin' happened while I was gone."

"I'd be glad to. What time do you want me come over?"

"Would now be too soon? I know I shoulda called

yesterday, but I clean forgot. Truth is, I wanna say somethin' in church tomorrow, and I look a wreck. I haven't had a decent haircut in months. The doctor gave the okay for Jason to go to church, too. It'll be our first time back, and I need to get this thing done, Matty."

"I'll be right over."

"Thank you, honey."

Matty hung up the phone and walked back to the desk. She hated to even touch the awful piece of paper, but she carefully picked it up by a corner and slid it into the desk drawer.

"I'll take care of this as soon as I can." Shep looked at her with big, innocent eyes. "I know. I have to go to the police. I will—just as soon as I can. Nothing bad will happen as long as I don't do any more investigating. I'll lay low for a couple of days and then bright and early Monday morning I'll take it to the police station. Right now, Willa-Mae and Jason need my help."

Shep followed her as she raced upstairs to brush her teeth and comb her hair.

❖

Willa-Mae must have been watching for her because she was out on the porch before Matty reached the end of the driveway.

"Thank you so much, honey. I sure do appreciate this. Come on inside and I'll show you what all needs to be done. It isn't much really—just the medicine he needs to take. I shouldn't be all that long, but you never know. Sometimes Rachel gets to gossipin', and you just can't shut her up."

Willa-Mae led the way into the living room where Jason was seated comfortably in his recliner. Behind her back, he gave Matty a little wink. She had a hard time suppressing a smile.

"Okay, here's his list of meds. He gets this here little blue one in a few minutes—nine-thirty sharp—and the white capsule thirty minutes after that. Make sure he drinks the whole glass of water. The doctor said that's real important. I should be home before he needs his next round a pills. Okay? Okay. I'm outta here. Behave yourself, darlin'." She bent down and gave her husband a kiss on the cheek. "Just call Rachel's if you need me for anything, Matty, hear? I'm sure it'll all be fine, but just in case I left the number here on the pad."

"We'll be fine, Willa-Mae. Take it easy, and enjoy a little relaxing time. I promise to call if anything happens—but I know that won't be necessary. We'll see you soon."

Matty gave Jason a hug and sat across from him on the old sofa. "You look wonderful."

The door banged open, and Willa-Mae popped back inside. "I almost forgot. He needs to get up and walk around. He shouldn't sit in one place for too long. He needs to move around a little. Y'all could even go out on the porch for a spell, if you wanted. It's a beautiful day, and fresh air does him so much good. Okay—I'm goin' now."

The door banged shut behind her. Matty and Jason looked at each other and burst out laughing.

"I heard that." She was back. "I left a little snack in the fridge for both of you. He likes to have it around ten o'clock."

"Please don't worry, dear. Matty and I are going to be just fine. I feel so good I just might jog on down to the barn and lift a few bales of hay."

"Jason Miller, don't you dare!" She caught the look between them. "Ha, ha. Very funny, you two. I just might take myself off for the whole day if you're not careful." And she waltzed out the door.

They heard the car door slam shut. Matty walked to the window and watched as Willa-Mae sped down the driveway. She turned to Jason. "She'll probably set a new world record for fastest trip to the beauty parlor and back."

Jason smiled. "She's a hoot, isn't she? But she's the best thing that ever happened to me. She hasn't left me for a minute since this whole thing started, Matty. I worry she'll work herself to death."

"She loves taking care of you, Jason. I think she'll be just fine. I'm so proud of her for the way she's handling all of this—especially the business at church. It isn't easy to admit you were wrong, especially in front of a whole church full of people."

Matty got up and went into the tidy kitchen to get Jason's medicine. She filled the waiting glass with water, carefully picked up the pill Willa-Mae had set out and walked back into the living room.

Jason took the pill from her hand and dutifully drained the glass. Handing it back to Matty, he said, "She's like a different person ever since she patched things up with Pastor Greg. I think a huge weight lifted when she forgave not only him but herself. She told you her story, didn't she?"

"Yes." Matty reached out and laid her hand on his arm. "She's carried such a heavy burden all these years—blaming herself for everything that's ever gone wrong. All the while, God wanted her to know how dearly He loves her."

"I believe she knows that now. Come. Tell me about you, Miss Matty. How are you doing these days?"

She longed to unburden herself to this dear man but was afraid it would be too upsetting for him. Instead, she filled him in on all the local news. Then they decided to take Willa-Mae's advice and walk out to the porch and get some fresh air.

Together they made their way outside. Jason sat in the old cushioned wicker chair, and Matty took the rocking chair beside him. It really was a perfect day. There wasn't a cloud in the sky. They sat in companionable silence drinking in the beauty all around them.

A strange car drove slowly past the house. Matty gripped the arms of the rocking chair. Could it be the person who sent her the letter? Was someone watching her? She swallowed and tried to focus on Jason.

"It's so lovely, Jason, but it's ten o'clock, and we have to go inside."

He laughed as they made their way inside. Matty glanced

over her shoulder as she pulled the door shut behind them. She poured them each a cold glass of water, filled two small bowls with the fruit salad Willa-Mae had prepared, picked up Jason's medicine and put everything on a serving tray. She and Jason were sitting back enjoying their snack when Willa-Mae streaked into the driveway.

"I'm back. How's everythin' goin'? Are you all right, honey? Can you believe I went off without my purse? I was just about there before I noticed. I know Rachel would let me slide, but I don't believe in that sorta thing. Oh, mercy, I really am gonna be late now."

She was in and out of the house and back in the car before either one of them could say a word. She gave them a wave as she shot out of the driveway. Matty offered up a silent prayer for safe travels. Jason just chuckled.

❖

Willa-Mae insisted she stay for lunch. "I made a nice salad earlier this mornin'. It'll fix what's ailin' you."

"There isn't anything ailing me, Willa-Mae."

"Well you do look a little peaked. Come on. Sit down and have some lunch."

Matty longed to get home, but she dutifully pulled out a chair and sat. She barely tasted the food. All she could think about was that sinister letter.

"Is there somethin wrong with the salad, honey?"

"No. It's delicious, Willa-Mae."

"Well, you've hardly touched it. Is somethin' else botherin' you?"

Matty looked to Jason for help.

"I think Matty might be a little tired."

Matty gave him a grateful smile. "Jason's right. I'm afraid I stayed up much too late reading last night. I was right in the middle of a good mystery."

"Well then, you get yourself right on home and have a little nap soon's we finish lunch.

It was mid-afternoon before Matty headed back home. Though it was still August, Matty felt a hint of fall in the chilly air. She crossed her arms and quickened her pace. The familiar, comfortable walk seemed somehow changed. A sinister presence lurked somewhere just out of view.

She felt a sense of relief when she reached her own driveway and relaxed a little. Still, she practically ran the rest of the way to the house. Shep was waiting by the door, eager to get outside. Unable to shake the feeling of being watched, she decided to let him out for a few minutes rather than go for a walk. More than anything, she wanted the safety and comfort of her home.

Once inside, she clicked shut the rarely used deadbolt and pulled the shades before settling down in Joe's recliner. Shep came to her and laid his head in her lap. She caressed his floppy ear and spoke softly—whether to him or Joe, she couldn't be sure. Perhaps it was more a prayer.

"I can't go on like this much longer. That letter has made me a nervous wreck. I've got to do the wise thing here. I can't help but think about all the mysteries I've read where the heroine takes foolish risks and I've wondered how she could be so stupid. Yet here I sit dithering about going to the police.

"It's just that I don't have anything substantial to go on—except the letter. I just need a little time to sort it all out. The letter just warned me to stop poking around. If I don't do anything for a couple of days, whoever it is will think I've decided to give it up. Or will they still consider me a threat? Oh, goodness. I don't know what to do.

"I do know I don't want to make things worse for Billy. He could be in danger, too. He looked so awful the last time I saw him. If someone were desperate enough, they could arrange to have him killed before he remembers something incriminating. If the police don't take this seriously, or if they take too long to find the real killer..."

She let the words trail off. Suddenly too exhausted to even think, she sat back in the big chair and closed her eyes. The phone rang just as she was drifting off. It rang several times before she could clear her head and walk to the little table in the hall.

"Hello." No answer. "Hello? Is anyone there?" Matty stood holding the phone to her ear. The only response was a dial tone. Caller ID flashed "unavailable." No help there.

"I wonder who it was?" Shep, apparently unconcerned, yawned from his place beside her chair. "Well, I'm sure whoever it was will call back later." She wished she felt as unconcerned as her words sounded. She couldn't shake the thought that the caller might well have been the same person who sent her the letter. Was he (or she) trying to see if she was home?

Before going upstairs, Matty checked to see if she had remembered to lock the door. She went into the pantry and opened the refrigerator door. After peering at its contents for a minute or two, she closed the door. The cupboard shelves looked equally unappealing.

She picked up her mystery book, flipped through the pages and put it back on the table. Back downstairs she pulled out the piano bench, sat down and lifted the cover. The keys had been silent since Joe's death. Fingers poised, she took a deep breath and gently closed the cover.

The phone rang, and this time she was out of her seat and in the hall before the second ring. "Hello. Who is this?"

"It's me, Mom—Jenny. Are you alright? You sound funny."

"I'm fine, honey." She breathed a sigh of relief. "How is everything on the Island?"

"We're fine. I just felt like I needed to call you. Are you sure everything's okay?"

"Yes. Of course. I spent most of the day at Willa-Mae and Jason's."

Matty filled Jenny in on all the news and then half listened as Jenny shared what was going on with the kids. The other half of her mind was turning over the idea of talking to Pete about Billy Taylor. He would certainly be able to give her good advice.

"Mom, are you there?"

"Yes, honey. I'm here."

"I asked you if you were still planning to come next month."

"I am. Of course I am. I'll let you know exactly when very soon. You've told me all about you and the kids. How is Pete? Why don't you let me talk to him for a few minutes. It's been ages since we've had a chance to even say hi."

"Oh, I'm sorry, Mom. Pete isn't here. He's at a big law enforcement conference on the mainland. He'll be home late Sunday night. Was there something special you wanted to talk to him about?"

"No, dear. Nothing special. I'll talk to him next time you call."

"Okay, Mom. We can't wait for you to come. Please plan to stay for a good long visit."

"I'd love to, Jenny, but you know I have Shep to think about, too. I'll have to find someone to take care of him while I'm gone."

"You can bring him with you. The kids are dying to see him. He'll have a great time swimming in the ocean and chasing rabbits in the woods."

Matty laughed. "I think he knows we're talking about him. He's sitting here looking like he's ready to go right now. I promise we'll come soon. I love you."

"Love you too, Mom. Bye, now."

Matty stood for a moment with the phone in her hand before hanging up. "Okay, big fella. Let's go upstairs and get you something to eat. First thing Monday morning I'll call

Pete at the office. He'll know what I should do."

Together they climbed the stairs.

~ CHAPTER 26 ~

By six-thirty Matty had given up any hope of falling back to sleep. She heard Shep whimper and looked down. He was sound asleep, his legs jerking as he chased rabbits in his dreams. Hoping not to wake him, she slipped on her robe and slippers and began to tiptoe to the door. He was awake and on his feet before she got to the head of the stairs.

"Morning, buddy. Sorry to wake you up so early. I couldn't sleep."

He yawned and shook himself. Matty smiled as she wrapped her arms around his neck.

After breakfast, while Shep made his morning rounds outside, she sat at the kitchen table with a second cup of coffee. Sleep had come quickly last night, despite her worries about the letter, but it hadn't lasted more than a few hours.

Once awake she began having imaginary conversations with her son-in-law, trying to get the words just right. When she wasn't thinking about Billy Taylor, she thought about Willa-Mae and what this day would bring. She prayed for grace and strength for her friend.

The sun shone brightly on this Sunday morning, and she had a hard time getting Shep to come back indoors. He ignored her calls, feigning deafness. She was forced to go outside and chase him down in her nightgown and robe, waving a dog biscuit in a blatant act of bribery.

Once he was settled and properly reprimanded, Matty raced upstairs to get ready for church. "It never fails," she said to no one in particular. "The more time I have to get ready, the more I have to rush around at the last minute."

She pulled into the church parking lot with a few minutes to spare. Slowing a bit as she walked toward church, she took a minute to breathe in the sweet, fresh air. Summer was beginning to fade. Fall came early to this farming community, and she wanted to savor these days.

It took a minute for her eyes to adjust from the bright sunlight to the darker interior of the church. She had no difficulty finding Willa-Mae and Jason. Her friend was sideways in what Matty had come to think of as their pew, eyes fixed on the entrance. The minute she spotted Matty, she waved her over.

"Come sit with us, honey. I want you to be beside Jason when I get up there to talk."

Matty sat down next to her and took her hand. It felt icy cold even in the warmth of the church. She gave it a squeeze. Willa-Mae returned the pressure. She sat on the edge of her seat, shoulders pulled back, head held high.

I have never figured out how word spreads so quickly,

Matty thought as she looked around. Every pew was filled. A few people were standing at the back of the church. Her own hands had gone cold, and she couldn't keep her legs from trembling.

The worship service seemed interminable. Finally Pastor Greg asked everyone to be seated. A hush fell over the congregation, and all eyes turned toward him. He looked at Willa-Mae and spoke softly.

"Before I give you the message God has placed on my heart, one of our members has asked to speak to all of you— her church family. I trust you will listen with open hearts."

He stepped down from the platform and extended his hand toward Willa-Mae. She walked toward him and took the proffered hand. He helped her up the steps and stood a few feet behind her as she stepped up to the pulpit. Matty held her breath and prayed.

"The first thing I wanna do is thank you for all you've done for Jason and me. Words can't rightly say how much it has meant to us." She wiped her eyes with her crumpled handkerchief. "That said, I don't think I need to tell any of y'all that I've been riled up over things here at church— things I thought weren't pleasin' to God. Now I don't say I was all wrong about that." A few folks looked at each other and smiled.

"What I do say," she continued, "is I was all wrong in the way I handled it. My heart wasn't right before God. I talked about the preacher behind his back. I got everyone else all riled up, too. Instead of listenin' to him and givin' him a chance to explain, I did everything I could to turn people against him. I'm ashamed of that.

"I got to know him real well when my Jason was so sick. For those of y'all who don't know, he was there every single day right from the get-go. I got to see his heart and the way he loves God. We talked, and we listened. I came to understand some things.

"He taught me about God's love and how He doesn't sit up there waitin' for us to mess up so He can lower the boom. You see—I was afraid if we did somethin' God didn't like, He would cause somethin' terrible to happen to us and our church. I was wrong about that. I don't say we don't suffer the consequences of the things we do wrong, but God isn't there waiting to beat us down. He's always there to make everything work out for our good.

"I've come to see it's okay if we don't see eye-to-eye on everything as long as we agree on the important things. The kind of music or the way we worship aren't those things. It's our hearts—our hearts bein' right with God. If we mess up, He'll tell us so—with love.

"I ask Pastor Greg, y'all and most of all God to forgive me. I'm gonna be here for worship service from now on. And I'm gonna try to see the beauty in all kinds of worship. I might even raise my hand a time or two." She turned as she spoke the next words, "And I hope we'll get to sing an old hymn now and then, too, cause they really are such a blessin'. That's all I have to say."

Pastor Greg took her arm and helped her down the stairs.

As she made her way back to her pew, someone stood and began to clap. Others picked it up, and soon they were all on their feet clapping. Willa-Mae sat and bowed her head. Jason wrapped an arm around her. Matty stood weeping and wildly applauding.

After his sermon, Pastor Greg closed the service with a hymn—"Blest Be the Tie that Binds." Matty closed her eyes and listened as the voices rose to fill the small sanctuary. Her heart felt too full for words. *Joe,* she thought, *listen to your church. This is what you prayed for.* She looked over at Willa-Mae. A beautiful smile lit her upturned face.

It took them quite a while to reach the back of the church. So many people came to speak a kind word or simply hug Jason and Willa-Mae. Art and Anna stood quietly waiting their turn. Anna gave them both a gentle hug, then stepped back behind Art. He looked down at his feet and said, "Just give us a call whenever you need anything from the store, Willa-Mae. I'll bring it to you myself. And don't worry about the mail. I can drop it off on my way home in the evening." They left so quickly, Willa-Mae barely had a chance to thank them.

They were just about to walk through the door when Matty felt a tug on her blouse. She turned around and was surprised to see Josh. Ellen stood behind him with little Ben in her arms. The boys were dressed alike in clean T-shirts tucked into freshly ironed jeans with frayed hems. Their hair had been wetted, parted and combed neatly to one side. Each wore a pair of old sandals.

"Josh, how nice to see you. Hello, Ellen." Matty gently patted Ben's cheek. He turned his head and buried his face in his mother's shoulder.

Willa-Mae, never one to miss a trick, turned to look at the little group. "Well, who do we have here? I don't think I've met y'all." She looked expectantly at Matty.

"Willa-Mae, this is Ellen. She lives just up the road from us. These are her two boys, Josh and Ben."

Willa-Mae extended her hand, "Well, nice to meet you, Ellen."

By this time Jason had stepped back through the doorway. "Hello, Ellen. My name's Jason." He patted Josh on the head. "Who are these big boys?"

"I'm Josh and that's Ben. He's shy."

"I'm happy to meet you, Josh. You too, Ben. Do you know, I'm just a little shy myself?" Ben turned his head just enough to get a peek at this new friend.

"We went to Children's Church," announced Josh. "I colored this here picture. I'm gonna give it to my Daddy."

"That's enough, Josh." Ellen gently pushed his hand down and looked at Willa-Mae. "I just wanted to say I was proud of what you done."

For once in her life, Willa-Mae was at a loss for words.

"I think me and my boys might come back here a time or two. I think I could feel comfortable in this place."

She took Josh's hand and walked briskly past them and out the door.

Willa-Mae watched them go. "Well, I'll be."

"Yes, indeed, dear," Jason said. "Yes, indeed."

❖

Matty had gently, but firmly, refused Willa-Mae's invitation to lunch. Both she and Jason looked done in—physically and emotionally drained. For once, she had gotten no argument.

The light on the answering machine was blinking when she walked in the door. She let Shep out and turned to push the button, hoping Pete had gotten home early and decided to give her a call.

"This is Crystal Hoyt. I got somethin' I wanna tell you. Today's my day off, but I got to take care of some things. I'll come by this evenin'."

Matty quickly dialed Crystal's number, but there was no answer. She let it ring a long time before hanging up. "I wonder what that's all about." She stepped outside into the fresh air and tried to put all thoughts of Crystal out of her mind for the time being.

The sunflowers in her garden nodded their heavy heads in the warm breeze. Daylilies lined the front of the house in a colorful mass of orange, yellow and white. The worries of the past few weeks and the waves of sorrow that often swept through faded a little as a sense of peace welled up.

Shep came trotting up to her—a big silly grin on his face.

"It's too nice to stay inside today, boy. Let's get some lunch, and then we'll go for a walk."

They walked down to the bridge and turned up the road

toward Buddy and Nancy's farm. They had missed all the big "doings" in church. Nancy called last night to tell Matty they wouldn't be there. Her youngest daughter had gone into labor, and she was driving to Petersburg to stay with her for a few days. Buddy would be joining them on Sunday right after he finished chores.

Matty couldn't wait for Nancy to get back home so they could sit and talk. She'd give anything to be able to tell her about the letter and the phone call from Crystal. Well, she would just have to wait. Truthfully, Pete would be the best one to talk to. By this time tomorrow she would know what to do.

The sun disappeared, and when Matty looked up, she saw a bank of dark clouds in the distance. "Time to head for home, Shep. It looks like we're in for another storm. We've had more than our fair share lately." She turned around and tugged on his leash. By the time they got to the bridge, dark clouds covered the sky and the wind had picked up. They just made it into the house before the first drops started. Within minutes it was pouring. Water cascaded off the roof and puddled in the driveway.

Matty went upstairs and put on a kettle of water for tea. She turned on the small light over the kitchen table and waited for the water to boil. Gusts of wind bent the tree limbs and drove the rain against the windows. The sunny afternoon seemed a distant memory. So did the peace that had calmed her fears. Now, with the rain and gloom, they came creeping back.

The teapot whistled, piercing the deep silence. Matty fixed her cup of tea and carried it downstairs. Shep lay sound asleep on his rug. *Must be nice,* she thought. *Some days I wish I could just close my eyes and never wake up.* Without bothering to turn on the lights, she settled into Joe's chair and sipped her tea.

What is it Crystal wants to talk about? Has she remembered something? What if she's the one who sent the letter? Or what if she's the one who murdered Karen? I've thought all along, just as Joe must have, that the person Billy saw is the one who killed Karen. Should I even let her in? But why would she call and leave a message if she had plans to harm me? That doesn't make sense. Oh, Lord, please help me with this.

She looked over at her sleeping companion. "You'd protect me, wouldn't you, boy?" she whispered into the darkness.

~ CHAPTER 27 ~

After picking at a light supper, Matty went back downstairs. She turned on the television hoping to get a weather report. The rain had let up a little, but was still coming down fairly hard. Every few minutes she got up and walked over to the window.

"I'm terrible at waiting," she mumbled under her breath. "I wish Crystal would just hurry up and get here already."

The news was over and still no sign of Crystal. Matty picked up the remote and scrolled through the menu looking for something, anything, to help make the time pass more quickly.

"Maybe she changed her mind. I wonder if I should call her. No—just be patient, Matty," she scolded herself.

Every time she heard a strange noise, she rushed over to the window. Her stomach felt twisted in knots. She switched off the TV and picked up her book. A few minutes later she slammed it shut.

"I'll bet she decided not to come after all and doesn't have the decency to call." Shep was wide awake now. "Sorry, buddy. I feel like I'm going to fly to pieces." Suddenly he was on his feet. He raced to the door and began barking furiously.

"It's okay, Shep." Matty walked to the door and took a firm grip on his collar. Above the noise of the wind and the rain, she heard someone knocking.

"Who is it?" she called through the closed door.

"It's me. Crystal."

Matty opened the door and let her in. "He won't bite, will he?" She stood in the entrance, trying to keep some distance between herself and Shep.

"No. That is, not unless there was some sort of danger," she couldn't help adding.

"Well I ain't here to hurt you if that's what you think. You said to let you know if I remembered anything, and I did. So here I am. Now get him to back off or I'll just go on home."

"I'm sorry, Crystal. Shep, it's all right." She petted his head to reassure him. "Please come in. It's a terrible night to be out and about."

"Yeah. Well, I'll just tell you what I come to say and be on my way."

"Please, sit down. Can I get you something? Would you like a cup of tea?"

"No, thanks. I'd just as soon get this over with and get on home."

They sat facing each other on the old sofa. Matty could hardly keep her legs from shaking as she waited for Crystal to pull off a red kerchief from her head; it was sopping wet from the rain. Finally, she began.

"After you left my place the other day I got to thinkin'. You asked me if there was anybody on the road that day that shouldn't a been. I told you the truth when I said there wasn't. But someone else *was* there. I never told about it 'cause it didn't seem important. It was nothin' unusual. I saw that person there lots of times."

Matty willed herself to be quiet and let Crystal tell it in her own way.

"I don't wanna make no trouble for nobody, but I got to thinkin' about ol' Billy Taylor sittin' up there in prison. It wouldn't be fair not to say somethin' if there was a chance he didn't do it."

Matty thought her heart would beat out of her chest.

"So I'll tell you who it was I saw, and you can do with it what you will. Just don't get me involved. I don't want no trouble."

Matty held her breath as Crystal spoke the name.

✤

Matty walked to the door with Crystal. She placed her hand on the younger woman's arm. "Thank you."

"Like I said. I don't wanna be involved in this. I always liked Billy. His old man was a real...well, you know. I did think he was guilty, but now you got me to thinkin'. Anyhow, I best be goin'.'"

Rain blew in through the open door. The storm had intensified while they sat talking. Crystal leaned into the wind as she rushed toward her truck. Matty quickly closed the door.

She walked slowly over to the old chair. She rubbed her legs to stop the familiar shaking. Shep came to her, and she absently stroked his head. "Is it possible? I just can't believe it. Maybe Crystal is making it all up to protect herself." She reviewed everything she knew, and suddenly it all began to fall into place.

Shep started up and ran to the door—a repeat performance of just a short while ago. Matty saw the kerchief on the sofa as she got up to go to the door. She could hear a faint knocking. "Hush, Shep. It's all right. It's just Crystal."

She grabbed the kerchief, opened the door and nearly fell over when she saw Donna standing there. Her first impulse was to slam it shut, but she simply stood there unable to move. Donna pushed past her and walked into the little foyer. She looked disheveled, so unlike her usual immaculate appearance. The placating demeanor was gone. Her eyes bore into Matty's.

"You know, don't you, Matty?"

She could hardly hear through the thrumming of her heart in her ears. "I don't know what you mean, Donna?"

"If I wasn't sure five minutes ago, one look at your face when you saw me made everything clear. Crystal told you she passed me on the road the day Karen was murdered, and you've figured the rest out."

Donna strode into the room and began to pace back and forth in front of the fireplace. Water dripped from her raincoat onto the braided rug. Matty followed, Shep close at her heels.

She stopped her frenetic pacing and turned to face Matty. "I've been following you around ever since I found out you went to visit Billy Taylor in prison. You've been a busy lady. I knew you were talking to Mr. Goss the day you literally ran into me at the nursing home. It didn't take a genius to figure out what you were up to. I'll bet he had a lot to say about his favorite student. For some reason, he thought Billy Taylor could make something of himself. Then you went back to the prison. But I didn't get really concerned until I saw you go to Crystal's."

"Did you send me that awful letter?"

Donna ignored the question. "When I saw Crystal's truck in your driveway this evening, I had to see for myself just how much you knew. You know you're a terrible liar, Matty. Your face is an open book."

Matty stared at her, trying to process what was happening.

"Can we sit down? I've got to talk to you—explain what happened. I've got to make you understand."

"Understand? What is there to understand, Donna? You killed that poor girl and let an innocent man sit in prison for thirty-six years."

"You make it sound so awful—so premeditated. It wasn't like that. Please listen to me, Matty." She sat on the edge of the sofa and motioned for Matty to join her. Hesitantly, Matty took a seat on the far end. She unwound the kerchief from her hand and put it on the seat beside her. She motioned to Shep, and he came to her, never once taking his eyes off Donna.

"You don't need protection, Matty. I'm not going to hurt you."

Anger had taken the place of fear. Matty sat staring at her, waiting.

"You know I lived in that old trailer park up the street when I was growing up. What you can't know is how awful it was. From the time I was a little girl, I was treated like an outcast—the one all the other kids made fun of. My clothes, what little I had, were someone else's cast-offs. My daddy spent most of his time in a drunken stupor, and my dear mother wasn't much better. I had to—"

"Donna," Matty interrupted, "I understand you had a terrible childhood. That doesn't excuse what you've done."

"Hear me out, Matty. When I got to high school, I was determined to make something of myself. I was a good student, but I wanted more than that. I wanted to be part of the 'in crowd'—to be looked up to and have a boyfriend. I did my best with the clothes I had and tried so hard to get the others to like me."

Matty shifted and let out a long sigh.

"I'm sorry to bore you with all this," Donna's voice had a decided edge to it now. "I'm trying to make you see things as they were."

"As they were, Donna? Or as you perceived them?"

"You don't know. You weren't there." Her voice grew

shrill.

Shep stood, and Matty heard a low rumble in his throat. She grabbed his collar and gently pulled him back into a sitting position.

"You've never been on the outside looking in. You've had such an easy life."

Matty checked the retort. "Please, Donna. Let's get on with this."

Donna picked up the stray kerchief and smoothed it out. "The best thing that ever happened to me was when Karen decided to be my friend. She was the most popular girl in school. Everyone followed her lead. I was part of the group as long as Karen wanted me to be. The first time she asked me to write a paper for her I understood why she had befriended me. But I didn't care. I finally had what I'd wanted all my life—to be accepted. The only thing lacking for me was a boyfriend.

"I had a secret crush on Karen's boyfriend Tommy. He was perfect as far as I was concerned. We got to be good friends, but I knew he loved Karen. He was heartbroken when she broke up with him. We talked all the time. He even took me to the movies one afternoon. I figured once he got over Karen, he would start to like me. She didn't care about him the way I did. She just used him like she used everyone else." Donna balled up the kerchief in her hand, and Matty pulled Shep a little closer.

"The day she died, Karen told me she knew Tommy and I had gone to the movies. She told me not to get any ideas.

Tommy loved her, and she planned to get back together with him. She also told me we could no longer be friends. She said I had betrayed her.

"I was devastated, Matty. I felt like my life was over. I couldn't go back to being that stupid little nobody. I had to do something.

"So I hid outside the church while they had their meeting, hoping I could get a chance to talk to her and ask her to please forgive me. Then I had to wait till everyone else headed home. I was trying to catch up to her when I saw her meet up with Billy. I figured I'd have to wait for another time, but then they separated at the bridge. I saw Karen start up the path that cut through the woods and hurried after her. I had no plan to hurt her in any way. I just wanted to talk to her.

"She was walking so fast I had to run to catch up with her. I called her name, and she stopped. I begged her to forgive me. I told her Tommy and I were just friends—that there was nothing going on between us. I reminded her of all the things I'd done for her. I promised to do anything she wanted me to do.

"She stood there staring at me, and then she started laughing. She said, 'Who do you think you are, you stinking ragamuffin. You're nothing without me. Do you think I can't do those things myself if I want to? You were useful to me for a while, but I'm no longer amused by you.'

"She turned around and started walking away. I don't know what came over me. It was as though I was watching someone else. I was so filled with anger I couldn't think. I bent over and picked up a rock and smashed her in the head."

She was becoming increasingly agitated, twisting the kerchief long and tight, then wrapping it around her fingers. Matty felt her own heart rate quicken. Shep pulled a little against the restraint, but she held him close to her side.

"When I realized she was dead, I didn't know what to do. I ran away as fast as I could and didn't stop running until I got to the road. I saw Crystal coming toward me, so I tried to act like everything was all right. I passed her lots of times on the way home from school. I knew she hadn't seen me come out of the woods, so I thought I was safe."

"And you let Billy Taylor take the blame. You stood by while he was arrested, tried and sent to prison. For all these years you've kept silent while his life has been a living hell. How could you, Donna?"

Her voice quivered, and her whole body was trembling. She pounded her fist into her thigh. "I couldn't say anything. I didn't want to go to prison. Don't think I didn't feel terrible, but I kept telling myself that Billy would get out on parole in no time and everything would be all right."

"But that didn't happen, and still you kept your awful secret."

"After a while it got a little easier to push the whole thing to the back of my mind. I got a full scholarship to college. I met Philip, and we got married. We had three wonderful kids and now grandchildren. I've worked tirelessly to help others and do whatever I can to make up for what I did. I've lived a good life, Matty. Must all of that be taken away because of one foolish mistake?"

Now Matty felt her own anger rising. "One foolish mistake?" Her fingers tightened around Shep's collar. "You took someone's life, Donna. There's a man in prison for something he didn't do, and you could make that right. Maybe you've led a good life, but is Billy Taylor's life of no value at all? Didn't he have the right to make something of his life, too? What right do you have to decide your life is more valuable than his?"

Donna sat looking stunned for a moment. She set the kerchief aside and drew herself up. "Billy Taylor is a stupid good-for-nothing. He would have ended up the same way his old man did. What difference does it make if he's in prison? He never would have made anything of himself. The world's—"

Matty stood up, and Shep stood with her. She held him close. "Don't you dare say it, Donna. Billy Taylor was trying to make something of himself, but you took away that chance. I don't want to hear any more of your excuses. What do you intend to do?"

"I suppose the real question is what do *you* intend to do, Matty? Will you go to the police? I don't think you have any real evidence that proves I did it. Do you?"

"You're right, Donna. I probably don't. But I do have the letter you sent me. Perhaps the police can do something with that. I believe I can get Crystal to tell them she saw you on the road that day. I could even tell them everything you've just told me. But more than that, I believe you'll decide to do the right thing yourself. You aren't that desperate young girl any more. You're a grown woman with beliefs and values that won't allow you to live with this secret any longer."

Donna got to her feet and took a step closer to Matty, keeping a watchful eye on Shep. "Matty, I beg you. Don't do this! Think about what will happen to my family. This will kill Phillip. And what about the kids and grandkids? How will they be able to live with the shame? They'll all hate me. Everyone will hate me." She became increasingly overwrought, rubbing her hands together and pacing again. She stopped in front of Matty and grabbed her hand. Matty pulled it away, keeping a firm grip on Shep's collar.

"Please, please, let this thing be. I've done everything I know to do to make up for it. I'll work even harder. I'll go speak up as a character witness for Billy when his next parole hearing comes up. I'll do anything you ask. I can't lose everything, Matty! I can't!"

She staggered over to the couch and collapsed against the cushions. Moaning, she doubled over, as though in physical pain. Shep whimpered and tried to pull free. Matty calmed him, hesitated for a moment, then sat down beside Donna and put her arms around her. She rocked her gently until the crying stopped.

"Look at me, Donna." Matty took her by the shoulders. "This isn't easy for me. I wish there was some way we could simply walk away from this, but we can't."

Donna looked at her with swollen eyes and wiped her

nose with the back of her hand. Matty walked over to the hall table and pulled a couple of tissues out of the box. Handing them to Donna, she said, "I'll give you until ten o'clock tomorrow morning to turn yourself in. That will give you some time to talk to your family and get things in order. If you don't, I'll go to the police with what I have. I should probably call them right now, but I believe you'll do the right thing. You've lived with this far too long."

Matty extended a hand and helped Donna to her feet, walking her to the door. The rain had finally stopped. A full moon shone through a break in the clouds. She stood outside and watched Donna climb into her car and pull out of the driveway.

Back inside, she called to Shep and slowly climbed the stairs. She felt so weary, she didn't think she would make it to the top. It was too early for sleep, but she put on her nightgown and climbed into the big empty bed. Shep curled up on his rug. Matty pulled up the covers and buried her head in Joe's pillow.

~ CHAPTER 28 ~

Matty lay in bed waiting for daylight to seep under the drawn shade. She had slept fitfully, waking every hour or so and then struggling to fall back to sleep. When sleep finally came, she had vivid dreams—frighteningly real. Donna taking her own life, Billy being beaten in his prison cell, a young girl's bloody body and a leaf-strewn path.

She looked over at the clock—5:30. In just four-and-a-half hours she would know. It felt like an eternity. *Why did I pick ten o'clock?* She couldn't still her mind long enough to pray.

She agonized over her decision. Had she done the right thing? Was it fair to Donna's family? The very real possibility that they had run away in the night made her feel sick. Should she have called the police before Donna left to go home? She closed her eyes and whispered the only words she could think of, "Father, give us grace and strength to do what must be done."

By six-thirty she had bathed and dressed and tidied the upstairs. She had no appetite but decided to make a pot of coffee so she wouldn't add to the headache she already had from lack of sleep. She did a load of laundry and swept the kitchen floor. Fearful the noise of the vacuum might drown out the phone, she ran her dust mop over the wood floors.

The hands of the old school clock moved so slowly she checked to see if it was still running. She started to call Jenny but immediately changed her mind. "I don't want to tie up the line," she said to no one in particular.

Shortly before ten o'clock, the phone rang. Although she had been waiting for hours, Matty jumped when she heard it. Heart pounding, she picked up the receiver.

"Mrs. Amoruso. This is Detective Carson. I'm calling to let you know Mr. and Mrs. Johnson are here at the station in Petersburg. They asked me to call."

"Yes, thank you, Detective." She could hardly speak.

"We'll want you to come in and give a statement, if you don't mind. Would you be able to come in later this morning?"

"Yes, I can do that."

"I'll see you then. Goodbye."

"Goodbye."

Matty replaced the receiver. "We did it, Joe. It wasn't easy, and I'm so sorry for Donna's family, but we did it." She lifted her gaze heavenward. "Thank You, Lord."

She ran upstairs and changed into a skirt and matching top. As she slipped on her shoes, she saw Joe's sweater laying on the rocking chair. Hesitating a moment, she picked it up and held it to her face. His scent was fading. With great care, she opened the bottom dresser drawer and laid the sweater on the envelope that held a copy of their wedding invitation, right next to Jenny's white baby shoes.

✣

Matty walked down the steps of the old building that housed the police department and headed toward the nearly empty parking lot. Her feet felt almost as heavy as her heart. She wanted nothing more than to get home.

"Matty! Please wait."

She turned to see Philip Johnson hurrying toward her. If she were able, she would have run to her car and driven away as fast as possible. As it was, all she could do was stay rooted to the spot.

He hurried up to her. For a moment they stood facing each other, neither able to speak. Then they both began at once.

"Philip, I'm so sorry..."

"Matty, you don't need to apologize. That's all I wanted to tell you. I knew you would be upset. None of this is your fault."

Her eyes brimmed as she looked up into his face. His skin looked ashen. Sweat beaded on his forehead. "I wish it could have been different, for everyone's sake. But especially for you and your family. I'm thankful Donna decided to come forward. It took great courage."

Now his eyes filled. "It didn't come easily. When she told me what had happened, I couldn't believe it. It didn't seem

297

possible or real. My wife—a murderer?" He ran his fingers through his hair and took a step back.

"At first she was angry and bitter. She kept trying to justify herself and put the blame on everyone else—including you, Matty."

Matty reached for his hand. "I wouldn't blame you if you never wanted to have anything to do with me ever again. I—"

He squeezed her hand. "I've told you. This is not your fault. Donna and I talked all night. At one point we even considered running away. In the end there was only one choice. We knew we had to do the right thing."

"What will you do? What will happen to Donna? The detective wouldn't tell me anything. He said he couldn't discuss it."

His breathing was becoming labored, and he stared off into space. Matty withdrew her hand and rested it on his arm.

"We spoke with a lawyer early this morning. He went over all of our options, and we decided to forego a trial. Donna couldn't bear the thought of all the publicity. She's so ashamed of what people will think of her."

He stepped back again and put his hands up to his face. He took a deep breath and began to speak in a detached monotone.

"She has pled guilty to first degree manslaughter. The Probation Department will do an investigation and make a recommendation for sentencing. Both lawyers, ours and the prosecutor, will also make recommendations. Then it will be up to the judge to decide. The maximum sentence for that crime is five to 25 years in prison. Our lawyer said he thinks the judge will render a decision for five to ten years with the possibility for parole after one third of the sentence is served. He's certain Donna's exemplary life will give the judge cause to be lenient. For the time being she must stay in jail."

Matty nodded, not knowing what to say.

He ran a hand over his scruffy chin. "I know you must be concerned about Billy Taylor."

"It's all right, Philip. You don't have to tell me any more."

He kept talking as though he hadn't even heard her. "They told us the lawyers will go before the judge. Billy's lawyer will make a motion to release him, and the prosecutor will consent. He'll be coming home very soon, Matty."

"And you, Philip. What will you do?"

"I don't know. I can't think about that right now. I want to see my kids and grandkids. I don't know if I'll be able to teach...I want to be here for Donna."

He stood for a moment gazing into space, then looked at her as though he had almost forgotten she was there. "Oh dear God, Matty, I can't believe this is happening. It doesn't seem real."

Matty stepped toward him, but he backed away.

"I've got to get back in there, Matty. You take care."

"I will. You, too."

She stood watching as he walked across the parking lot, then she turned and got into her car. The August sun shone bright and warm through the windows, but a chill ran through her. She leaned her head against the steering wheel, feeling a jumble of emotions: relief, sorrow, and underlying it all, a deep sense of gratitude.

❖

Matty had just gotten out of the shower when she heard Shep barking. She dressed as quickly as she could, threw a towel around her wet hair and rushed downstairs. A shiny black Lincoln was parked in the driveway, and a man in chauffeur's livery stood at attention on her front porch. Before she could decide what to do, he rang the bell, something he had apparently been doing for some time.

She shushed Shep, pulled the towel off her head and ran her fingers through the curls before opening the door.

"Yes. Can I help you?" She grabbed Shep's collar before he could welcome this new visitor.

"Mrs. Campbell wishes to speak with you, ma'am. Would it be convenient if she steps in now?"

Overwhelmed, Matty opened the door wide and nodded. He turned smartly, went down the porch steps and opened the gleaming door. Beatrice Campbell stepped out, smoothed her skirt and nimbly walked up the stairs. Matty looked down at her rumpled capris and T-shirt and wished the floor would open up and swallow her. She spoke a few words of warning to her exuberant pet and kept a firm grip on his collar.

"Please come in, Mrs. Campbell."

"I see you're taking better care of that dog."

At a loss for words, Matty just nodded. Beatrice kept a wary eye on Shep and walked into the living room. Once seated, Beatrice got right down to business. She refused any offer of refreshment, saying she had a committee meeting to attend shortly.

"I have come about Billy Taylor."

Matty searched for something intelligent to say.

"I know all about this Donna Johnson. My lawyer has assured me that her story is, in fact, true. Apparently she knew things only the killer could have known. You can imagine my distress, Mrs. Amoruso. Everything pointed to Billy Taylor as the perpetrator. No one thought him innocent, I can assure you."

This is one of those times, Matty thought, *I wish I could just buck up and say exactly what is on my mind.*

"In any case. Never let it be said that I am too proud to admit when I've been mistaken, although as I said, there was every reason to believe Billy Taylor murdered my daughter. I am grateful to you for your efforts to find the truth."

Shep had grown weary of the whole business and snuffled softly at Matty's feet.

Not one word of apology or regret. Instead she's waiting for me to fall all over myself with gratitude. Come on, Matty. Have a little gumption.

Matty sat up straight and took a deep breath. "I think, after all that poor man has been through, you might at the very least offer your apologies to Billy Taylor." She could feel the blood rushing to her face, but she kept going. "He never had a chance for a fair trial once you got involved, and you single-handedly kept him from getting paroled. He has suffered for thirty-six years for something he didn't do."

Steely blue eyes stared at her from across the room, and she could feel herself wilting. She fought to hold back the tears, determined not to let this bitter old woman see her cry.

Beatrice got to her feet. "I must be going now, Mrs. Amoruso. I've said what I came to say."

Matty sat stunned as the older woman walked out the door.

~ CHAPTER 29 ~

Matty stood at the farmhouse window watching the two men walk toward the barn.

"It hardly seems possible, Matty," Nancy said.

Matty turned to face her friend. "No, it happened so quickly. I can't seem to get my mind around it. I'm so thankful Donna pled guilty. And for Phillip's sake I'm thankful she got a fairly lenient sentence. She could be out of prison in a few years." Matty sighed and turned back to the window. "Although part of me wanted her to pay a bigger price for what she did to Billy. Not very nice of me, I know."

Nancy patted the seat next to her. "Come sit and have another cup of coffee with me."

The two friends sat sipping their coffee. The windows were open to let in the fresh air. They could hear the two men call to each other over the noise of the tractor.

"How's Billy doing, Nancy? Does he seem all right? He hardly said a word at lunch."

"I think he's doing about as well as can be expected. He's been through so much. We need to give him time."

"I don't know how to thank you and Buddy for taking him in. Once we knew he was going to be released, I couldn't imagine him being left on his own."

"That apartment has been sitting empty ever since Buddy's Mom passed away. The only time we use it is when the kids all come at the same time. Besides, Buddy can really use a couple of extra hands this time of year. There's so much work to be done. And that man knows a thing or two about farming. He hasn't forgotten, even after all these years."

Nancy set her coffee mug down and turned to look at the men. "He's no trouble at all," she said. "He eats all his meals with us, but right after supper he goes back to the apartment and watches a little TV before bed. Buddy's working him pretty hard, and he's good and tired by the end of the day."

"Has Pastor Greg come to see him?"

"Oh, yes. He's already been here a couple of times. They get along real well. Billy even said he wants to come to church with us this Sunday."

"I'm glad. He really is such a kind soul."

"He speaks of you and Joe often. Your going to the prison the night he was released meant a great deal to him."

"I admit I was a little frightened...well, not frightened. I guess nervous is more the word. I think his lawyer would have loved to turn it into a big media event, but once he got to know Billy, he decided it would be best to keep it as quiet as possible. I prayed all the way there that the press wouldn't find out. That's why we went so late at night."

Matty leaned back in her chair and continued, "There

were a few photographers hanging around the entrance, but we managed to get by without arousing suspicion. Billy was ready and waiting when we got there. He looked somehow smaller than I remembered. I was so happy for him. He didn't say much on the way here. He just thanked me and told me how much he loved Joe."

"He's going to be fine, Matty. We'll hold him in our prayers."

"I hope Billy will eventually be able to get a little place of his own."

"Matty, it's entirely possible Billy will be able to buy not only a place of his own but just about anything he wants. His lawyer has called several times since Billy got here. He wants to sue the state for compensation for unjust imprisonment. We could be talking about millions of dollars."

"Oh, Nancy with everything else going on I never thought about that. What did Billy say?"

A faint smile crossed Nancy's face as she shook her head. "He says he doesn't want anything but to be left alone. I don't think he can bear the idea of a legal battle and all the publicity involved. He's such a shy, timid soul underneath it all, Matty. We told his lawyer to let it go for now. There's time. Maybe Billy will reconsider once he's had a chance to adjust to all the changes in his life. For now he's just thankful to be free."

"I'm so thankful Joe saw what no one else seemed willing or able to see. Do you think he knows?"

"Yes, I do." She reached across the table and took Matty's

hand. "You look exhausted. Why don't you go on home and get some rest."

"I wish I could see him smile."

"Who, honey?"

"Billy. I've never seen him smile—not one single time."

"I'm going to go visit Mr. Goss tomorrow and tell him what's happened. I know he'll be pleased." Matty got up and carried her cup to the kitchen sink. "Then I leave in a couple of days to visit Jenny and Pete. I hope by the time I get there they'll have cooled off. They were both angry with me for not confiding in them. And you should have heard Willa-Mae. I thought she would burst a blood vessel she got so upset."

Nancy's boisterous laughter filled the room. "Never mind. They'll get over it. You have yourself a restful time and then come home to us refreshed."

"I'm looking forward to long walks on the beach. Shep's invited, too. I think he'll love the Island."

"You'll be driving this time?"

"Yes. We'll take it easy. The scenery is beautiful this time of year."

They moved to the screen door and embraced. "Love you, Matty. Take care. I'll be praying for you."

Matty couldn't speak. She gave Nancy one more hug and walked to the car. As she drove past the farmyard she saw Billy driving the tractor out to the fields. She tapped the horn, and he turned. When he saw who it was, he pulled off his John Deere cap, waved it in the air, and smiled.

~ ACKNOWLEDGMENTS ~

With deep gratitude:

To my Heavenly Father—the One who wrote my story with unimaginable love and grace before I ever drew breath. My heart's desire is that Your name be glorified.

To Ann Kroeker—writing coach and editor par excellence. You took all the faltering steps and kept them moving steadily toward the goal—with such wisdom, encouragement and skill. I absolutely could not have done this without you (apologies for the "ly" word).

To Charity Singleton Craig. You took this little story to completion. I am so grateful for your excellent work.

To my granddaughter Stephanie Savage. From your earliest years your artistic gift has amazed us. You have used it to bring such joy to so many. I am honored to have your artwork as part of this book. You took the pictures I could only imagine and brought them to life. I'm so delighted we got to do this together. I love you, sweet girl.

To my family, who didn't laugh when this old gal decided to write a book, but instead encouraged and believed. Dad and Mom (a.k.a. Grandma and Grandpa and Great-grandma and Great-grandpa), Scott and Susan, Stephanie and Stephen, Jared and Anna, Laura, Jacob, Grace, Todd and Sarah, Lauren, Hannah, Lisa and Dom, and Sandro (my newest little grandbaby, who can one day say his Grandma wrote a story)—you are a precious gift. How could I possibly deserve such grace?

To all the friends who read Matty's story in its early days and offered the gift of your time, encouragement, and constructive critiques: Lindsay Langton, Carol Graves, Darlene Steffenson, Jacquie Reed, Jennifer Dukes Lee, Susan Jones, Phyllis Cathey, Stacie Bell, Tonia Peckover, and my dear Mom. Words can't say how much your love and support mean to me.

To my brother-in-law Peter Chontos for your legal advice. It's nice to have a lawyer in the family.

To the women in my little Thursday morning prayer circle and my fellow "Bingo Moms." You are the precious sisters-of-my-heart. Thank you for all the prayers and for believing. Here we are.

It's been a long journey, and so many friends have offered encouragement along the way. Please know every word, every prayer, every listening ear has been a gift.

To Steve, my husband, dearest friend and love of my life. You have always believed so much more for me than I ever did for myself. Your love has never failed—not even when life was at its very darkest. Your faith has inspired and carried me when my own was so desperately weak. You are the very best of men. I love you forever.

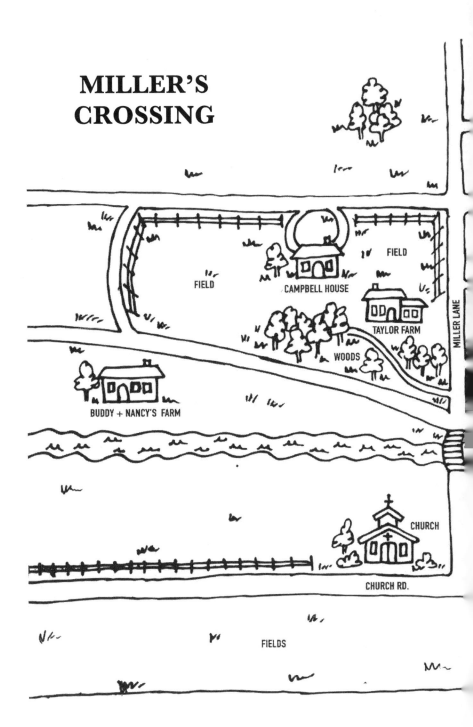

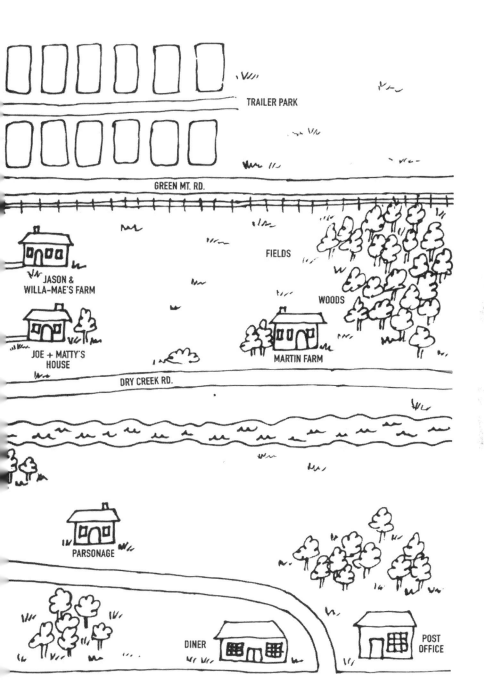

Made in the USA
San Bernardino, CA
09 January 2017